DORIAN GRAY

A NOVEL BY JOHN GARAVAGLIA

To Tom!
Live life!
Search for new sensations!
Be afraid of nothing!

John C. Garavaglia

ADAPTED FROM THE GRAPHIC NOVEL SERIES BY
DARREN G. DAVIS, SCOTT DAVIS AND
FEDERICO DE LUCA

11-25-19

BASED ON THE NOVEL
THE PICTURE OF DORIAN GRAY
BY OSCAR WILDE

Dorian Gray © 2017 Darren G. Davis & Markosia Enterprises, Ltd. All Rights Reserved. Reproduction of any part of this work by any means without the written permission of the publisher is expressly forbidden. All names, characters and events in this publication are entirely fictional. Any resemblance to actual persons, living or dead is purely coincidental. Published by Markosia Enterprises, PO BOX 3477, Barnet, Hertfordshire, EN5 9HN.
FIRST PRINTING, March 2018.
Harry Markos, Director.

Paperback: ISBN 978-1-911243-63-2
eBook: ISBN 978-1-911243-64-9

Book design by: Ian Sharman
Cover photography by: Stephanie Swartz
Cover model: JC Mason

www.markosia.com

First Edition

Those who find ugly meanings in beautiful things are corrupt without being charming. This is a fault. Those who find beautiful meanings in beautiful things are the cultivated. For these there is hope.
Oscar Wilde.

PROLOGUE

The artist is the creator of beautiful things.
Oscar Wilde.

LONDON, ENGLAND
April 7, 1890

Basil Hallward's studio was filled with the rich fragrance of freshly cut red roses his dutiful butler had picked up for him from the florist this morning. The light summer wind stirred in the trees in the master's garden, and through the door came the welcoming of the lilacs' sweet perfume. Basil loved to surround himself with such beautiful things. His sudden disappearance several years ago caused such public excitement and gave rise to so many outlandish assumptions.

Now he had been working on an important painting so he could reemerge himself back into the art world. He was genuinely proud of this one piece. So elated he even invited his very good friend, Lord Henry Wotton, to be the first to gaze upon to what Basil would think to be his magnum opus. Lord Wotton was also an admirer of beauty and, at the moment, was groveling over the portrait Basil had done. The painting was of a young man in his early twenties, and he was very handsome.

As the painter looked at the gracious and comely form he had so skillfully mirrored in his art, a smile of pleasure passed across his face, and seemed about to linger there. But he suddenly started up, and closing his eyes, placed his fingers upon the lids, as though he was deep in thought.

"It is your best work, Basil, the best thing you have ever done," said Lord Wotton lethargically. "You must certainly send it next year to the Grosvenor. The Academy is too large and too vulgar. Whenever I have gone there, there have been either so many people that I have not been able to see the pictures, which was dreadful, or so many pictures that I have not been able to see the people, which was worse. The Grosvenor is really the only place."

As the artist looked at the gracious figure he had captured in his painting, the smile pressed from his face and he hesitated for a moment.

"I don't think I shall send it anywhere," he frowned, shaking his head. "No, I won't send it anywhere."

Lord Wotton raised his eyebrows and looked at him in disbelief. "Not send it anywhere? My dear fellow, why? Have you any reason? What odd chaps you painters are! A portrait like this would set you far above all the young men in England, and make the old men quite jealous, if old men were ever capable of any emotion."

"I know you will laugh at me, Harry," Basil replied, "but I really can't. I have put too much of myself into it."

"But Basil," Lord Wotton laughed, "I can't see any resemblance. I don't see the problem. I didn't know you were so vain, but you flatter yourself. You don't look at all like this fine young lad."

"You don't understand me, Harry," answered the artist. "Of course I am not like him. I should be sorry to be so. There is a destructive quality about all such physical beauty. It is better not to be so different from others."

"Basil, I was wondering." Said Lord Wotton, walking across the studio toward the arrogant painter. "How did you meet this boy, and what is his name?"

"I went to a party at Lady Brandon's." Explained Basil, recalling the events if it had happened yesterday. "You know we poor artists have to show ourselves in society from time to time just to remind the public we aren't savages." Basil smiled. "After about ten minutes I ran into Dorian Gray—the good looking fellow you see before you." He gestured over to the portrait. "It was funny but from the moment Lady Brandon introduced us, I found him to be a most fascinating person. I had a strange feeling about our meeting—I knew he would have an impact on my painting."

Basil insisted that, thanks to Dorian Gray, his recent paintings were the finest he'd ever done and stated that the young man's personality had suggested a whole new style of art.

"Yet I'm sure Dorian Gray will suffer because of his good looks."

Lord Wotton was very surprised by Basil's gloomy prediction. He was eager to learn more about this mysterious model.

After a pause, Lord Wotton said, "You haven't answered my question, Basil."

"What is that?" Said the painter, keeping his eyes fixed on the ground.

"You know quite well."

"I do not, Harry."

"Well, I will tell you what it is. I want you to explain to me why you won't exhibit Dorian Gray's picture. I want the *real* reason."

"I told you the real reason."

"No, you did not. You said it was because there was too much of yourself in it. Now, that is childish."

"Harry," said Basil, looking him straight in the face, "every portrait that has ever been painted with feeling is a portrait of the artist, not of the sitter. The sitter is merely the accident, the occasion. It is not he who is revealed by the painter, it is rather the painter who, on the colored canvas, reveals himself. The reason I will not exhibit this picture is that I am afraid I have shown in it the secret of my own soul."

Lord Wotton laughed. "And what is that?" He asked.

"I will tell you," said Basil; but an expression of perplexity came over his face.

"I am all expectation, Basil," continued his companion, glancing at him.

"Oh, there is really very little to tell, Harry." Answered the painter. "And I am afraid you will hardly understand it. Perhaps you will hardly believe it."

Lord Wotton smiled. "I am quite sure I shall understand it, and as for believing things, I can believe anything, provided that is quite incredible. I must meet this Dorian Gray."

Basil got up from his seat and walked up and down the garden. After some time he came back.

"Harry," he said, "Dorian Gray is to me simply a motive in art. You might see nothing in him. I see everything in him. He is never more present in my work than when no image of him is there. He is a suggestion, as I have said, of a new manner. I find him in the curves of certain lines, in the loveliness and subtleties of certain colors. That is all."

"Then why don't you exhibit his portrait?" Asked Lord Wotton.

"Because, without intending it, I have put into some expression of all this curious artistic adoration, of which, of course, I have never cared to speak to him. He knows nothing about it. He shall never know anything about it. But the world might guess it, and I will not bare my soul to their shallow prying eyes. My heart shall never be put under a microscope. There is too much of myself in the thing. Too much of myself!"

"Poets are not so scrupulous as you are." Replied Lord Wotton. "They know how useful passion is for publication. Nowadays a broken heart will run to many editions."

"I hate them for it," cried Basil. "An artist should create beautiful things, but should put nothing of his own life into them. We live in an age when men treat art as it were meant to be a form of autobiography. We have lost the abstract sense of beauty. Some day I will show the world what it is; and for that reason the world shall never see my portrait of Dorian Gray."

"I think you are wrong, Basil, but I won't argue with you. It is only the intellectually lost who ever argue. Tell me, is Dorian Gray very fond of you?"

The painter considered for a few moments. "He likes me," he answered, breaking the silence between him and his very good friend. "I know he likes me. Of course I flatter him dreadfully. I find a strange pleasure in saying things to him that I know I shall be sorry for having said. As a rule, he is charming to me, and we sit in the studio and talk of a thousand things. Now and then, however, he is horribly thoughtless, and seems to take a real delight in giving me pain. Then I fell, Harry, that I have given away my whole soul to someone who treats it as if it were a flower to put in his coat, a bit of decoration to charm his vanity, an ornament for a summer's day."

"Days in summer, Basil, are apt to linger," murmured Lord Wotton. "Perhaps you will tire sooner than he will. It is a sad thing to think of, but there is no doubt that genius lasts longer than beauty. That accounts for the fact that we all take such pains to overeducate ourselves. In the wild struggle for existence, we want to have something that endures, and so we fill our minds with rubbish and facts, in the silly hope of keeping our place. The thoroughly well informed man and his mind is a dreadful thing. Some day you will look at your friend, and he will seems to you to be a little out of drawing, or you won't like this tone of color, or something. The next time he calls, you will be perfectly cold and indifferent. It will be a great pity, for it will alter you. What you have told me is quite a romance—a romance of art one might call it. And the worst of having a romance of any kind is that it leaves one so unromantic."

"Harry, don't talk like that. As long as I live, the personality of Dorian Gray will dominate me. You can't feel what I feel. You change too often."

"Ah, my dear Basil, that is exactly why I can feel it. Those who are faithful know only the trivial side of love. It is the faithless who know love's tragedies." Lord Wotton struck a light on a dainty silver case and began to smoke a cigarette. Then an idea came to him. "I just remembered."

"Remembered what, Harry?"

"Where I heard the name of Dorian Gray."

"Where was it?" Asked Basil, with a slight frown.

"Don't look so angry, Basil. It was at my aunt, Lady Agatha's. She told me she had discovered a wonderful young man who was going to help her in the East End, and that his name was Dorian Gray. I am bound to state that she never told me he was good looking. Women have no appreciation of such things. At least, good women have not. She said that he was very earnest and had a beautiful nature. I at once pictured to myself a creature with spectacles and lank hair, horribly freckled, and tramping about on huge feet. I wish I had known it was your friend."

"I am very glad you didn't Harry."

"Why?"

"I don't want you to meet him."

Lord Wotton raised his eyebrows. "You don't want me to meet him?"

"No."

The butler walked into the studio. "Mr. Dorian Gray has arrived, sir."

Lord Wotton smiled. "You must introduce me now." He laughed.

The artist turned to his servant, who stood blinking in the sunlight. "Ask Mr. Gray to wait, Parker. I shall be in a few moments."

The man bowed and went up the walk.

Basil looked at Lord Wotton. "Dorian Gray is my dearest friend," he said. "He has a simple and beautiful nature. Your aunt was quite right in what she said of him. Don't spoil or influence him. Your guidance would result very badly."

"Complete nonsense!" Exclaimed Lord Wotton, smiling and taking Basil by the arm.

The butler showed Dorian Gray into the room. The young man immediately sat at the piano, turning over the pages of a Mozart sonata. His boyish features struck both Basil and Lord Wotton. He was certainly handsome, with blue eyes and dark brown hair. He had an aura of purity and youth that enveloped him.

"You must lend me this sheet music, Basil. I want to learn it. It is beautiful!" Dorian announced.

"That entirely depends on how you sit today, Dorian." Basil replied.

"Oh, I'm tired of sitting and I don't know if I even want a life-sized portrait of myself." Dorian answered, and then he saw Lord Wotton. "I beg your pardon, Basil, I didn't realize you had company."

"This is Lord Henry Wotton, Dorian, an old Oxford friend of mine. I have just been telling him what a terrific subject you are." Basil said.

"I have a great pleasure in meeting you, Mr. Gray," said Lord Wotton, stepping forward and extending his hand. "My aunt has often spoken to me about you. You are one of her favorites."

"I am on Lady Agatha's bad list at the present," replied Dorian. "I promised to go to a club in Whitechapel with her last Tuesday and I genuinely forgot all about it. We were suppose to play several duets together—*three* duets, I believe."

"I will make peace with my aunt. She likes you very much." Wotton looked at him and was again struck by his youthful cherub appearance. Dorian Gray seemed curiously unspoiled by the world. He seemed to be good and pure.

It was at the moment that Lord Wotton decided not to pay attention to Basil's warning. And although Basil had cautioned

Dorian about his friend's scandalous reputation, Dorian ignored the artist as well.

Wotton's words had a profound impact on the young impressionable Dorian, while the model took his place on the well-decorated dais. He listened excitedly as the nobleman began to explain his theory of beauty.

"To me, beauty is the wonder of wonders. It is only shallow people who do not judge by appearances," grinned Lord Wotton. He looked at the young man. "Dorian, the gods have been good to you. But what the gods give, they cruelly take away. You have only a few years in which to live. Then your youth goes—and your beauty will go with it. Then you will discover that there are no more triumphs left for you."

Dorian frowned slightly at those words. But there was more to come.

"Realize your youth while you still have it," Lord Wotton commanded. "One day, time will catch up with you. You will become old and gray. There is such little time that youth will last. The common hill flowers wither, but they blossom again. But we humans never get our youth back. Our limbs fail, our senses go," he said, painting a scary picture for Dorian of old age.

"We degenerate into a hideous old age, haunted by the memory of missing out on passions that frightened us and temptations we never yielded to. Don't squander your golden days. Live life! Search for new sensations! Be afraid of nothing!"

Dorian listened intently, wide-eyed and silent. Basil also heard these dangerous words and worried about the impression they would make on his inexperienced young friend. But he was too busy putting the finishing touches on Dorian's painting to win him over or to stop Wotton.

For nearly ten minutes Dorian stood on the dais, motionless, with parted lips and eyes strangely bright. He was dimly conscious that entirely fresh influences were at work within him.

Basil painted away with that marvelous bold touch of his, that had the true refinement and perfect delicacy that in art, at any rate comes only from strength.

He stood staring at the picture for a long time, biting the end of one of his huge brushes and frowning.

"It's finished," he said proudly at last.

Then stooping down, he wrote his name in long red letters on the lower left corner of the canvas.

"Is it really finished?" Dorian murmured, stepping down from the platform.

Lord Wotton came over and examined the picture. It was certainly a wonderful work of art, and a wonderful likeness as well.

"I congratulate you, Basil," Wotton said to him. "This is the finest portrait of any man that has been created in modern times. Dorian, come look at yourself."

Dorian looked at the painting and blushed. The sense of his own beauty hit him like a lightning bolt. When he saw it, he drew back and his cheeks flushed for a moment with pleasure.

A look of joy came into his eyes, as if he had seen himself for the first time. He stood there, speechless by the sight of his portrait.

"Speak up, boy," Lord Wotton said, snapping Dorian awake from his silent reverie. "You'll hurt the man's feelings."

"Is that how I look?" Asked Dorian, not blinking even once at the painting. "It's so lifelike."

"Better than life," Lord Wotton laughed, approaching the painting for a closer look. "You and Basil will be the talk of the town."

"The brush seemed to dance, and I painted what I saw." Commented Basil, cleaning his brush with a rag.

The two gentlemen were excited with the finished masterwork; yet, a chill suddenly ran through Dorian. One day he would be old and wrinkled, his slender form would be gone, and his hair would fall out.

"He'll always look like that," Lord Wotton said, pointing to the painting, "but you, Mr. Gray, I'm afraid will not."

The words seem to hit Dorian like fists. Basil saw the saddened look on his inspiration's face. He frowned by the very sight of it.

"Some things are more precious because they don't last." Basil said, trying to perk up Dorian, but it was to no avail.

"Oh, poppycock." Lord Wotton scoffed.

"How awful it is," Dorian mused. "I shall grow old and horrible and dreadful. But this painting will remain always young. If it were only the other way! If only I were to be always young and the picture grew old. For that—I would give everything! I would give my soul!"

"You would hardly care for such an arrangement, Basil," cried Lord Wotton, laughing. "It would be rather hard lines on your work."

"I should object very strongly, Harry," said Basil.

Dorian turned and looked at him. "I believe you would, Basil. You like your art better than your friends. I am no more to you than a green bronze figure. Hardly as much, I dare say."

Basil stared at him in amazement. It was so unlike Dorian to think and speak like that.

What happened to him?

Was this Lord Henry Wotton's evil influence already at work?

"I am jealous of everything whose beauty does not die," said Dorian bitterly. "I know now that when one loses one's good looks, one loses everything. Your picture has taught me that. Lord Wotton is right. Youth is the only thing worth having. I find that I am growing old," he cried, "I shall kill myself!"

Basil was stunned by what he heard, but before he could speak Dorian went on.

"I am jealous of my portrait. It mocks me, Basil. I hate it! Why did you paint it?" With that, he flung himself onto the studio sofa and burst into tears.

"This is your doing, Harry." Said the painter bitterly.

Lord Wotton shrugged his shoulders. "It is the real Dorian Gray. That is all."

Dorian barely heard Basil's charge against Lord Wotton. He watched as the artist reached for a knife to rip the painting to shreds.

With a stifled sob Dorian leaped from the couch, and rushed over to Basil, tore the knife out of his hand and flung it to the end of the studio.

"Don't Basil!" Cried Dorian. "It would be murder!"

"I am glad you finally appreciate my work." Basil said coldly.

"Appreciate it? I am in love with it, Basil. It is a part of myself. I feel that." Dorian explained. "I didn't mean I wished you hadn't painted it."

"Well, as soon as it dries, it will be framed and sent to you." Basil said more gently.

Finally, Dorian calmed down. He couldn't keep his eyes off the portrait.

"I wish the picture would age for me." Dorian said with desperation in his voice.

"Remain as you are?" Lord Wotton said, arching an eyebrow and then smiling. "A fair trade."

"How about another gin?" Offered Basil, sauntering over to the bar, preparing a glass.

"All that hocus-pocus, endless conjurations, books bound in infant skin, pentacles of fire, and drinking blood of virgins." Lord Wotton prattled on, watching Basil refilling his glass. "Dorian wouldn't really barter his soul. Would you, Dorian?"

Dorian turned away from the painting. He stood there silent before Lord Wotton who was expecting on what the lad would say. A perplexed look stretched across Dorian's innocent and youthful façade.

"Would you?" Lord Wotton repeated the question, lighting a cigarette.

After what it seemed like forever Dorian finally answered. "Yes."

Basil shook his head. "You can't possibly mean that, Dorian."

Dorian raised his hand as if he were saluting. "With this, I nail my soul on the devil's altar."

After much chitchat, Dorian made plans to dine with Lord Wotton. Basil begged him not to go, fearing that the older man's encouragement would destroy his all-to-trusting friend.

"Don't go to the theatre tonight, Dorian," pleaded Basil. "Stop and dine with me."

"I can't, Basil!" Dorian replied, straightening his tie.

"Why?"

"Because I have promised Lord Wotton to go with him."

"He won't like you the better for keeping your promises. He always breaks his own. I beg you not to go."

Dorian laughed and shook his head.

"I entreat you."

The boy hesitated, and looked over to Lord Wotton, who was watching them with an amused smile.

"I must go, Basil," Dorian answered.

"Very well," Basil said, in defeat. "It is rather late, and, as you have to dress, you had better lose no time. Good-bye, Harry. Good-bye, Dorian. Come and see me soon. Perhaps tomorrow."

"Certainly," Dorian replied, walking out of the studio.

"You won't forget?"

"No, of course not."

Basil paused for a moment. "And…Harry?"

"Yes, Basil?" Answered Lord Wotton, donning his jacket.

"Remember what I asked you when we were in the garden this morning."

"I have forgotten it."

"I trust you."

"I wish I could trust myself," said Lord Wotton, laughing. "Come, Mr. Gray, my hansom is outside, and I can drop you at your own place. Good-bye, Basil. It has been a most interesting afternoon."

But Dorian did not heed his warning. And his life would never be the same. As the door closed behind them, the painter threw himself on the sofa, and a look of pain came into his face.

Basil licked his lips, ran his tongue along his teeth. He felt as if something had crawled into his mouth and died. And then, somewhere, far in the distance, he heard a faint cackling.

He quickly got out of the couch and looked around in confusion. Where the hell had that come from? Feeling vaguely uneasy, he wandered across the foyer.

The cackling continued as Basil drew closer to what seemed to be the source: the picture of Dorian Gray. But as he approached it, he only got within just a couple of feet, the laughter abruptly stopped. It was as if there was an intruder who suspected he'd been discovered and was trying to avoid detection.

"Somebody there?" Basil said, looking behind the painting and then around the room. "Parker, is that you?"

He should just be calling for assistance, but something stopped him. It wasn't just that the laughter had ceased. There was a palpable sense of emptiness.

He peered around the corner cautiously, aware that there could be some lunatic standing to the side, ready to stab him in the back.

But there was no one. The room was empty. The only thing staring back at him were the various paintings, and they obviously weren't posing any threat.

Basil took a deep breath, walked over to the bar and poured himself a drink. He was alarmed by how much his hands were shaking.

"You really care about that boy, don't you?"

Basil whirled, the sudden realization that he wasn't alone. Sweat was rolling off him in buckets. The glass was wobbling in his hand, the brandy slopping over the edges.

The voice was mirthful and otherworldly, and it chilled high to the bone, especially in the informal tone it was taking, as if the intruder and Basil were old friends. He stumbled to the middle of the room, spinning in place, trying to see everywhere in the room at once.

"Who said that?!" He demanded.

"Don't try to deny it. I see the way you look at him." The voice spoke in a demonic monotone.

"Where are you?"

"I'm over here."

Basil turned and faced Dorian's portrait. He stared into it.

"I…don't understand," he said, his throat closing up on him. He wondered if he was going keel over right there, before this intruder even showed himself.

"Did you think it was *you* who painted this portrait?" The voice asked, laughing. "'The brush just danced in my hands,'" it mocked him. "Before I came along your work was dull, uninspiring, and pedestrian."

"What do you want?" Basil shouted, his terror mounting, and he felt horribly weak for reacting that way. Sweat was dripping into his eyes. He rubbed them furiously to clear his vision, and then he lowered his hands.

"What do I want? I should be asking you that question."

"What do you mean?"

"The boy, Basil!" Urged the disembodied voice. "I can give you Dorian Gray. All you have to do is submit."

Basil backed away, shaking his head, positive now that either he was dreaming or going mad, or both. "Submit to what?"

Misty tendrils were emerging from the painting. Basil's eyes widened in horror, watching two clawed hands reaching out and pulling some foul creature into reality.

"Submit to me!" It growled, lunging at the terrified painter.

Basil fell backwards and crawled up against the wall. The monster prowled toward him, closer and closer. It gave him an awful grin.

"I can give you what you want." It enticed him. "All you have to do is accept me into your vessel."

Basil's breathing was erratic. He couldn't think straight. All he could see were images of Dorian being seduced by Harry's hedonistic lifestyle and vices. Getting up from the floor, Basil stared at the demon head on and gathered all of his courage.

"Yes," he said, "yes, I accept to be your vessel. I just want to be with Dorian."

The specter smiled, towering over its host. "I hope you remembered something hard to bite down on because the first time I crawl inside you hurts like nothing you can possibly imagine." Warned the demon, placing its claws on Basil's shoulders. "It's claustrophobic for a while, but once I settled in we'll both be breathing in synch before you know it."

Basil took a deep breath. "Then do it. Anything for Dorian."

The demon pierced its talons into Basil's muscle tissue, as he let out a painful scream. Taking advantage of the situation, the creature turned into smoky mist and entered Basil's mouth, slithering down his throat so it could take over his body.

The monster was right. It was the most painful thing Basil would ever experience. The pain was so immense, he fell to his knees and looked up at the portrait of Dorian and held his hand out as if the model was going reach out to him.

The last thing Basil saw before he blacked out was Dorian's innocent smile. But something wasn't right. For a moment he thought he could see something lurking underneath the canvas. Something that was twisting his work and colors.

It was monstrous.

PART I
A WILDE RIDE

CHAPTER ONE

For neither birth, nor wealth, nor honors, can awaken in the minds of men the principles, which should guide those who from their youth aspire to an honorable and excellent life, as love awakens them.
Plato.

17 YEARS AGO...

Wrapped in the womb, the baby listened to his mother's heart beating. It didn't sound like anything he'd heard before. The rhythm was off, fast but somehow excited. And it was racing.

Her screams still echoed in the amniotic fluid. Those sounds had scared him more than anything. He'd never felt an emotion so sharp, so jangling from his mother. The vibrations trapped inside her womb were less now, but still coasting through the liquid medium.

He felt distance grow between himself and his mother, something he'd never experienced in the nine months of gestation. Pressure constricted around him. His space had grown smaller in the past few weeks, but he'd accepted that. This was different.

He shifted, trying to find a comfortable position. He didn't like lying like this. His mother already knew that because he had let her know. Instead of being able to move, however, he felt he was pinned.

Then he felt a constriction so tight it hurt.

There had been some warning signs of that during the last few days, but he hadn't worried about it. Everything that had happened to him seemed normal.

He moved again, wishing she would sing to him. But his mother seemed to pull away from even more as he emerged into the light. A light so bright it blinded him. It hurt so much he let out a howl.

"Congratulations, Olivia," he heard a voice say, "it's a boy!"

Then the child recognized the next voice. "Oh, my God... he's so beautiful!"

It was a tearful proclamation of joy and love.

It belonged to his mother.

The doctor handed the newborn baby gently over to its mother, who welcomed the child in warm open arms.

"Have you decided on a name, Olivia?" The doctor asked her.

"Dorian," the child's mother said, smiling. "His name shall be Dorian Gray."

Dorian Gray IV's only memories were of shifting back and forth in the soft, protective confines of his mother's womb, dreaming of the gentle sounds she made. They were encouraging songs and tender coos that let him knew how much he was already loved. As she sang, he knew her hand would gently brush against her swollen abdomen then come to rest on his small, bulging stomach. Very soon he would look into her eyes and let her know he loved her, too.

He was six hours old when he opened his eyes to see her standing over him. A sweet proud smile was on her lips.

"You are so beautiful," she said, playing with the fringes of his already thick, brown hair. "You look so much like your father."

He recognized his mother's voice—it had comforted him for as long as he could remember—and he returned her a small smile in response. Her fingers danced across his tummy again, tickling him. He giggled, the chubby flesh around his eyes wrinkled as he reached to touch her long dark hair. She was beautiful but her bright blue eyes were welling up with tears. He didn't understand what was wrong with her, but in the nine months he grew inside her he had learned to deal with her shifting moods.

A second figure entered the room. When he spoke Dorian knew it was his father, a handsome raven-haired man with piercing blue eyes. He heard his soft voice, muffled and distant, many times before, but now there was anger in it Dorian had never known, and the words, which of course meant nothing to him, were spat out quickly, as if rushing through them would let his father get past the annoyance, whatever it was, and onto something more pleasurable.

"They won't listen no matter what I say and in spite of the proof I've shown them." The man said. His face was red and his knuckles turned white.

Dorian watched his mother circled her arms around his father, comforting him.

"That never stopped you before. You'll make them see. You know you will."

"I hope you're right, Liv, but you know how stubborn they can be. You should have heard them. They called me crazy."

He paced the room angrily, slamming his fist against a bright white wall.

"Sometimes I don't know why I bother," he unclenched his fist and dropped his arm to his side. "What's the whole point of talking if nobody listens?"

Olivia gingerly rocked her child. She knew with his work there came baggage. Most of it he carried it deep within himself, in the form of regrets, unanswered questions, and memories. He had gone to many places, done many things, a lot of them ugly, one or two perhaps unforgivable. But he'd succeeded in what he wanted to accomplish; he'd learned, and equipped himself.

"You know when you began to pursue this lifestyle you were going to meet some skeptics."

Her husband's anger faded. He turned to look at the baby, barely a day old. He had a lot of things to do today, and this was his first opportunity to study the boy closely. Olivia was right; Dorian looked exactly like his father.

"Dorian," he heard his mother say. But she wasn't addressing him, but the person who entered the room. "Come see our wonderful son. I was finally able to get the nurses away from him."

This should have been the elder Gray's happiest day. This should have been a time for celebration.

Dorian, Sr. came forward, wiping his brow. "They ran *more* tests, Olivia?"

"No," she replied, holding back a laugh, "all the nurses in the maternity ward crowded all around him and said he was most beautiful baby they have ever seen."

A smile suddenly appeared on the man's face. "Only a few hours old and he's already a lady killer. Way to go, Dorian!"

The baby giggled and stared into his father's eyes. The elder Gray was quite captivated by him and he thought the newborn was ready to say his first few words. But it turned out to be a burp.

Olivia knew as much as she prayed to God that one day she would cradle Dorian's own baby in her arms, tweaking its little nose, and gently pinching its soft, pillow cheeks, at some point in the next ten hours.

"Looks like he doesn't have any of your manners." Joked Olivia.

"Hey, in some cultures that is a form of respect."

"Would you like to hold him, dear?" She asked, gently holding Baby Dorian out to him.

Her husband faltered for a moment. "Oh…well, I don't…"

"It's easy." She smiled. "Just hold him like this and support his head."

Dorian, Sr. held his arms out and took the child from Olivia. He was very careful and brought him closer to his chest.

"That's right," Olivia guided him. "Think of him like a football. Don't cause a fumble."

"Ha-ha, very funny."

He looked down on his son with delightful eyes. It was the most incredible feeling in the world. There was little Dorian—a little hand to hold, and a little mind to mold. Most successful upper-class socialites only have children because they wanted to have heirs to their business empires. But Dorian's parents had him out of love, and that's what he was going to get from there on in. For that, Dorian smiled at his father.

The new happy family looked across the New York skyline, of which they had a splendid view. They stood there, taking in the fresh morning sun, feeling as if they could literally reach out and scoop up the entire city in the palm of their hands.

Dorian Gray III was smiling back at his wonderful son, but as with his mother, the infant could tell it was halfhearted. Dorian, Sr.'s deep, reassuring voice had always given him hope, but he sensed trouble now, and he started to cry.

"Don't cry, Dorian, everything is going to be so good for you." The elder Gray nuzzled his cheek until his son's tears sputtered out and were replaced with soft, happy giggles.

They called him "Dorian." That was his name. Dorian, Sr. was his father. And his mother was Olivia. They were his family.

His father carefully lifted him from the soft blankets and held him facing their wall-sized window in Olivia's hospital room to look out onto New York City.

Then he looked down on his child with his eyes filled with sorrow and worry. "My son, I don't know if you can understand me, but there are times that some things can't be explained. One day I'll be gone and you will have to take care of your mom. In the meantime I want you to know I love you very much and I will do anything for you."

"Do you have to go?" Olivia interrupted, taking the baby for his next feeding. "It's dangerous and you have a newborn son."

Dorian, Sr. heaved a world-weary sigh. "I have to, Liv."

"Why?"

"Because there's no one else."

Olivia lowered her head and kissed her son's cheek, then made a sucking sound against it. He giggled again, and her tears, thought long ago spent, began anew.

"It's not fair." She said. "You won't see him crawl or learn to walk. Is there some other way?"

Her husband shook his head. "No, I'm sorry. But he will walk. He'll even talk. And when he gets *there*—he'll do much more."

The baby cooed as his mother held him tightly, afraid to let him go. He heard her heartbeat quicken. It was not the same comforting, steady beat he had gotten so used to for all his short existence.

Things were not right.

He wanted to cry, to bring their attention back to him, but instead he sputtered and gurgled some meaningless sounds.

CHAPTER TWO

Have you ever lost someone you love and wanted one more conversation, one more chance to make up for the time when you thought they would be here forever? If so, then you know you can go your whole life collecting days, and none will outweigh the one you wish you had back.
Mitch Albom.

SIX YEARS LATER...

All of it was strange.

That was the first thing that Dorian noticed. The moment he stepped over the threshold, he noticed the furniture and door of the apartment. It was…it was metropolitan, somehow. Not that young Dorian standing there so neatly attired in his khaki shorts and red collared shirt would have known the word "metropolitan." Most six-year-olds hadn't used it in context, and couldn't even come close to spelling it correctly. To Dorian, it sounded like an ice cream flavor. In this regard, Dorian Gray IV who had celebrated his birthday the previous August at a big splendid party where his mother had made a marvelous fuss over him was no different. All Dorian was concerned at this very moment was the here and now. And what was here, and what wasn't.

He was here.

These people were very close family friends were here.

His mother was not.

The living room in which he was standing didn't seem even remotely involving. The couch alone must have cost over $5,000, and the cushions, which were made by the finest and most expensive fabric. He tried to sit on one and hadn't liked the way it had stuck to the underside of his legs.

The man and woman who were bringing the last of his things into the house, were speaking in hushed whispers to the woman name Miss Johansson—the "social worker," she'd been called—those people weren't paying any attention to him.

That suited him fine.

Perhaps he could simply reside there like a ghost, no one noticing him. When he was hungry, he could sneak food from the kitchen, presuming they had one, and otherwise be left alone.

He wanted that more than anything to be left alone by the man, who was practically a father to him. The man's son, Henry, has been Dorian's best friend since they were both babies.

The door closed, shutting out the outside world. The carpet felt like wood. It felt slightly moist under his feet, as if it had been just washed. Just to add to the assault, there was a lemony smell coming from all the wooden furniture. He stared down at his reflection on the coffee table. There were flowers arranged neatly on a small lacy thing in the middle of it.

"Well, Dorian," said the man, coming into the room.

He was a tall black man with a slight paunch. He clapped his hands once and rubbed them briskly together. The magician at Dorian's birthday party had done something similar, right before he'd produced coins from out of nowhere. He'd pretended he'd pulled them from thin air, but Dorian had spotted the sleight-of-hand. In a loud voice he'd explained every single one of the magician's tricks, to the irritation of the conjurer and the endless amusement of his mother. Her laugh still rang in his ears. He hadn't yet been able to grasp the notion that he would never hear that laughter again.

"Well, Dorian," the man said again, "would you like to sit down?"

"No, sir," Dorian said politely, addressing the older man as "sir," just as his mother had always taught him.

"Good lord, child," the woman said. "You can't just plan to stand there forever. Why don't you sit?"

He saw no reason to lie. "I don't like the couch. It's kinda stiff."

"Oh." She seemed vaguely disappointed. He felt as if he'd let her down in some way.

"Please, Dorian, call me George." Said the man. "I've known you since the day you were born."

"Okay."

He was studying the woman now. Her face was narrow and her hair was black and it shimmered in the light. She had a long neck and her hands tended to flutter toward it, as if she was trying to cool down waves of heat.

"I'm Lori," she told Dorian. She said this with a giant deal of gravity, as if she were revealing one of the great secrets of the universe.

"Okay," he said again.

The man clapped his hands together again. Dorian waited for a dove to appear or a coin to drop out of the air. None was forthcoming.

"Would you like to see your room, Dorian?"

"Can't I go back to my old room?"

"Dorian, dear," said Lori, and she took his hand in hers. Her hand felt cold, but smooth as if she'd put some sort of lotion on it. "I thought the social worker explained it…you'll be staying here with us."

"Can't we stay at my house?"

"But, Dorian, this is where we live. And this is where you're going to live now." George told him, trying desperately to sound upbeat about it. "We'll make a good home here for you."

Obviously George and Lori weren't getting it.

"I have a home," Dorian explained, politely but firmly.

"Dorian…"

"You know what you need?" Lori suddenly said briskly. She didn't clap and rub her hands. Instead she patted them on her knees. "Some nice, freshly baked cookies. Why don't you go get your things unpacked, and I'll whip up some cookies. Do you like chocolate chip?"

When Dorian nodded eagerly, she flicked a finger across the end of his nose in a playful manner.

"I thought you might." She rose as she looked over to the young maid at the kitchen. "Frambroise, pourrivez-vous faire cuire une fournee de biscuits aux pepites de chocolat pour Dorian ici?"

"Oui, madam." Frambroise snapped into attention, and began to gather the ingredients.

George just laughed and shook his head. Dorian shied away from the attractive young server who gave him a congenial smile. A black maid's uniform, complete with a pressed white apron, cuffs, and collar, flattered the brunette's slender figure.

Then Lori asked Dorian, "Is there anything else you'd like?"

"Yes, please."

"And what would that be?" She leaned over, hands resting on her knees. "What would you like?"

"My mom."

She winced at that, and George, trying to sound kindly but firm, said, "Dorian…you have to understand, you're going to live with us now."

"I don't want to," Dorian told him resolutely. He wasn't rude, whining, or crying. He couldn't have been more civil if he'd been ordering a meal in a restaurant. "I want my mom, please." He put in almost as an afterthought.

"She's not here, Dorian…" George began.

"Can I at least talk to her? Can you call her?"

"Dorian," and George took him securely by the shoulders. "Your mother…she's with God now."

"When is she coming back?"

George's lower lip was quivering. Dorian had never seen a grown-up cry, and the feeling made his stomach queasy. He didn't think it was something that grown-ups did.

George coughed loudly, took a deep breath, and said, "She's not coming back, Dorian."

"I want to talk to her."

"You can't. She…she went away…"

"I want to talk to her. Make her come back."

"Dorian…"

"**MAKE HER COME BACK!**"

The sound and agony that ripped from Dorian's throat terrified the child himself, because he couldn't believe that it was his own voice sounding like that. His eyes went wide, pupils tiny and swimming in a sea of white, and without another word he turned and bolted through the hall.

George turned to Lori and sighed dryly. "Well, *that* went well."

CHAPTER THREE

Life is a series of natural and spontaneous changes. Don't resist them; that only creates sorrow. Let reality be reality. Let things flow naturally forward in whatever way they like.
Lao Tzu.

Dorian sat on the floor in the middle of the room, his knees drawn up to just under his chin. The room itself wasn't terrible, but it didn't feel especially warm. In Dorian's room—his real room—all the furniture kind of looked like it went together. Here it seemed as if some random stuff had been stuck together in one place.

George had brought in the last of his suitcases some time ago. Dorian hadn't spoken to him. The truth was, he was embarrassed about his outburst and was quite certain that George was angry with him. So he had felt it wisest not to say anything and hope that, eventually, George would forget that he had shouted in such an inappropriate manner.

That's what his mother would have said. "In-ap-pro-pri-ate, young man," she would scold him, waggling her index finger in one quick downward stroke on every syllable.

George didn't try to strike up a conversation with him; he didn't seem to know what to say. So George would come and go from the room, grunting slightly and wondering out loud why

Dorian was packing anvils in his suitcases—which puzzled Dorian, who couldn't remember bringing any. The sun moved across the sky, the shadows lengthened and George stopped coming and going.

The day started like any other. Dorian hated homeroom almost as much as he hated being called Dorie. Unfortunately, he had to put up with both of these things every day. Everyone called him Dorie like he was some annoying blue fish in a Disney movie, and he *wasn't*.

And he hated homeroom.

It was mostly irritating because it had David Harrison in it. Dorian hated David Harrison. All he ever did was shoot spit wads at him and call him names with his stupid friends and called him a bastard.

Dorian hated that.

Especially the part about how his father left him and his mother.

It wasn't Dorian's fault that his father disappeared.

For this year, Dorian's homeroom teacher was a stupid man named Mr. Crumb. He had fake hair on top of his head that he kept saying was real, and he had a big moustache that was all gray and black. Dorian didn't like Mr. Crumb very much because he never made David Harrison and the other kids stop shooting spit wads at him, but he didn't think it was very nice to call Mr. Crumb's fake hair a dead animal.

Mr. Crumb was making the morning announcements. Dorian tried to pay attention to them, but Clarissa Simmons kept whispering to Serena Vincent right behind him, so he couldn't hear a thing.

He liked it better last year in Ms. Gruber's homeroom. Now there was a fun teacher.

Suddenly, the front door opened. This startled Dorian.

It apparently startled Mr. Crumb too; since he dropped the clipboard he was reading the announcements from. It hit the floor with a clatter that made Dorian jump a second time.

He grabbed his Spider-Man lunchbox. His mother had given him the lunchbox for the first day of school. Dorian liked Spider-Man because he always won in the end even when he wasn't supposed to or when bad things happened to him. His mother said when she gave it to him that she got it because he was her little hero.

So when the two men in the black suits walked into the classroom, the first thing he did was go for the lunchbox.

"I'm sorry, sir," one of the men in black said, "but I'm afraid I need to take Dorian out of class."

"Whadja *do*, Dorie?" David Harrison asked. He stretched out the word "do" so it sounded like a dirty word.

A bunch of other kids laughed.

Dorian really hated David Harrison.

He was also scared that something had happened at home.

"What's going on here?" Mr. Crumb asked. He bent over to pick up his clipboard.

"We were sent by a friend of Dorian's mother, sir. We've been instructed to pick Dorian up."

"Is something wrong with my mom?" Dorian asked.

One of the men in black looked at Dorian, then held out a hand. "Please, Dorian, you have to come with us."

"Is Mom okay?" He refused to get up from his desk until the men answered the question.

David Harrison put on a stupid voice and repeated, "'Is Mom okay?'" His stupid friends laughed some more.

The man hesitated for a moment and spoke again with great emphasis on the urgency. "You need to come with us *right now*."

Dorian got up, gripping his Spider-Man lunchbox.

The other man in the black suit said, "You won't need your lunch, Dorian."

"I'm not goin' without my lunchbox."

"Fine, whatever," the first man said. "Just come with us, please."

Mr. Crumb stepped forward. "Look, I can't just let some strange men walk into my homeroom and take one of my students."

The second man reached into the inner pocket of his jacket and pulled out a piece of paper, then handed it to Mr. Crumb.

The teacher read it. His big moustache drooped as he did so.

"All right, fine," the teacher said, handing the note back to the second man in the black suit.

The first man still had his hand out to Dorian.

"C'mon, Dorian, we have to go."

"Yeah, *Dorian*, we have to *go*," said David Harrison. His friends giggled.

Dorian muttered, "If I wanted any lip from you I'd jiggle my zipper."

David Harrison sat there dumbfounded. His friends laughed at the remark while Clarissa and Serena were asking each other, "What did Dorian say?"

For everyone else the clever comback was too quiet for anyone to hear—except for Henry, who gave Dorian a smile.

Henry didn't like David Harrison either.

Clutching the Spider-Man lunchbox to his chest as the men in black were leading him out into the school halfway, Dorian asked, "We're we going?"

"You'll see, Dorian."

Dorian didn't think that was much of an answer.

They went out the school's front door, which was supposed to be locked after homeroom started.

But if these two men worked for his mother, it wouldn't be the first time they'd done something they weren't supposed to.

In face, they weren't supposed to take him out of class like that. But they got Mr. Crumb to let them do it.

Dorian held the lunchbox tighter to his chest.

A big black car was parked on the street in front of the school, right under the red sign that said **NO STANDING ANYTIME**.

There was no ticket on the car.

Dorian knew something was happening.

Is Mommy sick? Am I in trouble? Did they find out something bad about Mom?

Or was it something even worse?

The second man in black opened the car's side door. The car was so big, Dorian had to climb into it like it was a stepladder. He almost dropped the lunchbox.

Dorian sat in the backseat while the two men sat in the two front seats.

"Let's boogie," the one in the passenger seat said.

"Why do you always say that?"

"Say what?"

"'Let's boogie.' It's so stupid."

"Will you just drive the goddamn car?"

"Hey, language! There's a kid in the backseat."

"Fine, will you just drive the *gosh darn* car, then?"

The big black car pulled out onto Main Street and they drove on for almost ten minutes. Throughout the whole trip the two strange men in the black suits were arguing about the phrase "let's boogie." It was a very odd debate between two grown men. However, the one in the passenger seat pled his case as he explained how boogie is a type of dancing, and in fact, dancing is a type of moving. Ergo what they needed to do was to move. It was simply a variation on "let's get moving."

Dorian wasn't paying attention to any of this. He was too occupied on whether or not he was in trouble. Then he thought about his mother. He hoped nothing bad happened to her. It always been him and her against the world, and if something did happen he wouldn't know what to do. He felt a dark cloud formed above him and there was no shelter in sight.

The car came to a complete stop in front of a skyscraper. The two men vacated the vehicle and helped Dorian onto the sidewalk. They escorted him through the double doors that the building's doorman held out for them.

The first man looked over to the receptionist at the registration desk. "Dorian Gray for George Lord." The man announced to her.

The receptionist glanced at the sign-in sheet and found the name. "Ah, right here. He has been expecting you, gentlemen. You just need to sign here."

"I'll sign for all of us," The first man replied, taking the clipboard from her, signed their names on the form, and brought it back to her.

The receptionist looked at the signature and gave them a small smile. "All right, you're good to go. Thank you."

The two men nodded in unison and brought Dorian to the elevator and his next stop was the Lords' penthouse—his new home.

The smell of fresh-baked cookies wafted from all the way in the kitchen and seeped through the doorway and wrapped the tempting fingers of their aroma around Dorian. For a moment he was sorely tempted to abandon his vigil, but he resisted. However, he did shift his posture so that he was sitting cross-legged.

Finally he heard footsteps again. He recognized them as belonging to George Lord. But he didn't bother to turn around. Then he heard George chuckling softly, and that distracted him. He swiveled his head and regarded his guardian, who was standing in the doorway, leaning against the frame, his arms folded.

"What's funny?" Asked Dorian.

"You just remind me so much of your father, that's all." Said George. "Same serious face. I'll show you pictures of him, if you want."

Then Dorian took a deep breath and let it out unsteadily. "My mom isn't coming back, is she?"

"No, Dorian," George told him, as gently as he could. "She was killed in a car crash. It was an accident."

"No," Dorian said flatly. "It wasn't."

"It wasn't?" Said George curiously.

Dorian shoved his hand into one of the bags and pulled out a stack of comic books.

"My mother and father were secret heroes. Like…monster hunters. And they were helping people, and a monster killed them." He held up an old issue, spine-rolled and tattered.

George picked it up automatically, flattening it carefully and looked at the cover. He frowned, trying to understand the image. It showed a hulking red man who had to be the devil wielding a cannon for a gun in his gigantic stone hand.

"*Hellboy*. You like these kind of comics?"

Dorian bobbed his head.

"And you think your mom and dad were like that? Why?"

"Because they were special. My dad didn't run out on me, and my mom was too special to get killed in a stupid car accident."

"I see," said George, very seriously. "That's an interesting possibility you've got there, Dorian. I'll have to think about that one."

Dorian nodded, and, satisfied that the conversation was over and went back to what he was doing…nothing.

After a while he went to the kitchen and had cookies and milk while Lori insisted that she would attend to putting away all of Dorian's clothes, just to help him feel more at home. George kept telling Dorian how pleased he was to see Dorian's mood improve, and how they were going to be great friends and a great family. Dorian's spirits improved with each bite of cookie and each sip of milk. It was the warmth of the freshly baked cookie versus the chill of the refrigerated milk, and the warmth won out, giving him a pleasant feeling in the pit of his stomach.

CHAPTER FOUR

*Behind every exquisite thing that existed,
there was something tragic.*
Oscar Wilde.

Olivia Gray was buried in a cemetery on Long Island. Dorian stood at the back of a small crowd of mourners. The turnout was immense for the funeral of such a prominent woman who was not a politician or a titan of industry.

The funeral procession began at the church, where a scowling minister gave a long and droning speech about how fragile life is and the enduring suffering of the grave. It was far, far worse than the sermon. At least in the church there was someone specific at whom Dorian could direct his frustration and anger, but now it was a slow march to the place where his mother's body would rest forever.

Rest, and rot, and probably be forgotten in little more than a month.

There were no more Grays except for his father, who no one has ever seen in six years.

Dorian watched the coffin that contained his mother was being lowered into an oblong hole. Some of the mourners were crying softly and a few of them looked at Dorian, as though trying to gauge his feelings. He desperately wanted to cry—he really did—because he realized that tears were expected and, more important, much appreciated. So he bowed his head, but no tears would come. The thing inside him, the thing that filled his body, would not allow crying.

This surprised George. The boy seemed paralyzed by grief, as still and silent as one of the marble angels at a nearby plot.

First his father abandoned him, and now his mother is gone, George thought, trying to imagine what Dorian must be feeling. *How is it possible he's not bawling his eyes out? For a boy his age, he sure is brave on facing this.*

Beside the grave the minister spoke again, but this time his remarks were brief and he recited his lines straight from the scriptures; by then Dorian was so set against the deaf old fool that he internally mocked the performance.

And then the words were done and the mourners each dropped a ritual handful of dirt onto the casket, and Lori had scattered roses atop it, and all that was left was the reality that Olivia was going into the ground.

Henry looked up to his father and asked, "Dad, why are they throwing dirt on Aunt Olivia's casket?"

George took a moment to find the best way to answer. "It means we're letting go to that one person from our lives."

Henry looked at him funny, not understanding his father's reply.

George saw his son's puzzled expression, elaborating, "It's a symbol of us returning to dust. From dust we were created and to dust we will return."

"You mean, 'ashes to ashes, dust to dust?'"

"That's exactly where we get that from."

"Oh."

It was the end of all things for Dorian's mother, and as he watched the coffin being lowered into the cold earth he could feel his heart descended to a lower place in his chest. He knew that it would remain there forever, just as his mother would remain here in the soil until the sun itself buried to a cinder in the sky.

Dorian wanted to scream.

He did not.

George took his arm and led him away from the grave, but once, for a fleeting moment, the guardian turned and looked back. Not at the grave, but at Dorian.

Dorian stood there for a long, long time, watching him go.

He wiped his face with his hands as if to cleanse it off more than tears.

A crowd of people, all of whom had spoken condolences to Dorian, began to walk slowly away from the gravesite. Dorian stood beside the Lords until the coffin was out of sight and then turned toward the Town car. It started to rain, and the wind was cold.

After a thoroughly depressing luncheon during which he had to be civil, pretending to remember relatives he had never met or couldn't recall, and was unable to have a private word with George. Then Dorian felt tears burning at the back of his eyes, and then his throat closed up as if a vise were tightening on it.

For the first time since he heard of his mother's passing, Dorian Gray cried.

CHAPTER FIVE

Live fast, die young, and leave a beautiful corpse.
Humphrey Bogart.

NEW YORK
PRESENT DAY

In his black combat suit, Dorian Gray—Pretty Boy to the other nine members of his elite covert insertion team—was spotlighted by a full moon that shone like a mighty alabaster beacon. He was tall and lean, and had a head of thick brown hair and open eyes that seemed incapable of hiding a lie.

He perched like a hawk on top of the building. The rooftops were by far the quickest and easiest way to get from one area or the city to another. He moved swiftly along the shadows. Slowly, Dorian scanned the train yard, searching for any sign of hostiles that he knew would be patrolling this sector. Finger on the trigger of his weapon, he was prepared to shoot at anything that moved.

Nothing did.

The aged structures, many decorated with old-world flourishes, offered hundreds of potential perches. Their roofs and windows would provide numerous vantage points for an assassin. And, with the many exterior fire escapes as well as a roof access hatches down to interior stairwells, there were literally hundreds of escape routes.

On clear nights like this one, the roof offered a good view. The city appeared quiet, but Dorian knew that looks could be deceptive. Who knew what was going on behind closed doors and in the murky back alleys?

Dorian lowered his night vision goggles from his forehead and checked the perimeter again—still nothing.

Nonetheless, in his gut, he felt a twinge of suspicion. He didn't know what cause it, but he had the feeling, that danger was imminent, and nearby.

Broad-shouldered yet tall and lean, a black stocking cap covered his shimmering brown hair, Dorian carried his submachine gun loosely in both hands, safety off, and his finger was on the trigger.

"Why are you always out front?" Said a voice in his com-link.

Dorian recognized the voice, which belonged to his stepbrother Henry Lord—his best friend and second in command.

Dorian held onto his earpiece. "We're supposed to be deadly, invisible, and soundless," he said in a low growl. "Emphasis on the *soundless*."

"What, you think a brother can't walk point?" Asked Henry, his voice was raised above a strained whisper.

Sliding his night-vision goggles up to his forehead, Dorian replied, "Give it a rest, Henry…"

Though Henry's kidding riffs could bring a welcome tension break, but now was not the time.

"You don't have to do this lone gunslinger act, Dorian." Henry said, with concern. "You should have brought backup."

"And let them have all the fun? I think not."

Henry remembered the last mission he went on with Dorian. Their team was a good ten klicks away from their objective until machine-gun fire erupted all around them.

Two of Dorian's men went down, and the rest dove, finding cover wherever they could. Pinned by two machine-gun nests, the team seemed powerless to fight back. The two nests were fifty yards ahead, one to the left and one to the right, catching the insertion team in a lethal crossfire.

Dorian rose and took off to his right, sprinting serpentine through the woods, screaming as he went, drawing the fire of both enemy positions.

Still, lungs burning, Dorian kept moving.

Behind him, his team was able to start returning fire, and the withering fusillade aimed at Dorian somewhat abated.

Circling around, Dorian came up behind the five men in the machine-gun nest on the right, and emptied the clip of his M-16 their way. The primary weapon and every other gun in the nest turned in Dorian's direction, and started blasting with no regard for any of their comrades who might still be drawing breath.

Hightailing it out, Dorian used the cover fire from his team to circle back into the woods. Two bad guys from the surviving machine-gun nest took after him—both of them were wearing green camouflage, one tall, and the other short.

Dorian easily picked them off like they were ducks at the shooting gallery in Coney Island. Doubling back to the machine-gun nest, Dorian found the other three shooters had retained their attention to his team, trying to mow them down. But Dorian took care of them before they could even pull the trigger.

Henry knew Dorian was the best soldier, but also the most dangerous. Not just to the enemy but also to his teammates... and himself.

Dorian could hear Henry scoff at the other end. "I know what you are capable of, man. But you need a babysitter."

Dorian smiled. "Why, Henry, I didn't know you cared."

"*Dorian.*"

"Fine, if it makes you feel better send over a squad to my position."

The first bullet whistled past Dorian's ear.

"HOLY SHIT!!" Dorian screamed, nearly toppling off his perch.

"Dorian? **DORIAN!**" Henry was going ballistic over the com-link system. "**Report.** What's your status?"

Dorian looked down to see several snipers taking aim. He couldn't help to smile.

"Now this party has officially started." He said to Henry, cocking his gun.

"Don't worry, buddy. Help is on the way." Henry replied. "Bravo Team, calling Bravo Team. Pretty Boy needs assistance."

I hate being called "Pretty Boy," Dorian snarled. *But not as much as being called "Dorie."*

"Let's go, people! Assholes and elbows!" Henry exclaimed through the private radio channel.

Dorian stood on the ledge, at the brink of precipice as he gracefully dodged the snipers' bullets.

The hostiles opened up at once, shooting up at Dorian. So much for his team being soundless and invisible—if they were going to get out of this scrape, they'd better get damned deadly damned fast.

He reached out and felt the empty air in front of him. No guardrail protected him from the perilous drop. Dorian heard the bustle of the traffic several stories below, and a flicker of doubt undercut his resolve.

It was a *loooong* way down.

For a second he imagined himself splattered all over the ground.

Dorian took a deep breath, steadied his nerves, and then cartwheeled along the edge of the roof, his heart pounding in exhilaration. The toe of his combat boot probed the corner, finding the top end of a broken rain gutter that plummeted several feet down to the rooftop next door.

"Hmm," Dorian murmured.

A crazy idea occurred to him. It was insane, but almost too daring to resist. He crouched beside the top of the gutter and tapped it with his finger to make sure it was sound and steady.

Probably.

He stepped forward, placing one foot upon the top of the gutter. He licked his lips nervously, took another deep breath, and pushed off from the ledge.

Whooooosh!

Dorian slid down the gutter like an extreme snowboarder. His blood was singing in his ears, and a hot wind blew against his face as he zoomed down the rickety slide. Gulls and pigeons bolted from their perches in alarm, startled by the young man's unprecedented descent. It rushed through him like an oncoming elevator as he tried to bail out as he reached the bottom, but he was going way too fast.

He jumped at the last second and with agility that would have sickened an Olympic gymnast, Dorian dodged the bullets and swooped low, hitting the ground in a crouch position like he was his childhood hero Spider-Man. He was smiling and threw up a victorious fist pump.

During times like these, Dorian followed three key elements: Acceleration, speed, and of course, emotional self-packing.

Unpredictability and adrenaline are the byproducts, but he remembered to drive is to feel and to love is to live.

After sprinting across the rooftop, he launched his body and caught the gutter of the next one, shimmying down the drainpipe till he hung just above the roof level of the next building over. Bracing his feet against the wall, Dorian pushed himself backward, until the drainpipe gave way, jogging from its building over toward its next-door neighbor, Dorian dropping onto that roof.

"There he is," said one of the gunmen, trying to get a bead on the intruder. "**SHOOT HIM!**"

Dorian stood his ground as gunfire erupted around him.

Not a single bullet connected.

Dorian wasn't even backing away. He simply twisted this way, that way, pivoted, and then leaned back as if he were a limbo dancer. With each movement, his confidence swelled all the more.

Two men emerged from an alley, and Dorian cut them down on the spot. Another peered out from behind an old train car, but Dorian blew the man away without blinking an eye.

"Report." Henry said to Dorian's earpiece.

Dorian had no idea how to respond to his request.

No, it was not a request. This was an order.

"Report *now*."

The panicked gunman fired with a submachine gun as he came. Bullets strafed up the flattop in Dorian's direction, whining off the concrete, and he threw himself aside, the rounds narrowly missing him.

Dorian came to his feet tugging the automatic pistol from his waistband, and returned fire. But he missed.

Then he emptied the clip, tossed the pistol aside, and lost sight of his target behind a cloud of smoke.

CHAPTER SIX

To survive war, you gotta become war.
—John Rambo.

"You just couldn't wait for the rest of us, huh?" Said a man coming out of the shadows, and several armored henchmen accompanied him.

Dorian holstered his weapon, knowing the stranger was not a threat. He turned around and gave the leader of the small militia a smile.

"I'm sorry, Henry," Dorian said casually, without the trace of a sincere apology in his voice. "It was a first-come/ first-serve ass-kicking buffet, and I got tired of hanging out at the bar."

A smile formed on Henry Lord's face, and a light chuckle had escaped from his lips. "Good ol' Dorian Gray. You always shoot first and never ask questions. Are you all right? Are you hit?"

"Nope," Dorian replied, grinning, "still untouched like a mafia don's virgin daughter."

"Thank you for that lovely image, Dor."

Henry had black hair cropped to the scalp, large brown eyes, and a quiet disposition. He was moving quickly in the shadows. Dorian kept a close eye on him as he advanced. Henry stopped in front of him and brushed him aside. He gazed over at the other side of the train yard. He was ever so vigilant.

"You think they'll come?" Henry asked Dorian.

Dorian nodded, automatically checking his best friend's temperament. Henry was standing ready on the blacktop, spare magazines at hand, and spare weapons as well.

"They'll come," Dorian said.

"Can we stop'em?"

"That's our objective."

"No offense, but what I heard from the—"

"That's our objective."

Henry shrugged. "All right, as soon as you see movement, blow them all to hell." He hefted his long gun. "I get a decent shot with this!"

One more time, for reassurance, and to give himself something to do, Dorian made the rounds of his fire team, checked their sight lines and kill zones, and made sure everything had an abundance of weapons and ammo. In a fair fight, against an adversary such as themselves, no matter how well trained and disciplined, he would have called the outcome no contest. His guys had ideal ground with anyone advancing up this sector wouldn't even come close.

Henry scurried back to his team, assuring Dorian would leave once he had tied his shoes.

"Everyone in position," he whispered loudly. "And remember, shoot to kill."

One of the agents indicated their objection to the order with the drooping of their firearms, but Henry's steely eyes said, *Don't argue. That's an order.*

The rookie exhaled, steeled himself. "You heard the boss," he said to his comrades, "let's saddle up."

The agents spread out in positions along the roof. Henry, naturally, had chosen the spot where he could fire the first fatal shots at the enemy.

They'd know the stakes now.

"I have a valid target," Henry announced, leveling his sniper rifle.

Dorian whipped his binoculars to his eyes and brought the approaching figures into focus.

"You're cleared to fire," Dorian said, and immediately a resounding boom filled the train yard around him, so loud he couldn't help flinching.

The shell didn't hit its target; it never came close. The rest of the team opened up, and Dorian was surrounded by the sound of spent casings rattling off the walls and floor. Every man here was a crack marksman, and this was point-blank range. The only pause in the murderous volleys was when someone had to replace an empty magazine. In the space of a few frantic minutes, they expended better than half their munitions…

…and found themselves with absolutely nothing to show for it.

A team in full body armor—it was hard for Dorian to tell who was who, there were so many of them.

Too astonished to be scared, the troopers gradually stopped firing. A couple looked to Dorian, hoping for a Plan B. In the countless number of times he'd played this scene out in his mind, it had never gone quite this way.

Dorian was hoping the hostiles hadn't made a radio call, either for reinforcements or to alert headquarters to the presence of the insertion team. But he knew that was a prayer that would likely go unanswered…

Henry and Dorian ducked low, still holding their drawn weapons, trying to shield themselves from the onslaught as all hell broke loose around them.

"Henry," Dorian shouted over the gunfire, "with me!"

Not waiting for an answer, Dorian crawled to his left, the enemy gunfire following him almost as closely as Henry, bullets whistling through the air, hitting the walls.

Henry asked, "What the hell are you *doin'*, bro?"

"I thought you said you liked it hot," Dorian said.

"*Bikini* women hot," Henry said, "umbrella drinks on the *beach* hot—not have bullets flyin' around my *head* hot!"

"I just can't take you anywhere. All you do is bitch, bitch, bitch."

With bullets whistling overhead, Henry was up to his chin in the mud. Feeling movement to his right, Henry glanced over to see Dorian ready to spring into action.

"You gonna move?" Dorian asked.

Another burst of gunfire shrilled past their heads.

"Actually," Henry said, "It's pretty cozy right here."

Bullets tore up the mud in front of them, flecking their faces with thick brown teardrops.

D O R I A N   G R A Y

* * *

The enemy scout gasped when he saw through the lenses of his night-vision goggles. He positively identified the subject as Dorian Gray.

"Better have a look at this, sir," he said to the aide-de-camp to the squad's captain.

The captain looked over the officer's shoulder at the horizon and recognized the face—it was indeed the man they all feared.

"I'd say he has a lot of nerve coming here like this," the captain said.

The aide-de –camp frowned. "I don't like it. The man is a menace."

The captain cocked his rifle. "Then let's do something about it."

Henry nodded, fixing the target in his mind. A second burst of weapons fire came. The instant it stopped, he was moving, the barrel of the gun coming up, his finger tightening on the trigger as he stepped forward again.

"Time to go, Dor," Henry said, replacing the magazine. But he didn't hear any reply. "Dor?" Henry called again. He turned his head to see Dorian charging at their assailants. "Crazy bastard."

Dorian broke from the shadows, sprinting after the two men in black, raising his gun and sighting down the barrel even as he ran, nothing that something about one of the attackers.

Then someone ran into him from behind.

The impact stunned him—his weapon flew from his hands, and he hit the ground hard with his chest, managing to turn just enough at the last second to catch the ground with part of his shoulder, too, so that he could use the momentum to roll to his feet.

As he turned to face his attacker, he heard the gunfire begin.

While his opponent was distracted, Dorian executed an arm bar and judo flipped the masked trooper. The enemy pulled out his sidearm in a last ditch effort to take out the most dangerous man alive. As soon as Dorian saw the gun, he grabbed the barrel and jerked it sideways, making the restrained commando shoot himself.

After scavenging the slain assassin for ammo, Dorian climbed up a service latter to get a bird's eye view on the rest of the hostiles. He was careful on not being spotted and made sure the light didn't catch his shadow. Dorian finally made his way to the top of the tower to see the melee being played out right below him.

Looking down, he saw five people dressed in all black and wearing face-covering masks. They were loaded for bear. Each of them carried at least two guns that Dorian could see, and a variety of other pieces of equipment he couldn't make out—it was all black on black.

Looks like I made it to the party, Dorian observed grimly. *Who's got the soda and chips?*

Deep in the shadows of the alley behind the building where the target was believed to be sighted, the security squad lined up behind their captain, waiting for the signal. He scanned the back entrance with the aid of night-vision goggles that cast the entire area around them in pale green. There was no reason to assume there was any sort of ambush waiting, but he last as long as he had because he operated on the belief that there was never a reason *not* to assure there was an ambush.

He surveyed the area a few moments more and then said confidently, "Clear."

Two of the shadows along the wall detached themselves and moved into a crunch toward the back door.

His men treaded cautiously side by side and they had their rifles at the ready, and balaclavas covering their faces. They all moved to the back door, but in the meantime, the scout had come in through the front, making certain that Gray didn't try to beat a retreat in that direction. They converged at the opposite side and slowly advanced.

Gunfire broke out in the alley behind the trains. There was a sighting of Dorian Gray over the hostile band. Vicious commandos, desperate to get away, opened fire on Dorian, who returned fire with extreme prejudice. The sound echoed off the grimy brick walls of the area. Bullets ricocheted off the rusted worn out cars. Frightened rats scurried for safety. Broken glass, cigarette butts, syringes, crack vials, and other debris crunched beneath the heels of the shooters.

Armed troopers converged on the murky passage, massing on both corners, just out of the line of fire. They exchanged hand signals and counted down silently before rounding the corner, their rifles aimed high and low. Dorian sprinted after them.

He kept his gun drawn and his eyes probed the darkness. His ears strained to hear which way his quarry had gone. For a few, frustrating moments, he was afraid that the fiery terrorists had given him the slip, but then he thought he heard some furtive footsteps ahead, just around a corner.

He signaled the men behind him to be on their guard. Adrenaline rushed through his veins, keeping him sharp. Dorian welcomed the extra edge.

Sure enough, the minute they rounded the corner, they were met with a furious hail of gunfire. Muzzles flared in the shadows. Bullets sparked off the walls, chipping away at the stonework. Dorian and his men pulled back, seeking shelter while returning fire.

"KEEP FIRING!" The enemy leader screamed.

Dorian heard him and, on top of a car, saw his enemy's figure rise, holding a machine pistol. A spray of automatic fire was coming right at him.

Little did Dorian know a commando had slithered through the defenses, and had a bead on him.

The targeting laser shifted all the way to Dorian. But the shooter was too late to realize his fatal mistake. He'd been thrown off by Dorian's size.

He had a submachine gun and managed to squeeze off a round before Dorian reached him. Dorian barely noticed as he grabbed the weapon's barrel, forcing it upward as the shooter squeezed the trigger on full auto. Bullets sprayed all over the place.

Dorian wrenched the gun from the other man's hands and shot him with his own weapon.

One of Dorian's men reached through the debris and sprayed up with his sidearm. A shooter's first bullet caught his shoulder, nailing him back against a wall. He felt the second bullet punch like a fist into his chest. The next three bullets were buttons that entered in a straight line down his chest.

Then another bullet slammed into his chest, a second blow almost on top of the first, nearly knocking the wind from his lungs.

One hit the arm he had thrown up over his face, leaving it feeling bruised and numb.

The third round sailed past his head and up over the Manhattan skyline.

The kid collapsed on the asphalt, struggling to catch his breath. He wondered what the assassin had been firing. Because it felt like several of his ribs were broken.

His chest was on fire.

"Cody's down!" Yelled Henry, and then returned fire on his friend's killers.

Dorian picked up Cody's rifle and dropped down on one knee, firing through the one shade of cover that was available, nailing two enemy soldiers that were rushing at them. Eventually those guys were going to try flanking. And then, Dorian figured, he and his comrades were screwed.

As if the hostiles had heard him thinking, a group of them came from his left flank—three of them, one firing a shotgun nearly took Dorian's head off.

As one, Dorian, Henry, and the rest of the team all swung left, firing as they did, all of them were ripping into the oncoming soldiers, making them dance with the impacts of the bullets, splashing the walls with fresh red blood. But there were always more where these came from. They were going to run out of ammo—and then what? Maybe scrounge weapons from the fallen.

The faction had taken casualties, *heavy* casualties, but they'd still managed to push what remained of the team into position two. And he wasn't worried. Not just because of the snarling hostiles—who fought as if possessed—but due to the fact that something even more dangerous was prowling the battlefield.

"I don't know about you, Dorian, but this is getting too hot for me." Henry said, exchanging rounds to the shooters at the other side.

Dorian gave out a loud sigh. He wasn't the kind of person who would cut and run, but this was getting too heavy.

"It's your call, bro," Henry commented, taking cover from an oncoming blast.

"You know what you signed up for, Henry," Dorian finally replied. "We stick to the plan. We're so close."

Henry stared at him with a dumbfounded look. "I like you, Dorian…but you're crazy."

"What can I say? It's part of my charm." Dorian replied, as he jumped up with his gun ready, facing the enemy.

He opened fire, and the front line of hostiles collapsed. Bullets whipped over Dorian's head, and slammed into an old team car. They were like insects blackening the air.

Shells burst on the ground, instantaneous blossoms of fire and shrapnel. Henry ran, shouting at the others to get back, get under cover, but the vast train yard was the size of a professional football field, open and flat and broad, and there was hardly any cover.

Sniper teams were taking roof positions around the train yard. Each team included two shooters one of which was armed with a thermal scanner. The scanners came online, and thermal images of three people appeared.

"Target is the tallest one in the middle." Henry said to Dorian.

Dorian muttered profanities to himself. If some damned sniper dispatched the mark before Dorian had a chance at him.

As for the rest of the assault force, Henry knew then they'd lost the element of surprise. No more time for subtlety. Time to shift into overdrive and apply brute force, to take down the headman before he could muster sufficient wits to resist.

"Suppressing fire!" The leader shouted.

"Yes, sir!" Came the response.

"Yes, sir!" Another trooper shouted. He signaled to the others and all the troopers let loose.

The other hostiles fired, hitting Dorian's advancing forces in all direction.

As the three kept firing, holding back Dorian's teammates, the leader turned to him.

His subordinates had finished reloading, slamming magazines home onto their weapons.

"Set!" A trooper shouted.

"Advance in teams!" The leader called. He reiterated the command in hand signals.

The aide-de-camp ordered, "Alpha team forward!"

They began to advance—and as they went they opened fire, ripping the place apart with long automatic-weapon bursts.

"We've got movement!" A trooper shouted, peering out a heads-up on his night-vision goggles. "Behind the compartment! Two targets!"

The leader signaled a halt, and ran to the trooper. "Identify!"

There was a moment's hesitation as he touched the goggles, zoomed in on the figures.

"It's Dorian Gray and Henry Lord," he said.

The leader frowned under his mask. Two targets *behind* the car?

So Gray and Lord were running, while the remaining members of their team stayed behind to keep the squad busy.

Okay. One kill at a time.

He pointed at the decommissioned car.

"Take those bastards out!"

Dorian and Henry ran through the flank, hoping to surprise the insurgents in a sortie. Dorian's youthful complexion showed a gleeful smile. Whereas Henry was wracked with fear as he constantly looked over his shoulder.

"You see, Henry," Dorian assured him, "smooth sailing all the way."

Before they could turn a corner, an urban commando stepped out in front of them.

"Oh, I wouldn't be so sure of that." The man said, cocking his rifle.

Dorian and Henry both stopped in their tracks, while two of the man's comrades materialized behind him and leveled their weapons at the perplexed youths.

Dorian was unaware that a sniper was lining him up in his gun sights. The one on the right got off a round, the bullet striking Henry in the chest, knocking him back.

Henry felt like a truck had hit him as he lay on the asphalt, the night sky above him, the stars twinkling their gentle laughter as he tried to draw a breath.

"You okay?" Dorian asked, kneeling over him.

Looking up at his friend, his vision slightly burring from the painful jolt the bullet delivered smashing into his body armor, Henry said, "No, thanks to you."

"I'm supposed to thank you, right?"

Henry clutched his chest, putting pressure on the wound. Bright red blood was smeared all over his shirt.

"A hero has but one life to give to his country." Henry laughed.

Their assailants had them surrounded. Laser pointers from their guns beaded on them. As the insurgents stepped into the light, Dorian and Henry discovered they didn't look like the run of the mill terrorists. They were a gang, but only wearing gear one might buy at Wal-Mart or any sporting goods store. They didn't wear any camouflage fatigues, but tattered jeans and oversized hooded sweatshirts.

The foot soldiers wore helmets that shrouded their faces all the way to the deep dark holes where their eyes should be. They were all armed the same way—with nasty-looking rifles whose snouts promised very big paydays. Affined to their barrels were bright lights that could see out through the night.

The leader came forward. He was dressed in black—all the way from head to toe. His face was covered with a protective helmet, but the only feature that was exposed was his eyes. He also wore combat boots, weapons and an equipment harness, and a pair of night-vision goggles rested on the top of his helmet. Dorian could see his eyes smiling and he was ready for that the man to start gloating.

"So you think you can just come right in and take me out, huh?" The man chortled at the ridiculous idea. Then he looked down to Dorian, who had a sour look on his face. "I heard you're the best there is, Gray. Yeah, I know about what happened at the woods, but if you were any of what everyone else is talking about you would be the one smirking right now. You disappoint me." Then he waved over to his men. "Waste 'em!"

Henry leaned over to Dorian and gave him a sly smile. "Sometimes two."

He reached into his pocket and pulled out four solid metal balls that had to be no more than at least two inches round. Then he threw them at the firing squad like they were ninja shuriken.

"Look out!" Screamed an urban soldier. "He's got a weapon!"

The group scattered and took cover. The small metallic spheres rolled on the ground before them. The terrorist leader looked at this display and scoffed.

"Get your asses up!" He ordered his men. "He's playing us for chumps."

His minions slowly got back to their feet; their guns were still trained on the intruders. The leader bent over and picked up one of the spheres. He expected them to be very light, but he felt something was rattling inside.

"Careful, sir." Said one of the gunmen.

But the boss waved him off and gave a small sneer. He looked over to Henry who was still bleeding from his wound and laughed in his face.

"Toys," the masked man chuckled, "you fight me with pathetic little toys. You think marbles are gonna safe you? This ain't no *Tom & Jerry* cartoon, boy."

Dorian groaned inwardly, whether by design or accident, them an had managed to hit another one of Henry's most sensitive parts. Henry's nostrils flared up and his eyes narrowed with anger.

"He did not just call me 'boy.'"

Dorian could see his best friend's hand tighten into a fist. "Wait for it…" Dorian whispered to him.

"Wait for what?" Scorned their captor.

Then came a disconcerting hiss all around them. The leader jumped and looked at the small silver ball in the palm of his hand. Something was happening. The top half of the sphere turned, exposing several secret compartments with little spouts on each side.

The man's exposed eyes widened in fear when the spouts suddenly popped out of the ball, and then released some sort of red gas.

"What the fuh…?" He gasped.

The balls exploded in this huge splash of red paint covering all the insurgents. Dorian and Henry took cover and watched the mayhem unfold. The gunmen covered their faces to shield them from the impact but it was no use. From head to toe they were soaked with cold, red paint.

One of the soldiers quickly removed his helmet because he couldn't see, and then threw it aside in a fit of rage.

"Dude, this is bullshit!" He whined, looking at his paint stained clothes. "That was totally unsanctioned and unfair!"

Dorian got out of his hiding spot and helped Henry to his feet. Henry was smoothing out his wrinkled shirt and wiping the blood red paint from his hands. Then Dorian walked up to the losing paintball team with a satisfied look on his face.

"Hey, I don't make the rules." He said to the sore loser. "I just make the difference." Then he and Henry exchanged high-fives.

The leader of the gang took off his mask and fixed his unkempt hair. He looked down at the broken shells where the paint was kept. He knew this kind of tech wasn't sold at the local five and dime. This was definitely a custom job. But he couldn't understand on how it was possible to harness all that firepower in such a small compact object. Then he looked over to see his two opponents laughing at him and his bewildered friends.

"This is why I hate playing with the rich guys." He muttered.

Before Dorian could react, there came the loud whirring sound of helicopter blades directly above them. Both paintball teams looked up to discover a NYPD chopper was hovering over their heads. Its floodlights caught them.

"Shit! Five-O!" Said one of the scared kids. He groaned at

that, cursed in frustration, his stomach churning—then heard the drumming of the chopper steadying, felt the wind of its rotors as it hovered over the yard.

"Damn!" Cried another player. "Just when the game was getting good."

"Attention to you kids down there." Exclaimed the pilot over the loudspeaker. "Leave the area. This is your last *only* warning!"

The other team's captain began to run. "Screw this! I just got out of juvie. That's the last time I'm hanging out with you guys again!"

"Fine!" Henry replied, running with Dorian. "Go cryin' home to Momma, baby!"

"I will!"

"Call you tomorrow."

The kid paused for a moment and said, "Okay."

As the other kids scattered in different directions, Henry looked over to Dorian was grinning like an idiot.

"Do you think we're going to get into trouble for this?"

Dorian's lips curled up to a disturbing smile. "Let's hope so."

For Dorian Gray, this was just another Saturday night.

CHAPTER SEVEN

*I'm really just a regular guy who has had
an incredibly blessed life.*
Bruce Willis.

The Lords' luxury penthouse occupied the top floor of a skyscraper in a ritzy uptown neighborhood in the Upper East Side that overlooked Central Park. It was consisted by the two top floors of the sleek high-rise. Flashy gold trim and black leather furniture advertised their wealth.

The Louis XIV couch—which Dorian had been afraid to sit in when he first arrived in the Lords' home for the fear that a museum guard would yell at him not to touch the exhibits—sat a beautiful wooden end table that looked to be as much an antique as the couch. It doubled as a cabinet, probably originally intended to store drinks or table linens or any of the kind.

An entire sitting room was given over to an entertainment center that included state-of-the-art CD and DVD players, shelves full of CDs and DVDs, half of which were of Dorian and Henry's favorite music and movies, a plasma widescreen television, and two very comfortable chairs.

There were also two small rooms with much smaller windows providing the same view as the picture window in the foyer. Each room had a desk, computer station, fax machine, phone, PDA (mounted to the computer), and an incredibly comfortable-looking leather chair from which to operate all of that machinery. These were Henry's parents' home offices.

The master bathroom was a lavish affair, all marble, with a claw foot bathtub and a tub-sized shower stall. Their favorite soaps and shampoos were stacked in the cabinet.

When he was younger, Dorian had gone through a phase of hating everything in his life. Now, he'd more or less made his peace with who he was and where he'd come from.

After his mother's funeral, he had to go through such a horrible school year. Every other child (with the exception of Henry) having somehow developed the idea that he was stuck-up, and determined to rub his face in the dirt—figuratively and literally.

In retrospect, maybe he had been a bit of a prick that year, or at least the last few months of it, since he was orphaned—bossy, selfish, and nasty, telling everyone what they should be doing for him. The Harrison boy hadn't listened too well, which was why the two of them were rolling around on the playground, beating the hell out of each other on a daily basis.

After several incidents, Dorian was taken to see a therapist to find a way to cope with the loss of his mother and the sudden extreme change to his life. George and Lori were with him every step of the way and they proved to be wonderful foster parents, and Henry had always been such a good friend to him. Dorian couldn't ask for anyone else to be his surrogate family. He felt like he was at peace, and over time he accepted the reality of his mother not being there for him anymore.

Henry grabbed a handful of popcorn and stuffed his face, and then chased it with an ice cold Coke. "Dude, watch this part." He said to Dorian, nearly knocking over his snacks. "The tiny guy is gonna flay the skin offa the big guy."

Dorian pointed at the screen and started laughing. "I've seen this before too…actually *twice*. Both times with you, and you don't have at least the courtesy of establishing a 'spoiler alert' before you ruin a scene."

"Don't you boys have anything better to do?" Said a voice from the kitchen. Dorian turned his head to find his stepmother Lori Lord wearing a very formfitting black cocktail dress. The ensemble was completed with a Cosmopolitan in her hand that she was rarely seen without. "If it's not video games or some gory piece of trash, do you ever engage in anything useful?"

Like topping off your Cosmo for the third time this afternoon? Dorian silently seethed.

In her younger days Lori had graced the cover on every magazine that has ever been published. Then she briefly transitioned into a short film career. One of them was a Segal flick—before he got too fat to kick. And now she spends her days organizing fundraisers and her own clothing line.

She's wearing more makeup than usual, Dorian saw. He saw tension in his stepmother's cheeks as she entered the room.

Dorian gave out a frustrating sigh. "I suppose we *could* get a bit of homework done."

Lori briefly looked at the television and quickly turned away when she saw a gruesome scene. "Uchhh! How can you watch this?"

"Don't tell me you're scared of this, Lori." Teased Dorian. "It's nothing but latex, CGI, and corn syrup with red dye #5."

Lori gave him stern look. Dorian recognized that look all too well. It was nearly identical to the one his mother had given him every time he would ever talk back to her or did something he wasn't supposed to.

"How many times do I have to tell you boys?" Lori said in a very disciplinary voice. "I don't want to see this garbage when I'm home."

"Sorry, Lori." Dorian apologized, taking the remote and stopping the DVD. "It's just a dumb movie."

Then he mentally followed with, *So was buying a diamond ankle cuff for your yappy Yorkie?*

Lori gave him a pleasant smile and proceeded to exit the room. "You are such a good boy, Dorian." Then she shifted her gaze to her son Henry. "I wish everyone is considerate as you."

Henry could see Dorian's eyes studying his mother. *Mom does look a lot like me,* Henry noticed.

Then Dorian suddenly felt a punch in his arm. He looked over to discover it was Henry who delivered the blow.

"Dude," he whispered to Dorian's ear, "stop pretending to be the good son!"

"Oh. I almost forgot, Dorian." Lori said, peering through the archway. "A package came for you this morning. I'm pretty sure it's that special edition *Grand Theft Murder* game you ordered."

"Oh, sweet." Smiled Dorian.

He got off the couch and briskly walked to the counter and found the tightly wrapped parcel right next to the fruit bowl. A look of excitement ran across his face. He had been waiting for this ever since he saw the demo play at last summer's E3 convention. All the top game magazines had built up the hype that this game would make *Splatter House* look like *Sesame Street*.

"All right, Dorian." Encouraged Henry, shifting around in his seat. "Open it up and let's kill some hookers!"

Dorian lifted the package. It was the size and width of a hardcover book. Then he looked at the return address, and he became puzzled.

Henry saw the expression on his friend's face, wondering what was the matter. "What's wrong, bro? Is it broken?"

"No," Dorian replied, inspecting the package. "It's from London."

"What? They give you a foreign game instead? I don't think you'd be able to play that on an American system."

"I don't think it's the game, Henry."

Henry gave Dorian a concerned look. "*Dorian…did you get drunk and order random stuff from the Internet again?*"

"No!" Dorian replied in defense. "I didn't order anything from London. I'm going to check my records and see what I may or may not have ordered."

"Okay," said Henry, turning the horror movie back on and taking a sip from his soda. "If you want anything I'll be right here."

Dorian took the package into his room, and began to track all the orders he made on every shopping site he visited in the last year, but it showed no record of a London purchase. He took a pair of scissors to open it. He carefully peeled away the wrapping paper to find a card. Dorian opened the envelope to see it was from his stepfather George Lord.

George often found himself socializing with people whose names and activities were the topic of articles found in every newspaper in the city, and they weren't always mentioned in the best light.

That made for some uncomfortable dealings, but George was used to easing the hurt feelings of the town's politicians, celebrities, and assorted power brokers. On rare occasions, however, he spoke bluntly at social affairs. Something told Dorian that this wasn't the usual care package.

Dear Dorian,

Sometimes opportunity unveils itself in the strangest places and thousands of miles away. I know, on occasion, you have asked about your family. You were so young when you lost your mother and of course, your father has long disappeared into the mists of mystery.

Dorian opened the package and pulled out an old skeleton key. It had to be at least a couple of centuries old, but it looked like it never aged. It was carefully preserved and it never lost its shine. Dorian studied it carefully and then looked through the box to see if there was anything else.

Nothing.

Dorian could feel his skin crawl. *Maybe there's a treasure map on the other side of the letter,* he thought. But to his disappointment, the back of the paper was completely blank. *Jeeze, George. If you're going to ask me to steal the Declaration of Independence I won't speak to you ever again.*

Dorian had known George Lord for his entire life. It wasn't too much of a stretch to say George was more of father to him. After Dorian's biological father left him, and his mother's death, George was the one who listened and encouraged Dorian to follow his own interests. With that in mind, Dorian continued to read the rest of the mysterious letter.

Not to be overly dramatic, but over the years I have told you what I can, which, sadly, wasn't much to satisfy your desire to learn more but in my recent land dabblings here in London, I came across a unique document. In my line it is quite common, but when I saw the name of Dorian Gray as its sender, I thought I would dig deeper.

As it happens, sixty years ago, your grandfather shipped a box from the Wotton estate to a property he owned in

New York. And here is the odd and occasion. This box never shipped until last month. It's now sitting at the Port Authority Yard. Before we auction off the contents to help settle your father's estate, I want to give you the chance to retrieve any personal family items you might find interesting. I am told this key might unlock the container and hopefully some of your family legacy.

Fondly,
George Lord

P.S. Please make sure Henry isn't late for school anymore!

Finally, Dorian had a clue to his father's mysterious disappearance. He was another step toward on finding out why his father had abandoned him and his mom. Then a sense of fright came over him on what he would find out. And even the possibility if he actually meet his dad.

It would be friggin' awkward. He concluded.

But if that scenario ever should come up, he would be ready. For years he thought about his father coming back for him. Always thinking on how he would react to such a scene.

Would he be angry?

Sad?

Or even glad that the only blood relative he had left would want to be part of his life.

But the first thing he would ever say to him would be, "I can forgive you for running out on me, but I can never forgive you for abandoning my mother."

This was pretty heavy for Dorian, and it wasn't even Monday yet. He wanted to go to the shipyard right away but they were closed on Sunday. This was so much to take in. He had to be careful on how he would want to approach this. Suddenly he felt like he was a character in one of those teen dramas that the female members of his class would watch.

"I just wanted to play a damn video game." He groaned.

CHAPTER EIGHT

The only greatness for man is immortality.
James Dean.

Morning bloomed brightly across the impressive Manhattan style, the rising sun shining on buildings that stood like sentinels. New York City was often called the greatest city in the world, and never did it seemed more true than on such a resplendent morning, when the metal buildings contrasted beautifully against the pale blue sky and the deeper lives of the surrounding Hudson and East Rivers, the city already awake and brimming with activity.

A bit north of Times Square, its streets already filled with men and women eager to start their day, just past the theater district of Broadway and its accompanying line of eateries know as Restaurant Row.

People were the life's blood of New York. This was never more evident than in Midtown during the morning rush hour on a cool September day.

Those beginning their workday thronged the sidewalks, jaywalked through stalled traffic, hailed cabs, climbed down steep steps into the subways, and glided overhead as the newly restored monorails.

Street vendors lined the sidewalks, hocking cheap wares—baseball caps, T-shirts, jewelry, small appliances—displayed on rolled out mats, merchandise almost all of which had "fallen off the back of a truck." Food carts squatted on corners, offering classics such as hot dogs, pretzels, and ice cream, as well as an astounding variety of ethnic snacks. Street musicians had their hats on the ground and their instruments wailing. Beggars held out their hands, importuning passersby.

The city's day started out pretty much like all the others. Manhattan was crowded with workers, shoppers, and tourists. Restaurants had opened at six for the breakfast crowd and wouldn't close again until long after midnight, their employees alternating eight-hour shifts. The museums and galleries opened at ten, while most theaters would begin their first show at noon.

There were, as always, complaints about the noise, about the traffic, about the sheer congestion of *everything*; but at the same time there was little talk of leaving. If you were born in New York you stayed there because you could never find another city that couldn't rival it. If you were born elsewhere, moving to it was more than a lifestyle change.

The sun had risen that morning—as it did every morning—by bubbling up out of Long Island Sound, climbing over the Chrysler Building, and casting its warmth down on midtown Manhattan. By dusk it would be finished and sliding quickly toward the Jersey marshes. If it sent down its warm anywhere else, New Yorkers were not aware of it, and cared less.

It was here, and it felt good. That was enough.

Dorian Gray had just one problem.

The boy had no sense of time.

No sense at all.

Times of meetings, appointments, tests…there and gone. His mind was filled with the simple joys of living each day to the fullest, and didn't do well with being bound by such inconveniences as deadlines. Timeliness was for lesser mortals.

Dorian didn't carry a watch; time on the scale kept by human society had little relevance to him. He had no real reason to hold, to conventions when it came to keeping a schedule. Which is not to say that Dorian was lackadaisical, or unconcerned with time.

He blasted up the avenue, slashing across lanes without signaling, or at least apparently thinking that blaring one's horn was an acceptable substitute for signaling. He sent a bike messenger crashing into a line of parked cars in a desperate swerve to avoid calamity, raced through yellow lights that were turning while he was still a block away, and the entire time had his radio blasting.

The 500 SL was a thing of beauty; with stylish black leather upholstery and polished maple trim elements. A powerful eight-cylinder engine walked beneath its snazzy silver hood, capable of going from zero to sixty in less than six seconds, with a maximum speed of over a hundred fifty miles per hour.

He pressed a button and the speakers erupted with explosive rock music. The car's sound system was as superb as its engine and handling, and the choice of CDs that Dorian was inspiring passionate about.

An expensive sports car with blacked out windows went speeding around the streets of downtown.

Stunt driver.
Close course.
Do not try this at home.
Dorian had seen all the commercials, and the warnings, and ignored each and every one of them.

Skyscrapers warped past Dorian in a screaming blur of steel and glass. His foot never eased on the accelerator.

He blasted past a row of parked cars, whose side windows nearly exploded in the sports car's wake. Dorian left Midtown behind in a matter of minutes. Heading east, he burned rubber along Main Street, racing recklessly through the early morning traffic.

Started drivers honked their horns and swore at the crazy son of a bitch seemingly risking life and limb as the racing luxury car zipped in front and around the other vehicles never slowing for a second.

"What the hell are you doing, you goddamn psycho?!" An angry motorist shouted at the kid who was driving a car that was probably worth three-years of his own salary.

A nonchalant Dorian Gray casually waved to him, only to be returned with a single finger.

Time herself is fickle, observed Dorian, turning the volume of his stereo to the max. Then he noticed the digital clock on his dashboard read 8:54 a.m. in bright green digits. He gave out a disconcerting sigh. *Always moving forward, never waiting.*

The car spun around the corner really quick. Pedestrians jumped out of the way in a panic. Dorian watched through his rearview mirror to see some of the people getting up from the ground, shaking their fists at him, and screaming profanities. He shifted his gaze back at the clock to find two minutes have already passed.

Yet it's said somewhere that punctuality is the thief of time. He admitted, before he drove down a very thin alley and found his way back onto the main street again. *My guess is that humorless 1st period math teachers armed with detention slips didn't coin that saying.*

St. Pascal's Academy was highly known as the school for the obnoxiously well to do. And also the notorious stomping grounds of their obnoxious offspring.

What resulted was a monument to wealth that beggared modern conceptions of the term but also exemplified rather extraordinary good taste. No expense had been spared in the academy's construction. It was considered something that the students might actually *enjoy*, more than a proclamation of excess. The main building was a towering four stories, allowing for a community view of the surrounding courtyard.

The school was an old and gothic building with ivy crawling up the front of the right wing. It is the most exclusive school in the city. The student body consisted of the sons and daughters of senators, attorneys, doctors, and many of the elite.

Adrian Singleton, Hetty Merton, and Geoff Clouston were standing by the school parking lot smoking. They were Dorian's friends, and they all had unlimited access to money, booze and whatever else they wanted. But what they valued the most was that all of their parents were rarely home, so privacy was always expected.

The sound of the warning bell rang and it caused Adrian to smile. "That's gonna be a C-note, G-Man." He said to Geoff, extending his hand and waved his fingers in anticipation.

"It's not over yet." Geoff replied confidently.

"Listen, junior," Adrian snapped at him, "the bet was that he would get here before nine and the bell already rang. Game's over!"

Then they heard a low rumble in the distance. Out of the corner of his eye, Adrian saw something that caused him to drop the very cigarette out of his mouth. It was Dorian's Mercedes roaring toward them, and it wasn't slowing down. was a Mercedes, glinting in the sunlight. It screeched up and stopped about two feet short of Adrian. He didn't take so much as a single step backward. He'd be damned if he gave Dorian Gray the satisfaction. He knew perfectly well that Dorian was behind the wheel; he wouldn't even let the chauffer drive it.

Dorian slammed on the brakes and turned the wheel to execute a double spin and set the car in park right in front of Adrian who was frozen with fear. Dorian screeched to a halt by the entrance to the school near the curb.

"Jesus!" Adrian gasped, thinking he was about to have a heart attack.

The door opened and Dorian emerged onto the sidewalk. He breathed the air, the smoky, earthly air, and smelled food and sun and sourness. The sunlight seemed harsher, somehow but it was still bright and golden. He could see giant buildings towering by and the trees, and hear the trembling, racing cars that choked the streets. Dorian saw Adrian hand over his money to Geoff, who was busy counting it.

"You were playing it close to the vest this time, Dorian." He said to the crazy stunt driver.

"Well, excuse me for being a good showman." Dorian replied, watching all of those greenbacks Geoff had in his closed hand that were waving in the breeze. "And you were gonna split that with me, right, dude?"

"Of course." Said Geoff, giving Dorian his share of the winnings. "Now, shall we?" He motioned over to the doors.

"Yes, we shall."

As soon as Dorian entered the school his watch alarm sounded off on 9:00 a.m. on the dot. Then he looked over to Hetty, who was wearing her hair differently today.

She saw him as golden and sunny. She would love to run her hand up and down the soft dark hair on the back of his arm. Then she would place her hand on his chest to feel his well-developed chest.

She was so different. She was so dark, all gravity, all earth. She lifted the shade do much. Sometimes when she was with him, she felt like one of those dark planets, invisible to the naked eye, until illuminated by the sun to become a star at night.

She was, indeed, hard not to adore. With that luscious red hair…with that exquisite mouth that could start as a pout that could crush someone's heart, then transform a smile that could send it soaring into the heavens. And those stunning green eyes that could evoke a spring day in the dead of winter.

Dorian looked her up and down, giving her a lecherous grin. "Are you part of my winnings, gorgeous?"

Hetty rolled her eyes at him. "Dorian, you don't have to be a douche like these clowns."

Adrian nudged Dorian. "Dude, heh, she called you a douche."

Dorian shrugged good-naturedly at her, and smiled as he admired the view of Hetty leaving. "Hey, at least I'm making progress."

"You'll be wasting your time." Warned Adrian. "I hear she's a tough nut to crack."

"I love a challenge." Dorian replied, walking through the hall. "But I'm not interested in nuts."

As he walked, all the girls turned their heads to stare at him. They were all enamored with him. He dated. No commitments, nothing that could be called a relationship, but he had no trouble finding attractive young women to share an evening with. No surprise there—he had the world in the palm of his hand. And he was handsome, as handsome as any leading man, and though he wasn't much of a dancer but he was socially adept enough to get through any reasonable social situation.

The girls that were standing in front of him didn't have the courage to talk to Dorian, except for one. Dorian wasn't shy. And he knew he was attractive. He just didn't see the point in calling attention to himself. Most women were turned on by his Mercedes, his $400 haircut, and the designer suits he wore on a daily basis (hint: they were not from Men's Wearhouse). He recognized the girl in front of him as Kari Jensen, the girl that sat behind him in political science. She had soft bangs across her forehead, parted in the center, nearly down to her dark eyebrows.

"Hi, Dorian," she said, twirling a strand of her long blonde hair, "are you going to the thingy tonight?"

Dorian looked confused. "'Thingy?'" He asked, trying not to laugh.

"That's the technical term for it." Quipped Adrian, as he opened his locker.

"Oh, thingy!" Dorian suddenly remembered, slapping his forehead. "The extra credit assignment for Haskins' class. It's an artsy-fartsy dance…uh, thingy."

"I bet Kari wants a thingy from you." Joked Geoff. "'Oh, Dorian, I want your thingy. I want it so-o-o-o bad.'"

Dorian flashed him a questionable look. "Sometimes I wonder about you, Geoff."

"Couldn't we just see that one ballet movie with Natalie Portman?" Suggested Adrian, rubbing his hands together.

"Yeah," agreed Geoff, "It's only worth watching for just the one scene she had with Mila."

Adrian rolled his eyes in revulsion. "Well, it least be better than the last play they did from a couple of months ago."

"*Macbeth* by William Shakespeare." Spoke Hetty, remembering the production fondly. "I went and seen it three times. Did you enjoy it?"

"Couldn't understand a friggin' word." Spat Adrian. "If that friggin' idiot wants to write friggin' plays why don't he learn how to speak proper friggin' English first."

Hetty heaved an aggravating sigh, shaking her head in disapproval of Adrian's childish outburst.

"Philistine." She said under her breath.

"Bitch."

Dorian laughed to himself as two of his closest friends went at it. Then his levity turned to dread when he remembered he had Mr. Haskins' English class. The old man had it in for

Dorian. Everyday he made Dorian an example by calling on him to answer the hardest answer in class and arranging him to sit where he could keep his eyes on him. Before Dorian entered the classroom he said a silent prayer, took a deep breath and plunged into the inevitable.

Why couldn't I see the ballet now instead of this class?

* * *

It was most of every student in New York's St. Pascal Academy thought was a typical afternoon in the life of Dorian Gray IV. A quick stop at a gallery, as he managed to get the phone number of the pretty receptionist. The he had an afterschool snack at a hip downtown bistro. A dash cut to the country club, where he decided *not* to play golf but instead chased the female employees around with his clubs. And it was concluded with a trip back to the Upper East Side, waving at passersby from the window of his Mercedes SL.

But this was all the beginning.

Dorian took out some of his frustrations by sparring with his ex-Navy SEAL trainer in the boxing ring at the exclusive gymnasium. It was regulation size, complete with springy floor and padded posts. The downside was that Dorian didn't really know how to box, so his trainer tended to pound the hell out of him and lecture Dorian while he did it. Dorian had private suspicions that his trainer was making the lessons harder then they needed to be, so he could take an extra shot at this snot nosed kid once in a while. Revenge, maybe, for some of the situations, Dorian had gotten him into. If that was true, Dorian couldn't blame him; but it didn't make the sparring any easier.

Former Sergeant Michael Steele didn't take any crap.

He was born with a different name in South Africa, and he was the fourth of five children, and the youngest boy, he had the misfortune to be on the wrong side of it. Shortly after his mother died, when he was sixteen, his father managed to secure a way for them to immigrate to the United States. Upon arrival, his father declared their name to be Steele, and gave all his children new names. They were now Christopher, Paul, Michael, Rachael, and Sarah, because those, their father said, sounded like American names, and he would hit them until they stopped. Not being fools, all the children learned quickly to think of themselves with their new identities.

In gratitude to his new home, Michael enlisted in the SEALs on his eighteenth birthday. Shortly thereafter, he was sent overseas to fight in Afghanistan. His father was happy that he did so. Christopher, who was three years older than Michael, moved to Boston and became a police officer, while Paul became a FBI agent. Rachael took up a career as a social worker, and as for Sarah, though women could serve in all branches of the military, she had no interest in doing so, preferring a career in sports medicine.

Michael Steele became alive for the first time in the desert. He had always succeeded academically, but mostly by rote. He was a fast learner, but he never had much enthusiasm for it. The two years of school he'd attended since immigration were difficult, as Michael spoke with a thick accent, which made him the target of teasing by his peers and made it difficult to derive any kind of enjoyment from the learning experience.

Combat though, he took joy in that, especially when that combat was against the enemies of the United States of America. And in the desert, nobody cared about his accent, except for a few idiots, and they all shut up once they saw Michael Steele in action.

It didn't take long for him to distinguish himself, and work his way up the ranks. He was leading his fellow soldiers into combat after only a few weeks, and his men would follow him anywhere. He had a natural charisma, and aptitude for tactics, and an especially fine ability to kill Saddam's foot soldiers.

Michael learned many things in the desert, but the most important thing was that, continuing to what his father had always taught him, life was neither precious nor sacred.

Life was, in fact, cheap.

If life were such a glorious, magnificent, wonderful thing, then it wouldn't be so easy to take it away.

If life were a great gift, then he wouldn't be able to kill a fellow human being with one hand, as he did often in Afghanistan.

After he was discharged Michael found work as a bodyguard and head of security for several high-class celebrities and politicians. Now his current job is to train some pompous rich kid how to throw a punch without breaking a nail.

"Cover," Michael said after sticking a jab into Dorian's nose. "Don't drop. Hands up. Jab-jab-hook-uppercut, jab."

Eyes watering from the jab, Dorian threw the combination.

Michael Steele flicked the punches aside and said, "You're dropping your hook. I got a clear line to your button. Again."

Dorian threw the same exact combination and apparently made the same exact mistake, as he was leading up the hook the former seal snapped another jab over his guard and into his mouth.

It was even harder than the last one.

Dorian started snapping a series of punches into his opponent's gloves, working up a rhythm, then added an MMA-style elbow just for punctuation.

"What's with the elbow?" Michael said.

"It's time to expand my arsenal," Dorian said, and threw another one. "Jujitsu, muay thai…"

"We're boxing here," Michael reminded his overzealous student. "Get your gloves up and fight like a…"

Dorian swung by with side punch, but Michael caught it and flipped him over. Dorian met the mat hard with a loud slam.

"Hey, you're not supposed to do that!" Dorian complained, rubbing his temples.

"Listen, Dorian," Michael said with authority in his voice, "I don't tolerate any bullshit in my gym. You're here to learn, not to screw around. I'm a former Navy SEAL, not a babysitter. If you continue to treat me this way consider this your last session."

Dorian unfastened his headgear and got up to face his mentor. "Come on, Mike, people don't fight like that anymore. I want to learn some new stuff."

"My gym, my rules." Michael said coldly, tossing Dorian a towel. "Go hit the showers, and come back if you're serious on listening what I have to say."

Michael walked out of the gym, without looking back at Dorian. The boy blotted the sweat off his face and smiled.

"I like this guy," he chuckled. "Maybe I'll keep him around for a little while longer."

CHAPTER NINE

I regard the theatre as the greatest of all art forms, the most immediate way in which a human being can share with another the sense of what it is to be a human being.
Oscar Wilde.

"I'd rather take Haskins' final than go to some lame ballet." Dorian grimaced as he struggled into his dress shirt.

"It might do you some good on seeing some actual entertainment besides those gory slasher movies you and Henry always watch." Said Lori, leaning against the door.

"I have never been to the ballet before, Lori." Dorian replied buttoning up his shirt. "I don't know what it's all about. It's just a bunch of people in tights prancing around the stage to classical music."

"It's not that hard," Lori assured him. "Just get listen to the music and get swept by the story."

"What story? There's no dialogue in ballet."

"Not all language has to be spoken."

Dorian got so distracted on tonight's event, he forgot how to simply tie a necktie. No matter how many times he had done this in the past, it was new to him.

Lori frowned. "What's wrong, Dorian?"

Struggling with his tie, Dorian replied, "I just can't get this to work."

Lori walked over to him and held the both ends of his silk tie. "Do you remember the thing George told you a long time ago?"

Dorian thought back to when George Lord helped him with his tie for his mother's funeral. He recited this story that would help him remember how to do it.

"Does it go; bunny boy, bunny boy…"

"No," Lori laughed, "that's for tying shoes. But it *does* involve a rabbit."

Then a smile came upon his face. "Now I remember," he said, laughing and taking the two ends. "The rabbit hops over the log. The rabbit crawls under the log. The rabbit runs around the log."

"One more time because he's trying to outsmart the fox." Lori joined in.

"The rabbit dives through his rabbit hole safe and sound."

"Safe and sound."

With the help of the story George had taught him, Dorian successfully tied his silk necktie into a well-executed Windsor knot.

"Thanks for the help, Lori."

Lori hid a knowing smile. She held his suit jacket ready for him to slip over his broad shoulders.

"Now you're ready for a night out on the town."

"Not yet," Said Dorian, pulling out a pair of sunglasses out of his pocket.

Lori shook her head and smirked.

Placing the glasses over his eyes, Dorian smiled. "Now I'm ready."

Designer sunglasses shielded his eyes against glare as he glanced causally out the floor-to-ceiling windows toward the city. His Italian suit fitted his body well, which made him look more slender than athletic. His hair was conservative but stylish. He attracted no serious attention.

Henry Lord shifted uncomfortably in the back of the chauffer driven Lincoln Town car. He always felt the way whenever he was riding with his father George. Henry would occasionally sneak looks at him, while fervently wishing that he were somewhere else—anywhere else—at this particular moment in time.

George Lord, for his part, has never glanced at Henry for at last twenty blocks. Instead he would be utterly absorbed in coordinating his day of meetings on his iPad. Henry's attempts at casual conversation had always been met with occasional grunts or nods, and not much more.

George radiated an odd mix of power and barely controlled anger. Henry had never been able to figure out just with whom his father was mad, exactly.

The world, it seemed.

He was frustrated at all he wished to accomplish…and able to focus only on failures rather than success. And Henry was often the target of his misplaced frustration. At least, that was what Henry chose to believe.

He had never forgotten his last birthday where his father had thrown a sizable bash, with a guest list comprised mostly of George's friends, with a couple of Henry's fair weather friends tossed in for appearances. It was more of a business opportunity for strategic meeting and greeting. But George had gotten himself seriously liquored up as the evening progressed. That was unusual for him. Visually, he prided himself on his total control.

Late in the evening, however, Henry had found himself alone in a hallway with his dad hanging with one arm on his son and speaking in a voice filled with alcohol and contempt.

"I look at you, Henry," he'd said, "and I see myself at your age…except without the potential for greatness."

Henry had gone to bed shortly thereafter, and hadn't come out for two days, claiming a headache. His father, mortified over what he'd said while in his cups, finally coaxed him out of his room with a snowboard he'd been coveting and a vacation at a ski resort in Aspen. It had been a glorious outing, but the circumstances behind it still rankled.

Dorian was almost relaxed in the leather upholstery of the luxury car as the chauffer drove him to the theatre. Dorian was vaguely annoyed with the driver, who was wearing his expensive uniform, but cheap grocery-store cologne with a name that implied a wild animal. Below its cheap spice and lime notes, Dorian could sniff the driver's natural smell, a scent redolent of putrid meat and canned sauerkraut. The tailored jacket and expensive tie filled to refine the man's appearance, serving only to accentuate the crudeness he would never overcome.

A huge crowd had turned out for the opening night of *The Firebird*. A line of eager theatergoers stretched around the block. Journalists and photographers were on hand to cover the premiere.

Dorian could think of lots of places he would rather be than the ballet that night. Curiously, most of them involved risking his life in another one of those thrill-seeking activities both he and Henry enjoyed. While another option was to laze around the TV watching very bad programing.

Yet as Dorian, outfitted in the best-looking clothes money could buy. Not the kind just anybody would get off the rack but tailor-made. He and Henry filled the void scoping out some of the promising talent—not the kind one would find on the stage but some of the hottest girls they had ever seen were stepping out of black stretched limousines and accompanied by men who were old enough to be their fathers. They were all elegantly dressed and wouldn't talk to you unless you have a very big bank account.

The Firebird ballet is a story of magic and love. It tells the story of Prince Ivan's journey to win the heart of his princess, but first, he had to get past the evil magician, Kostolei.

If it were like anything similar to *The Lord of the Rings* movies, Dorian and Henry would not be complaining. Too bad it wasn't in IMAX.

Dorian took his seat and was sinking into the plush upholstery when he sniffed the faint smell of vanilla and gardenia, the high notes of an expensive perfume. He looked at the girls' ankles, which stemmed up to perfectly long and creamy calves, then thighs, which knew no equal. His eyes ran up in tailored mini-dress to a tightly cinched waist and a décolletage that boasted two firm full, yet natural breasts. Dorian Gray could spot silicone a mile away and knew immediately that these were the real deal—they would be hot to his touch.

It wasn't the most comfortable seat Dorian had ever sat in. The cushion was threadbare, and there was a spring that seemed determined to lacerate his left thigh. But for all of that, it might as well have been a throne in Buckingham Palace for the sense of elation it gave him.

Dorian's face and body flushed with sudden warmth; the same expectant warmth he had come to associate with the theater, where, sitting so close to the stage, he could feel the nap of the immense velvet curtain, soft and heavy against his face, as if it imposed itself into the air. He did not want the curtain to open.

Dorian shifted in his seat and waited. Even though this is all recollection, even though it's all happening in a flash while a demented cackling was filtering dimly through his subconscious, but it still felt as it were taking forever. Finally, the orchestra swelled and the thick, red velvet curtain parted. Dorian took a deep breath and then grin and bared it.

Upon hearing the orchestra's music swelled Dorian snapped awake. He looked around the theater in a panicked daze and checked his watch to see that only five minutes have passed since the show began. He rubbed his temples and gave out an exaggerated sigh.

"Is it over yet?" He whined over to Henry, like an impatient child.

"Get your phone." Ordered Henry, who was checking out his Blackberry. "I just scored with 'plant' in *Words with Friends*."

An irritated audience member peered his head over between the two boys and shushed them. "That is the *third* time I told you to be quiet."

Henry gave the man a disaffected look. "Good, you can count."

"Well, you can count on me on meeting you in the parking lot after the show." The man snarled.

Henry's eyes widened and realized this disgruntled patron of the arts was not kidding. The vein on the guy's forehead was about to pop. Henry quickly turned his head and faced the stage.

"Did that just happened?" He whispered to Dorian.

"Yeah, that just happened." Dorian smirked. "So far it was the best thing I saw all night."

The star of the dance emerged on stage with such poise and grace. She was in a more elaborating outfit that made her stand out than the rest of the dancers. She was beautiful with a sense of innocence that glowed around her.

Dorian suddenly sat up in his seat and stared at her in awe. He totally forgot he was at a crowded theatre and it was just him and the pretty girl who was dancing on stage. He looked at her as if she was the most beautiful girl in the world. Slender, willowy, her legs impressively long, the dancer wore her long brown hair in a tight bun.

"Oh…" He felt the air leaving his body.

It was a pop-up book of bold wonderment. It is a respectful of fairy tale details but as an earthly touch and an often-amusing spin on minutiae. The stage was conceived with a forest of thick, ominous trees with spiky, finger-like branches topped with red leaves and spewing smoke.

Reality and fantasy began to blend all together; the barrier between them broke down. Dorian was no longer in his seat. He was floating out of it, reacting toward Sybil.

She stretched her hands toward him, laughing gaily, and then he was above her.

But Dorian knew this wasn't happening. He was caught up in the fantasy.

Broadway has its spectacle. Off-Broadway has a sort of charm. But this…glorified recital in the bowls of Soho is absolutely sublime. Her name is Sybil Vane. She cuts the air like a floating spirit shot from a cannon.

She danced across the stage as if she owned it. Sybil was beautiful. She had large dark eyes and a sensual smile; her face revealed every emotion she felt. She was grace under pressure and the perfectly calm, collected heart of a hurricane.

Something about the way she graced the stage, made Dorian felt if she was dancing just for him.

Tonight, though, was not a preview. Tonight was opening night. There was an additional charge in the air, and on intensity Dorian hadn't felt when he attended shows both on and off Broadway. He knew this was a make-or-break situation for some of the dangers. It was as if the entirety of Broadway is somehow spiritually poised, like a lion in the high weeds, waiting to see if the show would join the pride or instead become prey for the unforgiving fury of every theater critic in the city.

Dorian had remained on the far side of the street when he saw the theatergoers finally emerging from the ballet. He felt it would probably be better to wait until everyone had dispersed before approaching Sybil Vane. She would be doubtless be annoyed with him, and he didn't want to embarrass himself in front of her, and some of the audience members or the cast mates.

So he had leaned against the wall of the nearest building. The streetlight in front of him had a blown-out bulb, so he was effectively cloaked in darkness. From this vantage point he waited until he saw Sybil emerge from the stage door, another ballerina following her.

As she stood there and signed autographs for her fans, he ran through all things he was going to say to her. If there was any way to smooth this over—any turn of phrase he could come up with—he was determined to do it.

And then, as he prepared to cross the street, he saw a guy came up to Sybil. She threw her arms around him, and suddenly everything just hazed over and went away.

By the time the world came into focus and the thundering in his temple eased, both Sybil and the man, who was obviously her new significant other, were gone.

Dorian Gray adored Sybil Vane. There was no question in his mind about that. She was, indeed, hard not to adore. With that luscious brown hair…with that exquisite mouth that could start a pout that could crush someone's heart, then transform into a smile that could send it soaring into the sky…with those stunning green eyes that could evoke a spring day in the dead of winter…with that laughter as light as a meringue…from head to toe, the girl was as close to absolute perfection as any high school junior girl could be.

CHAPTER TEN

There are only two kinds of women, the plain and the colored.
Lord Henry Wotton.

There was a light breeze, but not one scrap of paper was blowing in the street.

He glanced up at the high, arched floor-to-ceiling windows, set like large jewels in the marble façade. The glittering attendees were clearly visible inside—Manhattan's wealthiest, most powerful, and most philanthropic—here to have a good time.

Those people lived in a completely different city...a completely different world...than the residents of Brooklyn or the Bronx. Dorian stopped for a moment, smiling and basking with the lifestyle and society reporters who thronged the sidewalk. He posed, allowing the photographers to snap his picture.

He smiled and charmed. There was a show to give. Applause and cheers and the flickering of dozens of flashbulbs washed over him. He kept his arms out and let it happen. When it started to seem self-indulgent, he let it go on a little bit more. He assured the paparazzi that each of his female acquaintances were just good friends. The truth was, as amazing as these women were, Dorian couldn't allow himself to get close to any of them. He enjoyed their company, and their quality and variety underlined his playboy image. Maybe he could have a serious relationship—someday. But, right now, he had to meet that ballerina.

Dorian and Henry dotted through the crowd of hangers-on and well-wishers were a smattering of real live innovators. Dorian caught sight of a soap opera actor.

"Nice to see you, man," he said.

Dorian gave him the high-five he wanted, and even managed to crack a smile for the cameras. Then he gave Henry a quick look when a gaggle of college-aged women clustered around him wanting pictures with him.

"Not now, ladies," Henry said, and hustled Dorian down the corridor.

"Let's get in there," Dorian said, gesturing over the entrance.

"You okay, man?"

"Aces," Dorian replied.

He shoved open the polished double doors and entered the foyer. The noise struck him first. The background music of the chamber quartet playing in the corner set the mood. The music was filled through the buzz of lively conversation. The clink of drinking glasses added soft accents to the music as soberly clad waiters offered trays of cocktails and hors d'oeuvres around the room.

Dorian strode across the inlaid marble floor of the foyer, into a high-ceilinged ballroom lit but a pair of immense chandeliers. Lavish silk curtains draped the gracefully arched windows. A hand-woven room-sized carpet softened the gleaming hardwood floor. Priceless paintings entranced the room's elegance, while gilded mirrors reflected the glittering spectacle.

The Whitechapel was a reasonably upscale rendezvous that was popular to New York's elite. Originally, Dorian had been concerned that he wasn't going to be able to put thoughts of what he saw outside the theatre behind him, but was now pleasantly surprised to find an increasing spring in his step as he approached the restaurant. During evening hours, an elevator in the front lobby operated express from the grand floor to the Whitechapel, and Dorian stepped into it feeling positively elated. Whether shellacking his confidence might have taken was all wasted away in a flood of good feeling that this evening would turn out well.

The Whitechapel was Manhattan's newest dining sensation. It was possible to spend a middle-class worker's monthly salary on a meal for six, if one went a little heavy on the wine. The food *was* spectacular. But it wasn't the cuisine that drew most of its clientele to the Whitechapel; it was the chance to be seen, and to let the world know that money was no object.

Prompted by the cheery ding of the elevator, he and Henry stepped out on the top floor and glanced around with uncertainty.

It was glittering place of white linen, crystal, and silver tableware, and the aroma of richly sauced dishes. A sculptured fountain with a peel at its center ran along one whole side of the establishment. There was a low murmur of conversation and the *clink* of spoons and forks against china.

There was an animated conversation already in progress between an expensively dressed, middle-aged man and the much younger women who was obviously his wife.

Expensive jewelry glittered on women in designer evening gowns, who were escorted by men in tailored silk suits and tuxedos. Champagne glasses clinked. Waiters wove through the party, offering fresh drinks and refreshments.

Through all the elegant guests, Dorian recognized Alan Campbell. Alan lived in the same building with him and Henry, and he was a successful video game designer. His last three video games were bestsellers, and rumors were speculating that two of such had been optioned for a film series and toy line.

"Hey, Alan," called Dorian.

Alan turned and smiled over to Dorian and Henry. "Hey, guys, come on over. What brings you here?"

"We had to come to the ballet for a school assignment." Dorian replied, taking a sip of his champagne. "How did you like it?"

"That ballet was brutal." Said, feigning a headache. "I thought that with a name like *The Firebird*, there would at least be some cool pyrotechnics."

"I just have to point that out in my essay review for Haskins' class." Retorted Henry, who pilfered a chocolate éclair from a passing waiter. "Right, Dor?"

Dorian didn't hear him. He was too busy looking through the crowd for the prima ballerina that had bewitched him. Then he felt a nudge on his arm.

"Dorian," Henry repeated, "did you hear me?"

Dorian snapped awake. "Huh? Uh, yeah."

Out of the elevator came Kate Windbrook and right beside her was the star of the show Sybil Vane. They both looked naturally beautiful, and also fashionable but not overdone.

There she was, Dorian silently announced. *Sacred. Total cornball, but there's no other word for it.*

Kate stepped into the already crowded restaurant, waving to someone she recognized. Sybil hesitated at the door.

Is Kate going to desert me before we even get inside? She wondered. *I don't know anyone here—except for some of the kids from school.*

Everyone applauded as the two girls walked into the restaurant. Sybil walked past Dorian, who was looking like he was struck by Cupid's arrow.

He struggled to speak as his eyes met hers. "I, uh, thought you..."

Sybil smiled and held up her arms for an embrace. Dorian was surprised that his pathetic opening line actually worked. So he spread his arms wide open to receive her.

He took a deep breath to steady his pounding heart, and then took two steps toward Sybil. That was as far as he got before a young man, with a timing bordering on the supernatural, swept in while Dorian was still a good five yards away, stepped in behind Sybil, partly obscuring her from view. He put his arm around her. Dorian gulped deeply, his Adam's apple bobbing up and down. Well, that was certainly all he needed to see.

"Isaac, you came!" She exclaimed, running past Dorian and into the arms of young man, giving him a friendly kiss.

"Well, I needed the extra credit!" Isaac Peterson laughed, giving Sybil a big hug.

"Charming." She giggled.

Dorian looked over to Alan, who was busy ogling an attractive female server catering a platter of shrimp cocktails. "What's her story?"

"I don't know." Alan replied, tapping his chin. "But I'm going to find out."

Dorian scoffed at Alan's response. "Not Tits McGee, Alan, that girl over there."

Alan looked over to see Sybil with Isaac. "Oh, you mean Sybil? I hear she's a junior—hangs with the emo set."

Then Alan let his eyes wander down the front of the server's dress. She had a nice, firm body. Alan was the textbook example of a "Harassanova." He thought of himself as the great lover Casanova, but the only reason a girl would ever consider on going out with him would be because she wanted him off her back. Alan was handsome in a delicate way, with high cheekbones and a narrow chin, and thick hair. Prettily pale, with startling green eyes. His body was as feminine as it was masculine.

"I wouldn't hurt you," said Alan, biting down on his lip. "I know I'm too big. You could be on top."

The server's head shot straight up and turned quickly to face Alan. Her hair flew wildly as she snarled at him. "What did you just say to me?"

Alan's jaw dropped and a bead of sweat formed on his forehead. "Oh, shit." He gasped. "Did I say that out loud?"

The server slapped him so hard in the face that it echoed throughout the whole restaurant. It was even loud enough to be heard over the music.

"Pervert!" She yelled at him, storming out of the floor.

Alan held his left cheek in pain, fighting back tears. "Didn't hurt!" He told her, as he tried to keep his voice from cracking.

Dorian moved through the sea of glitzy guests, shaking hands, smiling, clapping people on the back and laughing in all the right places and all at the right jokes. Dorian shambled on, grinning, shaking hands, and trading pleasantries. Then he grabbed another drink from a passing waiter. He downed his drink and slammed the empty glass down on a nearby table.

He was so close to Sybil, but then a gorgeous blonde stepped out in front of him. He had found that, in cases of hot women appearing and seeming to know him, this course of action usually worked better than the sheepish but more honest have-we-met routine. Typically he would remember their previous interactions as the conversation went along, and until then, he could shovel the B.S. as well as anyone. It was what worked for him.

So of course she threw him a curveball by saying, "Pleased to meet you, Dorian," and thereby proving himself to be the exact opposite of the typical groupie-wannabe who came up pretending to know him so she could get to know him. By approaching the situation in a straightforward and honest manner, she utterly destabilized all of Dorian's protocols, defenses, and strategies where women were concerned.

"Meet me?" Dorian repeated. The feeling of the conversation changed and he switched automatically into smooth-talking Dorian mode. She was worth knowing, that was for damn sure. "Wait, I'm sorry…we don't know each other? That ends now. Let's start with names, miss…?"

"Oh, we haven't met personally," the woman said, holding her glass of champagne, "but you know my sister."

Puzzled, Dorian asked, "Who is your sister?"

"Audrey."

"Audrey…?"

"Audrey-let's-not-do-it-in-the-shower."

With a flick of her wrist she threw the champagne right in his face. Several nearby guests gasped and stared at the scene. Dorian didn't even react; he just stood there and took it.

"I hope you rot in hell." Cursed the woman before she stormed out of the restaurant.

Henry, who had witnessed the episode, came to Dorian's side with a towel he got from one of the servers.

"Hey, Dor, you O.K.?" Henry asked, handing him the towel. "Who was that?"

Dorian wiped his face gently. "Wish I knew, but I'm a friend of her sister's."

He seemed to forget everything about Audrey-what's-her-name, and her brash sister. Only one young woman in particular caught his eye. She was not with his usual entourage, however, but instead seated out the next table. Sybil appeared to be alone, gazing into a compact and doing some touchups on her makeup. Then he saw a bevy of beauties gathering around her like a team huddle.

"How come you aren't checking out Dorian Gray, like the rest of the girls?" One of the dancers asked Sybil, as they scanned the crowd. "Look at him! You can see their heads turn to watch him as he walks across the room."

"And some of the men's as well." Sybil shot her friend a look out of the corner of her eyes. "That's one of the things I admire about you, Cecilia. Your keen powers of observation." She shrugged. "Word is, Gray's a pretty decent guy for a trust fund baby. What's not to like?"

Cecilia shook her head. "Whatever's attracting them, it's more than the money. He draws women like iron to a magnet."

* * *

Dorian made his way slowly through the crowds, circling Sybil, his eyes never leaving her face. She didn't notice him at first. It was the intensity of his gaze that finally alerted her, and then when she suddenly realized who it was, she stared at him in surprise.

There was something very different about him.

Something she couldn't quite figure out, but something strangely seductive all the same. She glided across the room who caught so much interest—everything seemed to slow down, men trying not to gawk and falling, women trying not to stare with equal lack of success, and the murmur of conversation and the clink of china and glassware subsiding over so slightly.

Dorian walked on over to the bar and Kate was standing there by herself. She gave him a smile.

"Hi," Dorian sweetly greeted her, "Kate, right?"

She smiled even wider. She wanted to talk to Dorian Gray all year and he came up to her. Kate couldn't help by staring at him wantonly.

It was a chance to talk to Dorian—and possibly to *flirt* with Dorian.

A chance to gaze into those soft blue eyes, to listen to his beautiful voice, and enjoy his radiant smile.

Kate Windbrook, don't get carried away. Is it our fate to meet, Dorian?

Sybil stepped into the crowded, noisy little room, watching Kate in the center, already helping herself to a glass of wine from a tray, playfully grabbing an hors d'oeuvre from the hand of some guy she obviously knew and popping it into her mouth.

She could see Kate's eyes flashing when she was talking to Dorian Gray.

"Dorian," Kate finally said, gathering the courage to speak to him, "I'm so glad you…"

"Your friend, Sybil…"

Kate paused in midsentence. A disappointing frown formed on her lips. "Oh. Yes. Of course." She looked over to Sybil and Isaac's direction. "They're just friends, but she…"

"You're a sweetheart!" Dorian said, grabbing a drink from the bar and began to make his move with the girl of his dreams.

Kate rested her hand alongside her face as a tear began to stream down her cheek. "Don't I wish," she said, before excusing herself to the ladies' room to reapply her mascara.

Sybil had sculpted features and piercing blue eyes that a man could take a headfirst drive into and never want to emerge. Add to that the fact that she not only had a body that wouldn't quit, but a body that no one would ever think of firing once it was in their employ. A couple of guys were standing off to the side, eyeing her with a drunken longing, although it was impossible to determine whether they would wind up hitting on her or just admiring her from afar.

That's my cue, Dorian thought gleefully. He gulped down the last of his drink and made his way across the room.

Dorian stood before Sybil, he cleared his throat gathering her attention over to him. She turned her head to see the man all her friends had been talking about all night.

Dorian had rehearsed on what he was going to say to Sybil since he left the theater. He opened his mouth, but the words didn't come out.

He was drawing a complete blank.

What the hell is wrong with me? Dorian panicked. *Say something, you idiot.* **Anything.**

Henry snapped his fingers in front of Dorian's face to catch his attention.

"Hey," he whispered, and nodded toward Sybil. "Say something."

Dorian squared his shoulders, which struck him as rather funny. Dorian couldn't have looked more serious if he'd been preparing to enter a ring with a maddened bull, armed with only a dishtowel. He approached Sybil, who saw him coming. She looked expectantly from Dorian to Henry and then back to Dorian, and Henry waited for his friend to say something.

And waited.

And waited.

The moment morphed from energy-charged to awkward. Sybil tilted her head slightly, expectantly, like a dog trying to pick up a high-pitched noise.

She reacted in a way that Dorian wasn't accustomed to. She stared at him as if he were some new virus that was attempting to intrude on her system.

Was his mouth as dry as hers? Was his heart pounding the same fandango? Usually he was so smooth. Now he was fumbling like a fool. A fool who was has fallen desperately in love.

He tried to speak, but the words reached his tongue, only to slide back and away to some black and distant place.

Desperate to have matters progress, Henry stepped forward and said to Sybil, "Hi. How are you doing?"

Sybil smiled in return. "Hey." She said conversationally, and waited once more for Dorian to say something.

It was difficult for Henry to get a read off her. It could be she was just being…or there might be someone interest. He needed Dorian to keep it going in order to tell for sure.

Dorian's jaw twitched once, twice more, which was good since it indicated that he was, in fact, alive.

"Man, you really tripped the light fantastic!" Dorian blurted out. Henry looked at him like he was a crazy man, and then he silently laughed. "Jeez," Dorian said, feeling embarrassed, "did those words really come out of my mouth?"

"Sweet." Sybil said, brushing the hair behind her ear looking a bit coy. "Odd. But sweet. Thank you…I think." Then she smelled something in the air. "What smells like booze?"

Dorian remembering the champagne incident from earlier, smiled. "It's my new cologne. It's Lindsay Lohan's new fragrance."

Sybil laughed softly. "I know cologne is made with some alcohol, but it looks like she used the whole damn bottle."

The words dropped from her rich red lips like diamonds and pearls. Her bright violet eyes twinkled from frames of long black lashes. She stared deeply, with the hint of a smile on a face rich in dramatic planes. Dorian saw it as an approving smile as he looked her over salaciously, then set his sights on her full mouth.

"Would you like to dance?" Dorian asked, offering his hand. "If you are not tired, of course."

Sybil gave him half a smile. "I dance five hours a day. I can go all night." She took his hand.

Dorian grinned. "That's what I like to hear."

Before she could take his hand, a shadow threw itself over them. Dorian glanced up to see a young man who had to be only a couple years older than him, and he didn't look friendly.

Then the man draped his arm over Sybil's shoulder. Dorian took a step back to see the man was staring straight at him with very cold eyes. Then Dorian sensed a feeling of familiarity between him and the girl.

"Excuse me, Sybil," said the well-dressed stranger, "but I believe you promised me the first dance."

Sybil forced a smile. "How good of you to show up, Jim. I thought you weren't going to make it."

"For you, I'd drop anything." He replied, taking her hand. "Shall we?"

Sybil looked wary and glanced over to Dorian, and then turned back toward Jim. "Maybe the next one," she said politely.

Jim frowned. "Fine." He replied, watching Dorian taking Sybil's hand. "Have fun." Jim said, feigning a smile.

"You're such a doll," Sybil said, kissing him on the cheek.

But the sign of affection didn't change his disposition. He crossed his arms and narrowed his eyes. Dorian felt that this guy was going to trounce him. Without further delay he escorted her to the dance floor and they began to dance the waltz.

Henry looked on, and couldn't believe what had transpired. Dorian came rushing out of the gate with that Rain Man stunt and then recovers with the trademarked Gray charm. Henry would give anything to be half as smooth as Dorian was.

Sybil would never have guessed he was such a great dancer. Guiding her to the center of the floor, Dorian held her and started moving in perfect rhythm, barely touching her, and his body was suggestive.

He is certainly good-looking, she thought.

She liked the way he kept raking back his thick, dark hair, liked the way it fell back over his forehead. She wondered what it would feel like to brush her hand through his hair.

Sybil's heart raced wildly. She could feel her resolve beginning to crumble. The touch of his hand made the back of her neck tingle. They were cheek to cheek. For a moment sexual energy flickered between them. His eyes locked on hers. He lowered his face, concentrating on her hair. She could feel the heat off his skin.

Dorian looked over at Sybil. His blue eyes lit up. He seemed so pleased. A lot had passed between them then, without being spoken. She moved closer to him.

"Who was that guy?" Dorian asked, turning his head to see Jim glaring at him like a pit bull. "Is he your boyfriend?"

"Worse," she replied, holding back a soft chuckle. "He's my brother."

INTERLUDE ONE
FROM THE JOURNAL OF DORIAN GRAY

April 13, 1890

One evening about seven o'clock I had felt this sudden determination to go out in search of some adventure. I felt that this grey, monstrous London of ours, with its myriads of people, its splendid sinners, and it sordid sins. There must be something in store for me.

The mere danger gave me a sense of delight. I remembered what Harry had said to me on that wonderful night when we first dined together, about the search for beauty being the poisonous secret of life. I didn't know what I was going to expect.

I went out, and wandered eastward. Soon I had lost my way in a labyrinth of grimy streets, until I passed a funny little theater with great flaring gas jets and ugly playbills. There was a strange man standing outside who was smoking a cigar, and he led me to a small private balcony where I could see the stage.

It was a third-rate curtain, colored in cupids and towers. And there were women who were selling oranges and ginger beer and nuts. Anyway, the play I've seen was Shakespeare's Romeo and Juliet. I thought it was a mistake on attending this ill production, but something had drawn me to this place.

The orchestra was absolutely terrible. Romeo was a stout elderly gentleman, with corked eyebrows, a husky tragedy voice, and a figure like a beer-barrel. Mercutio was almost as bad. They were as grotesque as the scenery, and that looked as if it had came out of a pantomime of fifty years ago.

But Juliet! Imagine a girl, hardly seventeen years of age with a little flower-like face; a small Greek head with plaited coils of dark brown hair, eyes that were violet wells of passion, lips that were like petals of a rose. She was the loveliest thing I have ever seen in my life. I could hardly see this girl for the mist of tears that came across me. And her voice—I never heard such a voice.

Her voice was wonderful and her beauty was unmatched. It was very low at first, with deep mellow notes that seemed to fall singly upon one's ear. Then it became a little louder. I couldn't stop looking at her. I hung onto every word she said.

In the garden scene it had all the ecstasy that one hears just before dawn nightingales are singing. There were moments, later on, when it had the wild passion of violins.

I love her. She is everything to me in life.

Night after night I go to see her play. One evening she is Rosalind, and the next night she was Imogen. I have seen her die in the gloom of an Italian tomb, sucking the poison from her lover's lips. I have watched her wandering through the forest of Arden, disguised as a pretty boy in hose and doublet and dainty cap.

She has been mad, and had come into the presence of a guilty king, and given him rue to wear, and bitter herbs to taste. She has been innocent, and the black hands of jealously have crushed her reed-like throat. I have seen her in every age and in every costume. Ordinary women never appeal to one's imagination. There is no mystery in one of them. They have their stereotyped smile and their fashionable manner. They are quite oblivious.

But an actress—how different an actress is why didn't Harry ever tell me that the only thing worth loving was an actress?

I was very desperate to meet her, so I paid a stagehand to have it arranged. He pushed through the door with a grunt, stepped over the velvet jacket and nameless frilly debutantes that belonged to who knew whom, ducked under the wind swing of an actress demonstrating a wobbly pirouette that she performed while drinking from a champagne glass, sidestepped a couple—who I don't know if it was a man and woman, or actually two women—passed a dozen other performers in various stages of undress and inebriation. I tried not to goggle at an actress wearing a very sheer slip that was smoking an opium pipe, and crept out of the madhouse before my sanity fled entirely.

I was almost indifferent to the debauchery around him. It became old hat and contempt of the excess. I sighed and procured a glass of wine from one of the caterers.

I discovered the woman who played Juliet's nurse. She had her skirts up around her waist and sat aside the young buck that played Mercutio. She certainly looked alive at the moment. Next to the wrangling coupe, the impresario nibbled the wrist of one of the makeup girls. He gave me an amused nod as if Pan to Bacchus.

Then we stopped at a door with Sybil's name on front of it. The stagehand opened the door for me and introduced me to the lovely Sybil Vane. She is so shy and gentle. She says I am like a prince. Since she doesn't know my name, she calls me Prince Charming.

I want Basil and Harry to see her perform. I don't have the slightest idea of how Harry would react or how I would describe Sybil. I would expect him to laugh, but I will tell him that Sybil is a genius.

I love her, and I must make her love me. I want to make Romeo jealous. I want the dead lovers of the world to hear our laughter, and grow sad. I want a breath of our passion to stir their dust into consciousness, to wake their ashes into pain.

Once my friends see her on the stage they will appreciate her talent. I'm going to rent a proper West End theater and introduce her to all the important critics in London. I will make my beloved Sybil a star.

CHAPTER ELEVEN

Now it was to hide something that had a corruption of its own, worse than the corruption of death itself—something that would breed horrors and yet would never die.
The eyes of the curse incarnate.
Oscar Wilde.

The next day Dorian and Henry drove to Newark for Dorian to claim his inheritance, which was located in a storage container at the Port Authority Container Terminal. More than five million containers per year are moved through the yard. That's more than fourteen thousand a day. Dorian could only think of it was a needle in a haystack.

It was a sunny, tranquil day at sea on the shipyard. It was indeed a very *lovely* day. Occasionally a bit of fog caressed the white caps of the blue waves, and then drifted away.

The two boys got out of the car and then proceeded to walk through the shipyard. Dorian carried the directions George had sent him, as he reveled in the cool breeze.

"You never said anything about Jersey." Henry said to Dorian. "I don't cross the river for anything less than Jets box seats at the Meadowlands."

"What about that time in Perth Amboy with the redhead and the cemetery?" Inquired Dorian, trying to make sense with this map.

Henry shot him a look. "We agreed never to talk about that. Besides, I remember that being your idea."

"Oh, yeah," Dorian replied, "that was fun."

The sun was still burning the early morning fog off the harbor, but it was clearly going to be a beautiful day. There was just a hint of a breeze in the air, and the sky was forming a bright blue dome over the city's skyscrapers.

Sweating longshoremen and stevedores hustled about the wharves. Most of them were loading and unloading crates, sacks, bales, and boxes to and from the holds of the heavily laden freighters docked along the river. Piles of lumber sat atop sturdy wooden pallets not to sprawling heaps of bagged sugar or bananas. Straining cranes supported slings full of cargo and contraband, sometimes swinging precariously over the heads of the hardhats below. Cargo checkers, armed with clipboards and ballpoint pens, scurried along the decks, trying to keep track of what was coming and going from every scow and rust bucket.

Dorian counted out the storage units as he walked north. The letter stated he was supposed to find storage unit 93 to claim his inheritance. He couldn't wait to see what was waiting for him.

Henry found the container in question in the back of the area. He pushed the dust off the storage unit, while Dorian noticed a lock on the door. It was very old and rust had covered some parts of it.

"Dad didn't say there was going to be a lock." Henry said, checking the directions again.

Dorian reached into his pocket and pulled out the strange golden key that was in the package George had sent him.

"Good thing I brought this along." He said, inserting it into the lock. It was a perfect fit.

"Do you really think there's gonna be anything worthwhile like stacks of 1930s porno?" Henry crudely asked.

Dorian hesitated for a moment as a look of fear ran across his face. "Nah, my bet's on some guy whacked by Tony Soprano."

Henry took a deep breath. "There's only one way to find out."

Dorian nodded and turned the key and before he could open the door Henry stopped him.

"Wait, Dor!"

"What?" Dorian turned to face him with fright.

"What if the door is rigged to a mechanism that is attached to a trigger of a shotgun facing at us?"

"Henry, what the hell are you talking about? Why would you say something like that?"

"I don't know. Something doesn't seem right about all of this. This is how some horror movies start out with."

Dorian narrowed his eyes. "As soon as we're done here, Henry, you're going to lay off the late night monster flicks." Then returned to unlocking the container.

"Dorian," Henry said, putting his hand on his friend's shoulder.

"What?" Dorian irritably replied.

"Be careful."

Dorian gave out an aggravating sigh. And opened the door to see what was waiting inside. His eyes were wide with wonder and words had slipped past his lips.

"Wow…"

"There *is* a dead guy in there?" Henry asked, slowly looking past Dorian's shoulder.

"Better." Dorian answered, never blinking.

"*Two* dead guys? Aw, man! Why couldn't we get lucky and have an entire shipping container filled with hot Russian chicks?"

"No," Dorian assured him, "but the stuff inside was unexpected."

Dorian and Henry turned on their flashlights and started to look around the container and examined several of its artifacts. Dorian looked around the area and saw they were a lot of weird weapons on the shelves. They looked like nothing he had ever seen before, outside of movies and television.

Were these even for real? This was the family legacy? Seemed more like a terrorist cell cache. Then he noticed some of these weapons were more steampunk in nature. *Or maybe something more like Downtown Abbey 007.*

"It looks like something out of *NCIS*." Dorian said to Henry, while he studied the strange weaponry.

"So does this make me Di Nozzo or McGee?"

"Mmm…Ducky." Settled Dorian, tossing back his head and laughed. Henry had seen him do that a million times.

"Screw you."

Then Henry noticed something at the back of the container. It was covered in a purple tapestry and his curiosity overcame him.

"And what's behind curtain number three?"

Dorian carefully approached the shrouded item. He reached forward and slowly unveiled the mysterious artifact. Henry watched with anticipation, wondering what was behind the tapestry.

"Well, we came all the way to Jersey." He said, rubbing his hands together. "Let's see."

As the veil was being lowered, Dorian could immediately tell it was a painting, and his eyes widened in horror. His grip in the purple tapestry tightened with fear and looked up at the six-foot tall picture that resembled a tormented damned member of the undead.

"Dorian," Henry gasped, putting his hand in front of his mouth like he was going to vomit. "Th-th-that's you!"

Dorian locked at the painting in front of him. He glanced into it and gasped, wondering who the hell that poor, grotesque bastard was staring back at him.

It took Dorian a few moments through the storage unit, as he let out a horrifying, sustaining scream resounded through the four walls.

PART II
THE IMPORTANCE OF BEING ERSTWHILE

INTERLUDE TWO
FROM THE JOURNAL OF DORIAN GRAY

November 7, 1908

I was walking home after dining with Harry over at his house, and I was wrapped in heavy furs, as the night was cold and foggy. At the corner of Grosvenor Square and South Audley Street, a man passed me in the mist. He was walking very fast and with the collar of his grey ulster turned up.

He had a bag in his hand.

The man was Basil. I was overcome with this sense of fear that nearly made my heart stop. I didn't want to speak to him so I tried hard as I might to avoid him, but Basil had spotted me.

He told me he had been waiting for me all night and he booked the midnight train to Paris. He wanted to speak to me before he left the city. He had a new exhibition and he wanted to ask me if I could loan him my portrait so it would be his principal piece.

I let him into my house and offered him a drink. He politely declined as I noticed the urgency in his eyes. I had a feeling that this wasn't a social call.

He looked at me sadly; telling me my reputation has been shattered. As if I cared about what everyone else is saying about me. I only cared about other people's gossip.

Then Basil mentioned a young royal son who had committed suicide in the Navy.

Lord Kant's son who married a prostitute.

And there was the scandal of Adrian Singleton, who had been convicted of forgery.

All of them were once close friends of mine.

Then Basil said if he really did know me he would have to see my soul. I led him up the stairs, feeling a terrible joy on sharing my secret. We walked silently up to the locked studio.

I asked him if he really wanted to know the truth. He replied, "Yes," with the utmost of certainty.

He was the only man in the world who was entitled to know everything about me. He had more to do with my life than he thought.

The studio was covered with dust and the carpet was full of holes.

Had Basil thought it was only God who could see the soul? I drew the curtain back to reveal the portrait he painted for me eighteen years ago and witnessed the expression on his face as he gazed upon it with horror and revulsion.

He saw in the dim light a hideous face on the canvas. It grinned wickedly at him. It took him a brief moment to realize the abomination in front of him was the rendering of my own grim visage.

The horror hadn't entirely spoiled the beauty of the subject. There was still some brown in the thinning hair and some red on the handsome mouth. The sunken eyes were still blue.

Basil seemed to recognize his own brushwork; the frame was his design. He was gripped with fear. He seized the lightened candle and held it to the picture. In the left hand corner was his own name, traced in long letters of the bright red.

He looked at me with the eyes of a sick man. He was utterly speechless, and sweat protruded from his brow.

He asked me how could this be, and I explained to him when he painted that portrait; he flattered me and taught me to be vain about my looks. Then he introduced me to Lord Wotton, who told me the only thing of value was beauty. The picture made me think I was handsome and I didn't want to lose my looks. In a moment of madness I made a wish.

Basil remembered but claimed it wasn't conceivable. Once I have told him it was my soul and ordered me to pray for repentance.

I glanced at the picture and suddenly felt an uncontrollable feeling of hatred for him. It had been suggested to me by the image on the canvas, whispering into my ear by those grinning lips. The mad passions of a cornered animal stirred within me. I hated the man who sat at the table more than I had ever hated anything in my whole life.

My eye fell on a knife that was lying on top of a chest. As soon as I got behind him, I picked up the blade and plunged it behind Basil's ear and stabbed him again and again. I didn't stop until I heard the dripping of blood on the carpet.

The most peculiar part was I felt absolutely calm. However, I felt haunted and longed to escape from my room of death and decay. I locked the door behind me and hid Basil's coat and bag.

Basil was scheduled to go to Paris on the midnight train. It would be months before his absence aroused suspicion. All the evidence could be destroyed by then.

All I needed was an alibi.

I put on my coat and hat, and went outside. After a few moments, I rang the bell. Within five minutes my valet, Francis, answered the door. I told him I forgot my key and asked him if anyone had stopped by the house.

Francis told me Basil was here but he left at eleven to catch a train.

The next day I summoned Alan Campbell to my abode. I wrote in a letter it was a matter of grave importance. I confessed I murdered a man and I wanted Alan to destroy the body. He refused and in my desperation I resorted to blackmail to get him on board.

CHAPTER TWELVE

Every saint has a past and every sinner has a future.
Oscar Wilde.

Finally home, Dorian changed into more comfortable clothes and spent the early part of the afternoon going through the artifacts he collected from the storage unit, and sorting them into piles.

Those items to donate.

And some junk to sell either on eBay or Craig's List to the highest bidder.

Then finally, some of the really cool stuff was just for him.

Going over his great-grandfather's journal for any mention of the painting, and finding nothing, unfortunately. But it gave him time to think about everything that had happened in the last two days, and to come to some conclusions.

The ones he'd reached so far.

Dorian lied on his bed and looked straight at the horrible painting, which was hanging on the wall. He held a crossbow in his hands and then drifted into another world.

When we are very young, we learn not to touch the stove. It's very hot. It causes great pain. We burn our fingers and never want to do that again. Human nature, right? Then why is it some lessons need to be learned over and over again? History is a great reset button. Some point to the karmic properties of reincarnation. That we are sent to learn a lesson, and when we fail, we enter some kind of metaphysical Moebius loop.

Forget reincarnation. Maybe mankind's affinity for generational amnesia is a bi-product of a fancy insect brain. Attracted to the light. We know it's bad for us but still we fly to close and…ZAP!!! We burn our transcendental compass forcing us to face down the challenges learned lifetime after lifetime.

Like a curse passed down from father to son.

Dorian was busy reading his ancestor's journal. He couldn't put it down. Everything his great-grandfather wrote was very haunting. Stephen King had nothing on this sick bastard. With each line the handwriting had become more passionate, the pen digging more desperately into the paper.

Without noticing, Henry walked into Dorian's room. "Dor, how can you keep that freak-show on—"

Dorian jumped up in an instant reflex looking startles and accidently shot the crossbow directly at Henry. An arrow *thwacked* into place, only inches away from his face.

Startled, Henry nearly fainted.

"Jesus Christ, Henry," Dorian screamed, "I'm so sorry. I didn't mean, I mean, uh…"

"Well, if *Halo* taught me anything, it's that your aim is for shit." Joked Henry, as he lowered his head under the arrow. "Thankfully. But I think I need to change my shorts." Then he picked up a random weapon to take a closer look at it. "These have got to be movie props. But I bet you could get at least two grand on eBay. Easy."

Dorian moved over to the doorway to pull out the arrow. When he did it left a huge hole. "I hope Lori doesn't have kittens when she sees the wall."

Henry scoffed as he picked up the pair of yellow goggles that were resting by the other weapons. "Won't even notice with that Mars Volta freak show above your bed."

He placed the goggles on and through the burnt orange tint he saw several yellow ghosts moving around in the room. Henry shook his head in disbelief. There was no way he was actually seeing ghosts floating around him and Dorian. He brushed it off with a smile.

"Dude, you got to check these out!"

But Dorian wasn't interested on Henry's discovery. His attention was focused on an antiqued yellow book.

"I don't think these are props." He said to Henry, picking up the book. "I was skimming this and it's all full of nasty shit." Then he shifted his gaze over at the ghastly portrait with embarrassment and shame. "The painting. That's my great-grandfather. If what he wrote in this book is even a quarter true…man, he was the poster child for Stranger Danger."

Henry cavalierly tossed the goggles on the table that aligned the lenses toward the portrait. "For your sake I hope you didn't inherit his cheekbones."

"He killed the guy who painted this picture." Said Dorian, his voice was serious and Henry's smile faded quickly. Dorian opened the journal to a section he was reading. "He slit his throat, Henry. He thought this guy Hallward was possessed."

"That's one way to kill art funding." Henry replied.

A sudden realization hit Dorian, and he hastily reached for his watch he rarely wore on his wrist. He winced as he discovered that it was nearly a quarter to one.

"Crap. It's late! I gotta meet Hetty!" He said running out of the room.

When the boys left, unbeknown to them something was still in the room. Through the tinted orange goggles something was stirring in the grotesque painting. The paint on the canvas rippled like a stone hitting a pond. Then it began to bubble as if a small fire was blazing behind hit.

A hand with sharp claws burst through the portrait.

It wasn't human in nature. It was demonic and it searched for the side of the frame with the utmost urgency. Its mate followed it and it grabbed hold of the other side of the picture. Then with one big pull the thing that lived in the painting entered the real world with an evil smile stretch across its gruesome lips.

* * *

Dorian sat quietly at a small café in the Greenwich Village. He was waiting for Hetty to meet him for their lunch date, but she was nowhere to be found. He looked at the clock on his cell phone to see he was five minutes late.

She probably thought I stood her up and she left, Dorian theorized, as he started to text her. And then he was filled with doubt. *But she would've waited a little longer than just five minutes.*

Dorian was so caught up in his lament he didn't notice the attractive waitress refilling his water. She felt a shiver when a hand was gently placed on her shoulder. It wasn't a threatening gesture, but a kind one.

"Excuse me," said the person behind her.

She gave him a polite smile as the gentleman moved past her and sat in the chair facing Dorian.

A sudden chill descended over the café. His goose bumps returned as the temperature inside the dining area seemed to drop fifty degrees in a matter of seconds. Dorian's breath frosted before his lips and he stared dumbfounded at the icy puffs.

What the hell? He thought in confusion. This didn't make any sense. *It's September in New York, for God's sake.*

"She's not coming." Said the man who was sitting across from Dorian.

Still puzzled by the inexplicable cold snap, he turned to see a stranger standing in the doorway. A long black coat cloaked the mysterious figure's bony frame. Dark blue eyes seemed to shimmer in the darkness, like a cat's. Jeweled rings glittered upon his fingers. More gems studded his shirt and sleeves. The man looked to be in his early thirties, and he had a big forehead.

Dorian was pretty sure he had never seen this guy before.

"Excuse me?!" Dorian jumped by the sound of the man's voice.

The strange man appeared before him and the contrast couldn't have been more pronounced. He was a lean and angular man with an expensive haircut. Dress and manner, as well as accent, suggested a European background.

He leaned forward, placing his elbows on the table and interlaced his fingers like he was going to pray. "Your date. She's been unavoidably delayed." He explained, pointing to Dorian's cell phone.

As if by magic, Dorian's cell phone buzzed. He looked at the screen to see it was a text message from Hetty.

Sorry D. Running late Gotta reskej. Kisses-H

Dorian shoved the phone back in his pocket. Then he looked at the strange man who was sitting in front of him. Was he a cop? Was he a process server? Or was he one of those guys from *To Catch a Predator*?

"I'm sorry, who the…"

"Manners, right." The man smiled warmly, his eyes crinkling up. He presented Dorian with a business card. "The name is Marlowee Diamond. And it has come to my attention that you have come into possession of several, we'll call them unusual items."

The man's eyes spoke of quiet intelligence, and his entire demeanor converged someone whose nature was to remain calm and collected no matter how stressed the situation.

Dorian didn't accept the stranger's card. "How could you possibly know what I own?"

"Let's say the extraordinary antiquities market is a very small, but chatty circle."

The stranger gave a sly, cryptic smile, as though, indulging in a private joke. The chill permeating the air suddenly ran through Dorian's blood. Even though he didn't know this guy from Adam, just being in the presence of this scary-looking dude made his skin crawl. His foggy breaths hung between them, and it occurred to Dorian that the freaky cold snap had arrived at the same time as the stranger.

"And I should care?" Dorian asked him.

Diamond looked very nonplussed, understanding Dorian's distrust. He dropped his business card in an empty glass in front of the young man. Dorian could see the card read:

THE GOETHE GROUP
RARE ART CONSIGNMENTS, ANTIQUITY
ACQUISITIONS AND AUCTIONS

"A brass tax man. I can appreciate that." Diamond gave out a soft chuckle. "I represent a group of investors, who might have a keen interest in acquiring your collection."

The stranger studied Dorian's expression. His feline eyes seemed to peer into the teenager's soul.

Dorian tilted his head to the side and let his eyes wander off. "Not interested."

Diamond's smile was thin, and his eyes were narrowed, as he felt a quiet wave of confidence came over him. "Can't blame a guy for trying. However, if you change your mind, you have my card."

Diamond rose from his seat and extended his hand over to Dorian. The uninterested young man remained seat as he begrudgingly accepted the stranger's hand and shook.

"A word of advice, Mr. Gray. Dorian." Diamond's words sent a chill down Dorian's spine. It felt he was being threatened by a mobster to keep his mouth shut on a crime he had just witnessed. "Understand what is you have before you decide one way or the other. *Ars longa, vita brevis.*"

"Yeah, yeah, I've seen *The Boondock Saints*, too. 'As shepherds we shall be' blah-blah-blah." Dorian waved him off, as he plucked the man's card from the drinking glass.

Then he glanced up quickly. The mysterious man had disappeared.

"What a friggin' weirdo."

CHAPTER THIRTEEN

To reveal art and conceal the artist is art's aim.
Oscar Wilde.

Dorian lied in his bed reading his great-grandfather's journal. The orange goggles rested on his forehead, wondering if he would put them on there might be a hidden message in the book.

The Saligia, Dorian observed, *it's like one of those books found in forgotten basements of forgotten libraries. And it was just as odd as the rest of the goodies from the container.*

Dorian was captivated on everything his ancestor wrote. He was beginning to think this was a diary of a madman. None of this was making any sense.

His namesake killed his best friend for God's sake. And he was blaming this on demonic possession? Dorian silently prayed that insanity didn't run in the family. He wanted to close the book, but he couldn't help to read the next part.

The Morbi are the sickness that infects the soul of mankind.

"Geez, what a load of crap." Dorian said, rubbing his temples. "But maybe it's worth a buck." Then he lowered the goggles over his eyes and watched in wonder to see the inked letters of the book began to swirl around. "Especially in 3D."

It was amazing. All the loops and swirls in his great-grandfather's handwriting were turning like rotating gears in a colossal machine. It reminded Dorian of the marijuana poster in Adrian Singleton's bedroom. It was one of those magic-eye pictures where you see a hidden image. Adrian's poster was to simulate what your vision was supposed to be like while being stoned. However, to Adrian's disappointment it wasn't the same.

Dorian relaxed his eyes to see the letters in the book were forming an image.

"Oh, boy, this is it. Here were go."

The image began to reveal itself.

It was a hand. It was a very strange looking hand that was reaching out to him.

Dorian became confused. "What the hell is this?"

Then he looked into the palm of the hand. There was something written on it. Something he couldn't clearly see. Dorian leaned in, trying to make out what the text said. Then his eyes grew wider.

* * *

Welcome, Dorian Gray.

Suddenly he heard something.

A deep-chested grunt, a soft football with the thin sound of nails scraping on floorboards.

Dorian crawled and turned. Whatever it was—the thing was just around the next turning. The fear drove him like the pain that sinks a trapped coyote's teeth into his own leg.

The hand flew out of the book and grabbed Dorian's face. The talons on its fingers were digging into both sides of his face.

"OH, MY GOD!!" Dorian cried, trying to break away from the creature's grasp.

Dorian swallowed hard. This whole thing was like something from one of those lame horror movies he and Henry watched. But this time Dorian didn't feel like laughing.

Is this for real?

With supernatural strength it pulled Dorian into the book, slamming it shut.

For Dorian time had lost all meaning. There was no sense of its passing. He did not know when it was—neither the day nor the hour—and only vaguely grasped where he was. He swam for what seemed like centuries in a sea of darkness that had no up or down. He was like one of those blind creatures that lived in the lightless depths of the ocean, moving through eternal nothingness, with no destination and no purpose. The only sound was that of his own breathing, which was low and deep and steady, and when he listened to it his consciousness faded back into sleep.

Dorian slipped off to another place.

There was nothing but here.

Here was not really a here, either. There was no sense of space, of points and lines and planes and time to reference. No light, no dark, no color, no texture.

Here was a state of being.

"*Dorian!*" A state of being with a voice called to him.

"*Dorian.*" Then it came from behind him.

He turned. He turned his self to another point of view. He turned to look behind.

There it was. Right behind him—the monstrous figure from his journey into the extra-cosmic fragment, so tall and spindly, and its large, flattened head with huge luminous eyes.

"*Dorian.*" It seemed to be swimming toward him. Struggling through gulfs of nothingness that swept against the figure like a surging current. It was impossibly strong and graceful, yet unable to breakthrough and jam Dorian.

Most of him regarded this with detached disinterest, but a small part of him somewhere deep inside was very concerned.

Then Dorian blinked, or maybe the creature blinked, or maybe one of their minds shuddered. Suddenly the strange entity was much closer, standing right before Dorian, gently sweeping its long, thins arms and oversized hands in a sculling motion, as if it were treading water.

The fierce, glowing eyes were so close, were burning right into Dorian's, and there was something so familiar there.

"*Dorian.*" The voice was not really a voice. It was a reassurance.

"*Dorian, meet me at the great constant.*"

It did not come out as words. It was a concept and Dorian understood perfectly.

Another blink and it was distant again, swimming against that invisible, reprehensible current. It started to break apart, slowly at first. Little pieces of black shipped off the edges of the silhouette, carried away into the void. Then more and more of it melted away until it had dissolved like a sand castle overrun by the tide.

Or a structure vaporized by an extreme blast.

The eyes were the last to go.

Dorian seldom felt calm. It wasn't often his racing mind stayed low and patient of its own accord.

But it did now.

He contentedly drifted into the nothing.

The crowd noise hit him like a thing alive. He was like a sponge taking in water, except he had an endless capacity for absorbency.

Dorian was spiraling in orbit.

That's how it seemed. He was held in some kind of astral reserve, in a between-place. There were no-man's-lands between the dimensions, twilight zones of non-definition between the various levels of the astral world.

Dorian thought of many things, in a mild, nonjudgmental sort of way—he was in a detached state, in more ways than one. His body was in a kind of time-space loop, his body and his soul as well.

One time he opened his eyes to see an empty room and the scantly golden light of the afternoon sun. But then he was transported to smoky plane, much like a forgotten corner of Hell.

Dorian heard a low growl.

He looked around. Wondering if an attack was imminent.

It squinted way too close and too loud—in fact, it was almost whispered in his ear. He heard long jaws click together, and he knew a beast was right behind him, ready to attack. Dorian whirled around and lifted his hand to ward off the attack, but it didn't come—at least not at that instant.

Dorian bounded to his feet and looked for an escape route. There was none. In every direction, all he saw was foggy mist and haze.

The owner of the hand stood before him. The demon was raging in his face and it was smoldering with a bright blue flame and spittle dripped from its sharpened teeth. Chains held the monster and it was the only think that kept it from tearing Dorian apart. Dorian fell backwards as he looked at the creature in terror.

"This is your refuge of failure!" The monster roared.

The voice was like a whisper in the dark. It was similar to the touch of a spider crawling on the back of someone's neck. To Dorian, this was a damn big spider, and it was standing right in front of him.

Dorian could smell its rancid breath, but then he saw its eyes had receded from blue fire to almost human. It looked at him with such familiarity.

"Dorian?" It said, recognizing him. The demon sat back on its haunches and it shrank in size. "Dorian Gray?"

The demon was changing into a human being. His wardrobe was from the Victorian era and he wielded a cane.

"I never suspected you would open the damnable book again." The man said, dusting off his waistcoat. He offered his hand to help Dorian off the floor, but something wasn't right with this boy. "Good God, you're not Dorian. Well, at least one with which I am familiar."

Dorian was still frightened. And he thought the guy he met at the café was creepy.

"I…am Dorian Gray." He said, taking the man's hand.

The man studied the features of Dorian's face and smirked. "So you are." He offered a broad smile and placed his hand on Dorian's shoulder. "And I am Oscar Wilde. Sorry for all the vulgar theatrics, but you never know who wanders into the pages of a cursed tome."

"I don't understand."

The man who called himself Oscar Wilde gestured for Dorian to walk with him through the misty netherworld. "Of course you do. You're a Gray. This is your calling. Your legacy."

Dorian gave the man a perplexed looked. "Am I dreaming? What's going on? Where are we?"

"So many questions." Wilde said with understanding. "You'd think you were abandoned at birth. That's it! You're a new generation. Your father and grandfather must be dead."

He tapped his cane forward and a small shower of sparks and the tendrils of blue smoke wispily framing a portal. Dorian found himself in a large mirrored training room. Along the walls were many of the weapons Dorian found in the container at the shipyard, and many others. Wilde shed his overcoat and pulled a sword from his cane.

"When one hides from his keepers in a book dedicated to the Seven Deadly Sins, one remains slightly out of touch. What year is it?"

"2012." Dorian answered.

"It must be glorious." Wilde said, tossing Dorian a rapier.

Dorian caught it very carefully. "Not if you still have an essay due on Friday."

"Then I shall be brief." Wilde circled Dorian with his sword. Then he thrust at Dorian, who awkwardly deflected the parry.

"What the hell, dude?"

"Hell, indeed, Dorian." Confirmed Wilde. "Or some Faustian construct of it." Then he leaped into the air, flipping to make a difficult target, and Dorian missed his shot—missed him by a nanosecond.

Dorian stared at awe. "No way."

Wilde landed behind Dorian and flicked his rapier, cutting the boy's ear.

"Ow!" Dorian cried, grabbing his ear in pain. "Jesus Christ! What is your deal?"

"My book about your great-grandfather," ignored Wilde, "critics marveled at its social commentary. It wasn't. It was a warning. A warning about the Morbi."

Pissed off by his bleeding ear, Dorian executed a leg sweep at Wilde. The well-dressed man faltered and flashed a smile.

"Excellent. You have the family skills."

Dorian brushed it off. "Your gums keep flapping, and nothing comes out."

Wilde smiled at him wryly. "Then let's accelerate the lesson."

He transformed into his demon form and took a large swing at Dorian who ducked and rolled.

"The Morbi—they feed on greed, avarice, power, lust." The Wilde demon growled, while Dorian took cover. "And no one embodies that more than the rich and famous."

Dorian burst out laughing. He couldn't help it. Of all the stupid foolishness he had ever heard, this was the most absurd.

"Listen, buddy," Dorian's grin disappeared, crossing his arms, "if I wanted someone to jerk me off, I'd go over to Times Square. It would only cost me twenty bucks."

"There is no need for such filth, Mr. Gray." The Wilde monster scolded the unbeliever, grabbing Dorian by the neck and slammed him into the mirrored wall. The sword flew out of his hand, and he found it very hard to breathe.

The demon looked into his eyes, setting his soul on fire.

"Yours is a cursed family, Dorian Gray. However, yours is one family who chose to fight back."

Dorian looked around and found a shard of glass lying on the floor. He picked it up and charged at the demon that swatted him away like a fly.

"In this book you shall find a list of names." The Wilde demon instructed him. "They, like your family, have been plagued. Fed upon by these insidious creatures. They solicit the whims of the deepest darkest desires and exact a heady price."

All the mirrors in the room showed different parts in history. Dorian glanced around the mirrored room, a chill tightening his skin as he imagined it. He stared at everything that was going on behind the looking glass. He watched his great-grandfather stabbing Basil Hallward—the artist who painted the portrait—repeatedly until he was dead. Then Dorian looked over to see a Morbus demon from the 1920s encouraging a man to jump out of window during the stock market crash. The young Gray winced in horror to witness a sad girl hanging herself in the 1950s, and then it shifted to Dallas where Lee Harvey Oswald had John F. Kennedy in his crosshairs while a Morbus hovered over him.

The Oscar Wilde demon tried to stomp on the prostrate Dorian who rolled away just in time.

"Your father and grandfather found ways to free some families in hopes their own curse might be abated." The demon revealed to him. It saw Dorian was picking up its discarded cane since it was the only weapon within reach.

"But alas, the Morbi are strong, they are immortal, and they are insatiable."

Dorian swung the cane at the demon with all his might, but it broke on impact. The creature shattered and in the middle was Oscar Wilde smiling and primping his hair.

"Kind of beautiful symmetry in it." He said, putting his arm around Dorian to guide him out. "Each family has a totem. Call it an heirloom that binds a Morbus to it."

"Totem?" Dorian said, hearing it ring a small bell. "You mean a cursed object like when Sam found that lucky rabbit's foot on the second season of *Supernatural*?"

Wilde paused for a moment and stared at the young descendant of his former acquaintance. Wilde briefly wondered about all this had to do with a dismembered animal's limb, and why it would be considered good fortune to carry it around with them.

It sounded very barbaric.

"I haven't the foggiest what you are talking about, young Gray." He replied, clutching his cane. "However, if you think you can associate this into something that is easier for you to comprehend, then yes. You can't possibly destroy the Morbus, but destroy the totem, you can free the family."

"Like the painting?" Dorian asked.

Wilde nodded. "Like the painting.

* * *

Dorian bolted up in his bed with a start. The book closed with a thump. He was sweating and seemingly out of breath as if he finally broke the surface from swimming up the depths of the ocean. Then he quickly twisted around and stared at the painting.

A ghostly fist clobbered him right in the face.

Morbi had emerged from the painting. Dorian fell out of bed and peered over the sheets to see it was Basil Hallward—the man his ancestor murdered over a hundred years ago. Now he was here to exact his revenge on his killer's descendants.

"Did the poofta warn you about me, Dorian Gray?" It asked the frightened boy.

Dorian scrambled and picked up the crossbow he was fooling around with earlier. He took aim and fired. The Basil Morbus easily dodged the arrow and it bounced harmlessly off the painting.

"Kids today." The demon seethed. The words seemed to pummel Dorian. He staggered back against the doorframe. "No respect for the arts. I guess he didn't tell you everything. I can give you whatever you desire, Dorian Gray. May it be women…"

With the snap of Basil's talons a vivacious blonde appeared out of nowhere. She was beautiful with bright blue eyes and creamy white skin. Dorian was amazed by her, but then started to think that this was a dream. The sweet fragrance of lilac had entered his nostrils and he figured that dreams didn't smell this good.

Abruptly, the woman turned to him, grabbing his head with both hands and pulled his mouth hungrily to hers. Her kiss was searing passion, and as he felt her body move against his, already seeking out that old instinctive rhythm, he knew he wasn't going to pass up a chance with her.

Suddenly he felt a tongue flick against his ear. He turned, finding a beautiful woman standing there. She was tall as he was, and slender and Asian. She pirouetted for him, giving him a view of the complete package, obviously knowing she could turn the head of everything male in the room with her skimpy outfit.

"My friend, Kimie," the blonde said. "Hope you don't mind?"

Dorian grinned, looking at the woman. "Not me. I always thought three was company."

The new girl joined the other, and they sandwiched Dorian with their taut bodies, doing a slow grind. He was dancing, losing all stiffness, and feeling darkly entwined with the music's somber throb. He was vaguely aware of a warm, cupping sensation and looked down to see the blonde rubbing him. She looked up at him, opened her mouth and clamped her lips over his. When her tongue drove into his mouth, he felt as if his entire body had been penetrated by something moist and fiery and tart. The petite Asian was slowly running her hands over his backside. Dorian plunged into the sensations of asphalt being smoothed by a steamroller. She turned him around and thrust her tongue in his mouth.

But the girls weren't just kissing. They were whispering to each other.

They were conspirators in a sexual plot!

His mind reeled in a grove of blossoming lime trees, when she spoke to him, as if she were in a close up on a giant movie screen. Then all their mouths met in a passionate kiss. Dorian felt a pair of hands sliding over his naked torso, but couldn't tell if they belonged to the blonde or Miss East. The girls seemed to have blended into one.

He kept feeling the seduction of feminine flesh pressing in against him from both women. He knew he wasn't going to be able to take much more of this without some kind of relief. From the way both women breathing deep and looking at him, he knew the same was true for them as well.

Basil watched perversely from the shadows, rubbing himself as he enjoyed the show. The blonde winked at him as she put on a show for him with Dorian and Kimie. Pulling out a handkerchief to dab the sweat from his brow, Basil cleared his throat.

"If that isn't enough for you, I can give you more money than you can ever dream of."

With a gesture of his hand, the women were turned in to piles of money. Dorian jumped at the sudden transformation and suddenly found himself frozen in place to see his entire room was filled with gold, jewels, and cash. He probably had enough money to buy New York—not the city but all the five boroughs.

Dorian picked up a wad of cash and flipped through the many bills. They were all legitimate. Unmarked, no forgeries, this was real.

Basil stroked his chin, deep in thought. "No, you have enough money as it is already," he said. "What do people your age want these days? Aha! I know. You need something that goes with your vanity. How about your own reality series?"

Dorian was surrounded by sudden bursts of white flashes. He held up his hand to cover his eyes from the piercing lights, hearing several voices from both sides. He opened his eyes to see the paparazzi snapping pictures of him and a camera crew was following him around. At the other side of his room there was a wall of television sets that recorded his every movement.

"Dorian!" Called one of the reporters. "Is it true you and Vanessa are an item?"

Then another one said, "What was like working with Spielberg? Can you talk about your role in his upcoming movie?"

"Who are you wearing this season?" Asked a fashion reporter.

"Is it true that you were one of the sperm donors for the Octo-Mom?"

"Is it true you only take your shirt off for $10,000 in publicity photo shoots?"

"When are you going to man up and take the paternity test?"

"What do you have to say about the D.U.I. charges against you?"

Dorian started to feel claustrophobic. All these strange people advanced on him and there was nowhere to run. They closed him in a corner and he couldn't breathe.

Hearing the snapping of Basil's fingers all the reporters and camera operators vanished.

"The sneak peak is over," the demon said, crossing his arms. "All this can be yours. What do you say?"

"Yeah, that sounds great," Dorian said, watching the being passing itself off as the great painter Basil Hallward smile. "You mind if I sleep on it and have my people call your people?"

The demon's smile quickly faded. Basil took Dorian by the neck and pressed him hard against the high-rise glass of his bedroom window.

"I offered you unlimited wealth and pleasure, and you spat in my face." Basil growled easing his grip on Dorian.

The window was starting to crack and Dorian was hyperventilating. The window shattered and Dorian was now dangling in sixty stories in the cold night air.

"Hmm…on second thought," Basil said, letting go of Dorian's throat finger by finger. "You've just woke up and you can't think clearly."

Dorian could feel the hand letting him go.

"Maybe some fresh air would help." Basil said, throwing him out of the window.

Dorian felt a scream tear itself from his lungs. The involuntary shriek was lost to the howling of the wind whipping past his terrified face.

All his life Dorian Gray took a lot of senseless risks and lived in the fast lane. Now for the first time ever, he found himself going so fast it scared him.

CHAPTER FOURTEEN

Every portrait that is painted with feeling is a portrait of the artist, not of the sitter.
Oscar Wilde.

Dorian shot upright, his heart thumping, skipping beats, and a sheen of cold perspiration covered his body. His hands frantically dragged up the bed sheets, using them to wipe the blood off his face.

He quavered, the silent cry on his lips, and then fell back into the pillows. His heartbeat paced down and then he looked at the sheets.

No blood.

It was only a nightmare.

The thunder boomed overhead as the storm finally struck with full force. The deafening blast jolted Dorian—

—Who sat up abruptly in his bed.

"WHOA!"

He looked around in confusion. The bizarre dimension where he met Oscar Wilde was gone, replaced by the familiar sights of his own room in the Lords' penthouse apartment. Moonlight filtered in through the window curtains. Blinking to clear his eyes, Dorian glanced at his alarm clock. It was almost four AM, and the demon was nowhere to be seen.

"Damn," he murmured.

That was one hell of a dream.

For some reason, he felt as if he were in the middle of an arcane haunted house story. He was just waiting for Vincent Price to come out of the shadows to give him a long overdramatic monologue on how the dark spirits are at play.

The mirror in the bathroom was no kinder than the one in his room, but Dorian stood before it, shirtless, barefoot, hair wild, fists clenched at his sides. He looked into his reflected eyes, rarely blinking, and it seemed to him that he could see through those eyes, that they were windows instead of mirrored reflections.

"God," Dorian said softly, his voice weak and desperate.

He started to turn away from the reflection—and then turned back again. His image had distorted slightly.

As he watched, his human face distorted even further—the demonic visage of his ancestor's portrait seemed to push out, like a man pressing his real face against the lineaments of a rubber mask.

Dorian touched his fear and leaned closer to the mirror. Perhaps his mind was playing tricks on him.

And then the skin of his face began to ripple, as if liquefying. His clear complexion broke out into hideous boils and his hairline was receding as parts of his scalp fell apart in large clumps.

It was no longer the reflection of Dorian Gray, but the true image of his very own soul.

"Jesus!" He yelled and suddenly smashed his fist into the mirror, which exploded into a thousand shards.

"What the hell is happening to me?" He breathed.

But he feared that his plea to a forgotten deity and the renewal of his own discarded faith had come for too late. He stared down at the mirrored fragments scattered around him on the floor. Each one seemed to reflect its own perverse distortion of him.

He saw a black car that was not a hearse but it sure as hell looked like one. A grim-faced man drove large and heavy, with shaded windows and it in a dark suit.

Young Dorian was only remotely aware that he was being carried. His mind didn't process time or moment or action with any clarity or cogency. He felt like he was floating. When he heard voices he did not know whom they belonged to. His mother's voice was that of a stranger. The other voice—people were calling him Basil Hallward—is equally unknown to him. Dorian was beyond the point of associating people with reality, because nothing was real.

This was all a dream.

A nightmare.

He knew that, because it must have been a nightmare. These were not possible in the real world...they belonged in dark dreams.

Dorian understood this. Just as he knew that the black car and Basil Hallward likewise do not belong to the waking world.

He thought these things without knowing that he was thinking. His mind was twisted into crooked shapes and self-awareness had been washed away with black rain.

All that belonged to him was the darkness. He could feel it spread through him and closely around him, and as he sunk into it Dorian heard his mother's voice singing an old lullaby. He knew that he should remember the words. But he couldn't, and couldn't find a way to care.

The blackness was so soft and smooth and it covered everything…

Thinking back, remembering now with a cruel clarity those things that were fractured dreams into him as a boy, Dorian threw his arm across his eyes in an attempt to deny, even to himself, that he wept.

At five years old Dorian Gray was a thin boy. Not yet strong, not yet the muscular specimen he would become, but pale and carefree. He was dreamy as a poet; lost in frequent reveries whose particular naïve he shared with no one.

Except for his mother. Olivia Gray knew all of her son's secrets.

Dorian lay with his head on her lap, his dark curls lost against the intricate embroidery of her gown as if he were still, years after his birth, enmeshed with her. Olivia sung a comforting song to him. Dorian lay with his eyes closed, listening, flowing in and out of dreams, guided by the melody, and the promises hidden in the words.

One image in the broken piece of glass was Dorian the boy, in his mother's arms.

Another was the boy standing in the rain at a cemetery in front of a freshly dug plot.

Another fragment of him had him cavorting with beautiful girls and living a life in total excess and not worrying a single thought on the consequences.

And one fragment, a sliver no wider than a knife and equally as sharp, lay on the floor between his bare feet and when Dorian looked down at his reflection He did not see a man, or a boy.

He saw the hideous face of the painting that hung on his bedroom wall.

Dorian closed his eyes and beat the sides of his temples with his fists. "Please," he begged. "Please…"

But all that answered him was the dark.

Twice Dorian tried to go back to bed with the promise of losing himself in sleep, but each time he was out of bed within a few minutes, pacing his room with nervous energy, sometimes muttering to himself. Fear was a clawing thing that tore at the walls of his chest.

He stood in the emptiness of his room and tired to decide what to do. He wished he had some of the good stuff Adrian had. Losing himself in the velvet dreams would help, but it was too late and too early to call his friend.

Whiskey, he thought.

A lot of whiskey might do the trick, and so he hurried to George's liquor cabinet, filled a tumbler to the brim with his stepfather's scotch and gulped half of it down. He choked and coughed, but the warm burn inside his chest felt good. He took a second gulp, and a third, then refilled his glass and went back to his room.

In Henry Lord's dreams, the Yankees were sweeping the Red Sox for the World Series in straight shutouts. Derek Jeter was making people forget that Babe Ruth had ever existed, and he had front-row field-level seats for every game, right behind the Yankees dugout. He watched A-Rod whiff a fastball straight up into the air. He knew from that moment of contact it was coming for him, and he leaped to his feet, eyes on the ball, gloved posed to grab it.

But he started to lose it in the sun. He squinted his eyes as he'd been taught, but he couldn't filter out the wicked glare.

Then he heard a loud noise that rumbled the stadium.

He stood his ground, still determined to catch the ball, but the sun's radiance grew brighter, unbearably so, and next to it in the sky, bigger than anything he'd ever seen up there.

Henry's dream popped like a soap bubble and he became instantly and totally awake. One part of his mind automatically cataloging everything around him while his active consciousness came up to speed.

He was in his bedroom in his parents' apartment, where his friend Dorian Gray lived across the hall.

It was night.

Then he realized that something wasn't right. He got out bed to investigate.

The whiskey didn't help Dorian at all. All it made him was hungry. He remembered the leftover pizza that he and Henry had ordered earlier and decided to snitch a few pieces. Still alert from his vivid dreams, he tiptoed through the dark hallway. He didn't want to wake anyone else up. He was still surprised that the sound of the mirror breaking didn't send everyone running to his room.

Henry must've had a few before he hit the sack, joked Dorian, finally bringing a smile to his face. Then his smile disappeared when he saw a silhouette down the hall.

His fears had returned at full blast. He wasn't having a nightmare—he was in one.

At the end of the corridor, the figure stood motionless. Dorian rushed it, ready to inflict damage, when he realized about halfway to his destination that it was Henry, looking very apprehensive and very sleepy.

"Dorian?" Henry queried muzzily. "Is something wrong?"

Dorian shook his head. "Couldn't sleep."

"Oh." His stepbrother still looked just as apprehensive, and only slightly less sleepy. "And so you were going to attack me?"

"Not you," Dorian blurted, and then shrugged with a little laugh. "Just a burglar. Which is," he added quickly at Henry's look, "not so funny."

Henry frowned. "Is there a burglar in the house, Dorian?"

Dorian firmly shook his head. "No, Henry, it's all clear. Go back to bed."

Henry cocked his head. "What are you going to do?"

Dorian smiled sheepishly. "Attack. The rest of that meat-lover's pizza."

"Not if I get there first," Henry shot back. He darted around Dorian and loped down the hall.

"Henry!" Dorian shouted, tearing after him.

Dorian could have easily outdistanced his stepbrother. There was not a human alive he couldn't best in a skirmish. But he fussed and fumed all the way to the kitchen for Henry's benefit, only to find him pulling out two plates and the prize—the half eaten box of the infamous meat-lover's pizza.

Dorian sat at the table and watched Henry place several slices into the microwave. The sauce was bland. The cheese was stale. The pepperoni tasted like ham, and the crust wasn't cooked all the way through.

Henry had ordered from Antonio's again. Dorian had told him time and time again not to order from Antonio's, but Henry just didn't listen to him. Dorian didn't know why. Not only was their pizza the worst in the city, their drivers were terrible, too. By the time the pizza arrived, it was ice cold.

Still, Dorian thought, *it was pizza.*

And they ordered the pies on Wednesday, so they got three for the price of one. Maybe that was why Henry always ordered from Antonio's.

Watching Henry's boyish grin as he stood eagerly in front of the microwave door, counting down the seconds when it would be pizza time made Dorian forget about the vivid nightmares. For the first time tonight, Dorian smiled.

Dorian was in some ways a delicate flower. Henry had learned to keep him watered and positioned so the sun would hit him in the right ways. He thought that his parents knew some of those ways too. Henry also wished that Dorian was not quite so high maintenance, but maybe that was just the price of being part of his entourage.

Beside Dorian's bed the alarm was buzzing gently. His entire body was shaking and his legs were wrapped in the light blanket. It felt as if he had just sprinted miles.

Dorian was wide-awake, blinking against the sunlight that was pouring on through the window. For one delirious moment, he thought that the sun had come out at night, and then his mind settled down as he realized that, no, the night had passed. And to his very great surprise, he had not woken up dead.

He lay there, trying to catch his breath, his eyes open for fear that closing them might send him back into the dream. But the images were still with him, as real as if he had actually been there. There was no forgetting them.

CHAPTER FIFTEEN

Art imitates life and, sometimes, life imitates art. It's a weird combination of elements.
Bruce Willis.

Dorian bolted up again in bed scrambling to hold on to anything, and nearly pulled his mattress cover off.

Henry peeked into Dorian's room carefully. "Hey, don't shoot. It's only me." He said, waving his arms in defense. "Breakfast is ready." Then he noticed the terrified look on his best friend's face. "You okay?"

Dorian wiped the sweat from his face. "I'm…I'm coming!"

Then he sat on the end of his bed staring intently at the painting and the Saligia was on his lap. Dorian did a double take on the painting. Something about it was different. It seemed slightly less grotesque. It was as if the scarred visage was healing.

He took his time under the shower, muttering darkly that the spray wasn't as powerful as he like. Truth was, what he liked was a fire hose at full pressure, enough to scour his flesh the way it could be used to flay paint off a wall. He started as hot as he could bear, which wasn't quite hot enough to burn, then went for cold, that wasn't satisfactory either. The immersion left him tingling all over, totally raw and feeling better.

After he finished dressing he looked at the journal wondering what he had gotten himself into. He wanted to blame this damned book for all those nightmares he had, but then he got a weird feeling that he was being watched. He turned his head quickly to see who was spying on him.

All he saw was his grandfather's painting staring back at him. He carefully approached it and looked into its painted eyes. He waved his hand back and forth, wondering if the eyes would follow the movement.

Dorian snorted, "What the hell is this, *Scooby-Doo*, or something?"

"Dorian, come on!" Yelled Henry. "We're gonna be late!"

"Coming!" Dorian replied, grabbing his backpack and closing his door in a hurry.

When he left the room, a ghostly tendril formed around the painting.

Dorian chewed his lip, trying to decide how much of the day's events he wanted to reveal to Henry. He desperately wanted his feedback, but Dorian knew full well it wasn't going to do any good to get his best friend involved with his business when all he had were questions and fears.

He finally resolved to keep silent until he had a better idea of what was what. Beginning all his confusion off of Henry would make him feel better, but it wouldn't help solve anything.

So why freak him out unnecessarily?

They would both be better off if he kept his mouth shut.

Dorian just hoped Henry would always be patient and understanding on what he was going through.

He barely stayed awake in Mr. Haskins' English class. Actually, only a few were looking at the old fart anyway. Most of the twenty kids were studying either their notebooks, or the window, or the floor, or the clock in the hopes that it would move faster.

Mr. Haskins sighed.

When he decided to be a teacher, he knew it was going to be an uphill struggle. Most of these kids would rather be playing with their Xboxes or checking their Facebook pages, or text messaging each other from across the room.

Dorian was restless.

He sat at his desk, staring into space.

What's the matter with me? He wondered.

He stayed in his seat, gaze fixed on nothing in particular.

"What's Dorian's problem?" Hetty asked Henry. She twirled her long red hair around two fingers as she spoke. "I checked him out a couple of minutes ago to listen for his breathing, just to see if he was still alive. Finally he blinked, so I guess I don't have to give him mouth-to-mouth."

"Oh, you poor thing," Henry taunted her, receiving a playful scowl in return. "I bet he's tired. He had a helluva dream last night."

"Was it that bad?"

"I don't know," Henry answered scratching his head. "He wouldn't talk about it. I guess he was so worked up he thought he was still dreaming and tried to attack me."

Hetty's eyes were almost the same size as Felix the Cat's. "Dorian tried to beat you up?"

"He thought I was a burglar."

The fear in Hetty's eyes was now replaced with concern. "My God. I hope he's okay. Did he at least write his essay?"

Henry frowned, shaking his head. "Nope."

Hetty winced as if she was getting a flu shot. "Talk about going from bad to worse." Then she shifted her attention over to Haskins' lecture.

"When contrasting Marlowee's interpretation with that of Goethe…" Looking out over the mostly apathetic faces of kids desperate to get out of his class as fast as possible, he let out a long breath and walked in front of Dorian Gray. "Mr. Gray, am I keeping you awake?"

Dorian groggily opened his eyes to see his teacher giving him a very mean look. Dorian straightened his back against the rest of his seat and waited for the Haskins to deliver the forthcoming fury.

I so don't need this right now.

"Not only do you come to class without your essay. But you waste my time with your inattention." The class clamored over at Dorian and watched Haskins taking the warpath. "You may be the belle of the ball amongst your fellow miscreants, but I see you for what you really are. After school, Mr. Gray, and bring your #2 pencil."

* * *

While walking down the hallway after class, Dorian still felt sluggish and tired.

"He busted your balls good, bra." Teased Geoff, who felt amused on Dorian's humiliation.

"Ease off, Geoff," said Henry, "my brother from another mother had a tough night."

"Really?" Asked Hetty, trailing back to walk with Dorian. "What was her name this time?" She playfully taunted, being able to make her brooding crush smile.

Geoff gave her a smug look. "Gotta be that Sybil chick from the dance. Musta worn her out…she wasn't in art class today either."

Dorian grabbed Geoff by the front of his shirt. There was a crazed look in his eyes.

"Whaddaya mean?" Dorian shook Geoff.

"Mellow out, Gray!" Geoff protested. "I'm just saying that you performed the signature cuddle-scuttle on her this morning."

"Dorian! Let him go!" Hetty said, trying to pull him back. She was panic-stricken, wringing her hands and her pretty face was wracked with worry.

"Hey, just putting two and two together." Answered Geoff. "Now are you gonna let me go, or are we gonna have a problem?"

Dorian released him and made a break for it through the school's emergency exit door down the hall.

Geoff gave out a pleasing grin. "I sure showed him."

Hetty rolled her eyes. "Geoff, sometimes you have the tact of a carnival barker."

Dorian arrived home and flopped on the couch and turned on the TV. But he was caught off guard by a sound that was coming from his bedroom.

Sometimes the smallest things can set you off. And sometimes they grow like gremlins when you feed them after midnight.

Dorian opened the door to his room and the first thing he saw was his great-grandfather's portrait.

It was much different than the way he left it.

The picture had changed and it looked exactly like him without all the ugliness, scars, and lacerations.

Dorian felt he wasn't alone. Out of the corner of his eye he could see something sitting on his bed. He turned around slowly to see the monster from his nightmare was right in front of him.

Clear as day. And it was smiling at him.

Basil Hallward sat on the bed as if he had been waiting for Dorian all day. Dorian watched as the Morbus' clawed hand patted the bed as to beckon him to sit next to him.

Basil's lips twisted into a cruel smile. "Let's have a chat about Sybil Vane."

PART III
A WOMAN OF NO IMPORTANCE

INTERLUDE THREE

October 29, 1929

Chaos was reigning in the office. Paper and ticker tape was flying around like confetti in a child's birthday party. Workers were bundling paper and dashing around in a mad rush. One man that was dressed in a three-piece pinstripe suit with a high collar, and a watch with a chain, strode calmly through the area.

The man's name was Dorian Gray II.

Wish upon a star. Rub a magic lamp. Pitch a coin into a well. Tie flags to the Kalpatharu Tree. Every age, every culture has a means of finding the easy way to achieve the heart's desire. All are empty promises.

The dagger of realizing your every desire is not what was gained but the awareness of what has been taken. Only then we see its true face.

Of lust and gluttony.

Avarice, greed and pride.

No one ever wishes for bliss.

Dorian stopped in front of the closed office door of Cyril Vane. He didn't bother on knocking so he let himself in. Vane was at the end of his very large office. He was a slim man in his early fifties, but fatigue made him age for two more decades.

He sat behind the desk with his head buried in his hands. To the side was a small sculpture of a ballerina in mid gette.

Dorian recognized the lovely piece of art that was created by Edgar Degas. It was known as the *La Petite Danseuse de Quatorze Ans*, or *The Little Dancer of Fourteen Years*. The statue was modeled after Marie van Goethem, who was a student at the Paris Opera Ballet. The sculpture stood two-thirds life size, and it is dressed in a real bodice, tutu and ballet slippers. It even had a wig of real hair. All but a hair ribbon and the tutu were covered in wax.

When the *La Petite Danseuse de Quatorze Ans* was shown in Paris at the Sixth Impressionist Exhibition of 1881, it received mixed reviews. The majority of critics were shocked by the piece. They compared the dancer to a monkey and an Aztec and referred to her as a "flower of precocious depravity," with a face "marked by the hateful promise of every vice" and "bearing the signs of a profoundly heinous character." She looked like a medical specimen, they reported, in part because Degas exhibited the sculpture inside a glass case.

Then it appeared once again at a gallery not very long ago. However, this was not the real statue, but a smaller replica the artist must have commissioned for Vane. Now it was staring at Dorian Gray right in the face. For a brief moment Dorian could feel something sentient encased in the statue. His eyes met with Vane, who somewhat knew why this strange man was here.

Dorian walked toward the sculpture. "I hear Degas sculpted this just for you." He said to Vane, looking at the porcelain ballerina very closely.

He looked at the dancer's face was horrifically anguished. Blood had pooled around her shoes and dripped along the glass dome that surrounded it.

"It means nothing anymore." Vane replied, his face was haggard and defeated. "Destroy it."

Dorian donned his goggles. "Like the families you destroyed? You know it's not that easy."

Through the orange lenses Dorian could see the Morbus standing behind the Degas sculpture, and it was pointing to the chaos in the other room, smiling broadly. Then it noticed Dorian and it gave him a threatening snarl.

Dorian pulled out a Japanese katana sword from his overcoat. The blade had been forged five hundred times to remove all impurities and it was blessed by a Shinto priest. The Morbus moved to disarm him, while Vane opened the window behind his desk.

Dorian closed on the Morbus, and with stunning speed he knocked the creature back. Dorian had the samurai sword, but the Morbus was able to evade the fury swipes. The creature seemed to anticipate every moved Dorian made, no matter what he did—and he used every trick he knew—the monster seemed to predict it, blocked him, or to avoid the cut completely.

Back and forth they raged, arms flashing, weapons making only minor strikes—but with the sword, even a glaring blow to the shoulder was excruciating painful. One struck just at his wound made Dorian grit his teeth with agony. Forcing himself to counterattack.

He slashed his sword, cutting the demon's left arm, but only slightly, but enough that the blood flecked a shiny crimson.

Dorian met the creature, sliding into a martial-arts kata, the sword flashing in his hands as he let his natural skills take over. He carried the sword up high, hands tilted back to put the point down. At the last minute he stepped aside, avoiding the Morbus. He whipped the sword around in a blinding arc, slashing it across the chest and it retaliated with a vicious claw slash.

Dorian was being driven back by the Morbus' attack, the creature laughed nastily, and Dorian suspected it was only toying with him. It was getting harder by the second on blocking the Morbus' attacks.

Dorian's arms were beginning to feel heavy as he tried to slash past the demon's blur-fast defenses. He managed to nick the Morbus' right ear—but that gave the demon an opening and it crackled Dorian glancing across his right cheekbone, laying open his skin and sending a thrill of pain that reverberated to the core of his being.

Normally Dorian could detach himself from the pain, but that one was hard to ignore. He groaned and slipped to one side, almost losing his footing. Blood was slicking his neck, running onto his fingers. It was becoming difficult to hold onto the sword. It seemed to double in weight every few seconds, as Dorian's arms trembled with fatigue. Sweat trickled, and it mixed with blood.

In a flash, he saw his opening, as the Morbus reeled back. Dorian stepped in, slashing at the demon's exposed arm.

The sword blade cut entirely through the Morbus' arm at the elbow. Dorian drew back, regrouping, not letting the triumph touch him yet.

The severed hand spun through the air, turning to ash and blowing away almost at once. The demon stared at its stump, awe and disbelief straining its pained features.

Dorian took a fresh grip on his sword and stepped in to deliver the finishing stroke that would literally part the creature from existence.

Dorian wasted no time, pulling all his strength into a swipe across its midsection. He had expected the sword to grate on bone, to hang on sinew, and to tear through muscle as it cleaved the Morbus in two.

Only the sword passed clearly though the monster, slicing it nearly in half.

The Morbus' upper body separated from its lower, toppling backward. Startled at first, a sudden confident smile lit its features. Smoke and mist leaped from its two halves, taking the place of the intestines and internal organs that Dorian had expected to see come spilling out.

The mist pulled the Morbus together again like rubber bands, and the two halves of its body joined into one once again with a rushing windy WHOOSH!

Dorian couldn't believe his eyes. He sliced through the damned thing like an onion, and now it literally pulled itself back together and all its injuries had been healed.

The demon gave Dorian a sadistic smile and then faded away from reality.

Dorian held his stance, knowing that this wasn't the end. The creature was toying with him. It was waiting for him to make a mistake. And when he does, the Morbus will deliver a killing stroke.

As Dorian walked back across the room, he sensed something rising up behind him. None of his natural senses told him of the coming attack. It all come from the combined skills he'd honed fighting this particular enemy for so many years.

Dorian whirled, swinging his sword across the demon.

The Morbus creeping up on him from behind moved with agile suppleness away from the blade.

Before Dorian could pull himself back into proper form the demon slammed into him, knocking him back thirty feet.

Dorian tumbled over the tables and chairs, unable to stop his headlong sprawl until he smashed up against the rear wall of the office so hard the drywall caved in. He tried to push himself to his feet and reach for his sword, but his body ache all over from the impact, and the Morbus was on him too quickly.

Seeing the great Dorian Gray panting for breath, increasingly on the defensive, the Morbus grinned in murderous glee and moved in for the kill.

Dorian struggled with the demon, as the Morbus watched with delight to see Vane stepping up on the windowsill. His training and the special senses he'd developed, which had helped keep him alive this long, told him it wasn't over. But the grim reality hit him that it *was* over.

"Too late." It laughed at Dorian's face. "You've failed again."

Dorian knocked the demon aside and ran over to Vane. "No! Don't do it!"

It was too late. Cyril Vane jumped out of the window and fell to his death, landing on top of a Ford Model-T.

The Morbus released Dorian and vanished in a puff of smoke. Dorian ran toward the window and looked at the body where a small crowd was clamoring.

"Damn it." Dorian cursed loudly. "Goddammit!"

Flexing his body as he watched, he checked himself to make sure that the Morbus' attack had only resulted in some sore muscles and bruises, nothing that would hamper him. It always took time to find the demons and set up a means to execute them. The attacks were much shorter than the recon and research went into an operation. Attending to these details always gave him too much time to think, and too much time on his hands.

Dorian Gray II lowered his head in defeat, and decided to evacuate the premises before the authorities came to investigate Vane's suicide. Dorian carried no grudges with the police department; however, he didn't like to stick around for questioning.

CHAPTER SIXTEEN

Skepticism is the beginning of faith.
Oscar Wilde.

Henry climbed onto Dorian's bed and forcibly closed the book while Dorian was still reading. He shot up with fright.

"If you only paid this much attention to chemistry, you wouldn't be pulling a C." Henry yanked the book away from him.

"Jesus Christ, Henry!" Dorian screamed. "Don't you friggin' do that!"

Henry smirked. "Which makes copying off your paper problematic." Then he tossed the book onto the floor. "So that is why my plan is sublime."

Dorian took a moment to calm down. "Henry, the stuff in this book. It's mind-blowing. Did you know…"

Henry moved over to Dorian's drawer across the room and pulled a random shirt. "Did you hear? I said *sublime*." Then he tossed the shirt at Dorian. "Now I'm not gonna study. *You're* not gonna study. So we're gonna go see Dextrose Coma playing at The Barca Lounge."

Dorian and Henry were standing outside the Barca Lounge, taking in the cool night.

The world wakes up for day in a certain way; there's another way it wakes up for night. The New York night was beginning to wake up. Cars honked, sirens wailed, music blared from radios, and all of it was given a kind of backbeat rhythm by the change of traffic lights, the pulse of cars going by.

People were gathering for the club; others were walking by with their kids, on their way to a video arcade, laughing about the money they'd waste. Couples walked by on dates, each with an agenda they didn't even know they had. Just following impulses, desires, lusts, of wishful longings.

In this part of town, a line of people stood waiting in the cold night to enter the trendiest nightclub in all of Manhattan. Ambient noise from behind the double steel doors excited those waiting to get in as a mixture of heat and deep hues could be felt coming from inside. The sound that was coming out of the club turned Dorian's bones into icicles. The highly polished doors gave those waiting something to do as they cloaked their reflections, their skin, at least briefly, colored a light shade of silver.

The large space filled almost to capacity with gorgeous girls and well-groomed men. In the center of the rectangular room was a dance floor made of metal, and its silver sheen made the lights dance and reflect that much more rapidly.

About an hour later, the club was in full swing. The line in front stretched around the block, leaving the silver-hued would-be patrons shivering in the cold evening.

The walls were vibrating in the Manhattan nightclub. The music was cranked to the max and the DJ was still trying to coax even more decibels from it, just to make sure that no one would have their proper hearing by morning. The pulsating lights added an eerie, disorienting feeling to the atmosphere… not that it bothered the people who were writhing to it in fits of primitive enthusiasm.

The club's sign—The Barca Lounge—glowed eerily in blue and purple neon. It was a familiar sight, a landmark for Dorian's eye. The line out front wound halfway up the block—another familiar sight—that proved the establishment's popularity as the best club in New York. There were many, of course, and many more had come and gone over the years, along with every incarnation and reincarnation of the movement. Everything else seemed to change, every aspect of the city and even the world.

However, it didn't affect this very nightclub in this part of the city.

Not The Barca Lounge.

For Dorian and so many like him, the club was a sanctuary. A cultural anchor one might say for the strange ship that they were all elected to sail. Not simply the next big thing in the club craze.

Dorian thanked God for that.

In a pop society that changed in eye blinks, where every other week brought some new version of Eminem-like hatred excused as the language of a culture or facile teeny-bopper tramp-glamour divas with tight, shiny leather pants and blonde hair who couldn't even read music, the symbolism of The Barca Lounge never wavered.

Here Dextrose Coma reigned, as he had since he first hit the indie scene.

There were no Jonas Brothers.

No Taylor Swift.

And absolutely no one was catching "Bieber fever" in the club tonight.

It would be at least an hour's wait, and Dorian and his friends were four years shy of the posted requirement: **YOU MUST BE 21 OR OVER TO ENTER.**

But it was fortunate for Dorian to have friends in high places. With names like George, Abe, Jackson, and Grant he could pretty much get in anywhere. However, his best friend Benjamin was the most popular around these parts.

He stood at the curb, tapping his $300 limited edition sneaker as dusk lengthened over the city. Dorian's favorite Manga artist designed the sneakers. Dorian had been a loyal fan since he found an old tattered Hentai graphic novel that got him through when he was suffering from puberty. Distant sirens could be heard in this murder capital of the east coast, mixed with the collision of music pouring into the street from other clubs. At a strip bar just a block away, a former mayor had picked up prostitutes to smoke crack with. After doing jail time, he'd been re-elected.

Friggin' politics, Dorian thought with an amused sarcasm.

If he peered between the high-rises just right, he could see the Chrysler Building juxtaposed against dilapidated row houses that provided area heroin addicts with their shooting galleries.

Come on, hurry up, he thought, still anxiously tapping his foot.

Hetty Merton stepped back into the shadow of the nightclub, and stared across the street. A glimmer of light behind the streetlight offered promise.

Dorian, are you here tonight? She silently called out. *Dorian, do you think about me?"*

She straightened her red-orange hair, pulling a lock of it down over one eye. It was sexy that way. At home, she had pulled it back and tied it, then changed her mind and let it fall free. It hanged all free and wild.

For you, Dorian.

She had been thinking about him all week.

Obsessing? Well, maybe.

But what else did she have to think about? Homework?

The way he brushed against her in school. And then he acted as if it had been an accident. Some accident. He probably felt her up. Those blue eyes on her face, then on her rack. Those soulful eyes had penetrating her more times than she could count.

Talking to her so softly, so sensually with that dreamy voice of his. Teasing her, flirting with her, brushing her hand as they stepped into their first class.

She remembered each time he touched her. Each time.

And then she could feel his eyes on her as she led the way into the classroom. She knew what he was looking at. She knew he was enjoying what he saw.

She had been thinking about Dorian so much. Tonight she just couldn't bear to sit home alone. That's why she decided to get dressed. Wearing the sexiest top she owned. She knew Dorian liked this top. She saw him staring at her perky breasts, fondling them with his eyes.

They're for real, Dorian, she teased. *No Wonder Bra for Hetty. No way. No bra at all. You'll find out.*

She got dressed for him. She'd been thinking about doing this since last week. It wasn't just the stuff she bought from Adrian. The weed just helped to clear her mind.

Are you looking for me, Dorian? She called, like a siren luring sailors to crash their ships on the jagged rocks. *I'm here, I'm right here across the street. Waiting. Waiting for the right moment. Just catching my breath.*

"Over here!" Hetty tugged him by the hand through more pressing bodies.

She wore a dark waistcoat over a plain black silk blouse, and a long black skirt with a slit accenting her long, shapely legs; her straight red hair touched her shoulders, high cheekbones highlighting a heart-shaped face made even prettier by an effervescent smile and startling blue eyes.

Hetty shot up both fists in triumph. As Dorian passed through the crowd, a wave of dizziness swept over her.

Steady, girl. Don't blow your big chance now.

She pulled her hair down over her blue eyes. Cleared her throat and wondered if her breath was okay, and then wished she had sprayed on a little more perfume.

Be friendly, Dorian, she begged. *Be nice to me. Be glad to see me.*

Henry looked over to Dorian, who was checking out Hetty. However, she wasn't alone. She was with Adrian and Geoff, who were both waiting impatiently for the rest of their party to join them.

Henry gave them a successful smile. "Told you I'd get his sorry ass out of the apartment."

Dorian greeted Hetty with a quick hug and she responded with a soft kiss on his cheek.

"What can I say—I love the nightlife, I've got to boogie."

Hetty's eyes gleamed as she pulled Dorian in through the door, guiding him toward the dance floor. By the entrance, two hulking doormen who looked like they could have been professional wrestlers kept watch. Their chiseled faces looked anything but happy.

Dorian thought about blowing them off immediately. If the brawler twins had any real power to prevent him from being there, they would have already used it. Dorian had no illusions about what probably went on at the club. He had cruised after-hours clubs before.

Drugs, drinks, and dirty sex.

It was truly his kind of place.

The sound system was awesome, the deep basso throbbing of the band stepping, just short of torment. Lights glittered and flashed overhead, cool neon lights that barely lit up anything.

Now Dorian and his friends were getting their I.D.s ready for the two bouncers who stood in front of the door. The kids saw the much bigger bouncer before he saw them.

He stood at the front entrance, all authority and muscle, and tried to stop them as they headed for the door. His shirt was stretched tightly over his massive chest, and he had the look of a thug, but one who might knew more than most things do. He seemed to be blocking access to whatever was beyond the door behind him.

Dorian stared at the overstretched shirt the bouncer wore. It had to be at least a size too small.

Good god, he observed, *does he shop at Baby Gap?*

There were three types of bouncers: the ones who manned the shi-shi bar, the kind who handle private parties, and there was the nightclub doormen. The bouncers for each event can be distinguished by the folds of flesh known as hot dogs on the back of their neck. The private party bouncer would normally be a one-hot dog doorman. The shi-shi bar bouncer has two hot dogs folding up on each other. And finally the club bouncer—a mature bouncer in his prime can maintain up as many as eight hot dogs. It's a sign of status amongst fully-grown bouncers. And it takes years of high-caloric eating to achieve this majesty.

Judging by the man's size, this bouncer was on the verge on getting a baker's dozen of hot dogs on the back of his neck.

"I need I.D.," The oversized man told them.

They wouldn't answer and they wouldn't stop. The bouncer wasn't particularity fond of trouble, so he tried raising his voice.

"Hey! Nobody goes inside 'til I see—"

Then as if by magic, Dorian produced his driver's license in front of the big scary man's face. The bouncer stared at the impetuous rich kid who flashed him a smile. The hard-bodied man seized the license so he could inspect it. After a brief moment he raised his eyes at Dorian.

"I need the girl's too," the bouncer said with a low growl.

"Of course," Dorian replied casually.

He looked over to Hetty, who was a bit intimidated by the burly man. Dorian put his arm around her for comfort.

"Hey, it's okay, Hetty." He said to her, smiling. "He just wants to see your I.D. That's all."

Hetty gave him a smile, reaching down her pocket for her wallet. Whenever she was with Dorian she felt safe. He was always there for her, and she liked that.

"Come on, come on." Said the other doorman who was handing out the bracelets. "Quit holding up the line. People are waiting!"

Dorian waved Henry over. "Hey, Henry, go right ahead."

"Thanks, Dor," Henry said, showing the bouncer his I.D.

Hetty took her license out of the wallet and gave it to Dorian. He sent her a smile, showing all of his beautiful white teeth.

"Atta girl." He said, giving it to the strongman.

The bouncer checked Dorian and Hetty's I.D.s while the other was putting a pink band around Henry's wrist. It was the kind of wristbands that were reserved for attendees who were underage and designated drivers. Dorian noticed Henry was wearing the yellow goggles around his neck.

"Dude, why'd you take my goggles?" He asked Henry.

Dorian waited for a reply but he was cut off by Geoff and Adrian's conversation in the back.

"Wasn't this Dextrose guy from St. Pascal's?" Geoff asked Adrian.

Adrian snapped his fingers. "Dexter VandenBraun, class of '09! He was a friend of my brother's." Then he started to laugh. "He was voted most likely to end up in rehab!"

"*Henry*," Dorian said with more conviction, "why did you swipe my goggles?"

Henry placed the goggles over his eyes and struck a pose. "I thought it would give the evening a kind of Flaming Lips Laserium vibe."

Dorian felt like he was moving upstream against a strong current. His gut wrenched as the diabolic stench hit him. Like sulfur and rotting blood. Only it wasn't the smell in the air but it was all in his mind.

Dorian pushed through a metal door, stepped out onto the landing over the cavernous room—a room far, far bigger than he could ever imagine. It was impossible to tell, for sure, how far it was down to the floor. It was a vast chamber with many lights and others sorts of glows in it, yet dark for all of that. The farther wall wasn't visible at all—the light flecked dimness might've gone on forever. The lights only dented the darkness, didn't illuminate must past their small circles. Smirking, thudding dance music played from somewhere with the walls.

He started through the coatroom, cutting through level after level of tables and bars. At one table, two girls in their early twenties looked up at him—and their eyes began to glow at they watched him pass. He heard their flirtatious whispers, their giggles—and he felt a bit uncomfortably undressed. He sensed they had quite literally undressed him with their eyes.

Muffled music trebled in volume when Henry followed them in through the door. A few quick turns down a few corridors, and they were in the middle of the jam-packed club. The throng of stage light bathed figures danced wildly to the loud pumping beats.

The club was stating the night off with some classics from 50 Cent, DMX, and some Wu Tang. Right now everyone was singing along to J-Kwon's one-hit wonder "Tipsy."

Dorian always preferred the material that founded the movement rather than the generic popped up fluff that was now ending it. Salvos of blinding white strobe lights turned the dance floor into shifting freeze frames.

Tanned skin and clothes of this season's popular fashion.

They were young and they had such smooth flawless complexions.

They had wide eyes that never seemed to blink.

In cages high overhead, girls danced through with playful expressions, in varying states of undress, couples kissed voraciously in secluded corners. Waves of grinding music made the air concuss.

Dorian felt immediately at home.

A lot of kids were squeezed into the bar at the back, while even more watched the action from the balcony above, lounging at tables set for two. Dorian could feel his senses growing even sharper, his mind groping across the room. The Barca Lounge was busy tonight, as usual—noisy and crowded with its mobbed dance floor, loud music, and general confusion of conversation and fun. Even though he was with his friends, Dorian felt strangely distant from it all.

He'd been in many places like this over the course of his life. And through the fashions and music, the language and etiquette might have changed over the years, there was still that seductive play of light and shadow across the floor, across the walks; there was still that entirely crush of too many bodies packed into too small a space. Even now he could smell it—that throbbing heat of human flesh pressing in on him from every side. And he closed his eyes, surrendering to the temptation.

Yes, he'd been in places just like this many times before. Waiting for women.

Slowly he opened his eyes.

Surrounded by people, he felt utterly alone. Surrounded by laughter, he felt weary with an age—old sadness. He looked around at all the young faces, so full of innocence and recklessness and life.

Dorian clasped his hands together, his jaw tightening in a grimace. *Why did I even come tonight, anyway?*

The DJ spun behind an assembly of sound equipment that would just about have sufficed for a show at Madison Square Garden. There were other famous faces at the club, too—Hollywood types who got a kick out of being close to someone with a real alter ego instead of a bunch of pretend ones, mostly, but the occasional athlete, as well. Mostly what jumped out at him as he walked in he felt like he had walked into a frat house party. Everyone appeared to be convinced that there was a certain way they had to act, and they were acting that way. Young women pretended to be to see who could most wittily insult their friends' favorite things while also competing to see who could drink the hardest and fastest.

The noise was deafening. It thundered not from exhaust or enigmatic engines but from the speakers that pounded out the latest top-ten hits by singers who couldn't sing and musicians who couldn't play instruments, but who by dint of artful aesthetic deceit and elemental prehistoric rhythms had succeeded in convincing a large proportion of the under-thirty population that sounds they generated were worthy of approbation.

Space for a dance floor had been cleared upstairs. The DJ was busy, the room was rocking, and the place was packed. The music, the color, the sights, the lights, and the veneer of sophistication were so different than any club Dorian had ever set feet in.

Spotting a member of the opposite gender who might or might not be dancing by herself, Adrian abandoned his friends to their own devices as he made his way out onto the dance floor. Set free, Dorian let the tide of music and youthful humanity pushed him in the direction of the bar.

The music had begun to numb not only his hearing but also his consciousness. Both began to echo and fade, intensify and rebound. He felt—odd.

Had he sipped or consumed something packing an unadvertised surprise?

Then his attention was focused over to Geoff, who was desperately showing off his "dope" breakdancing skills on an unsuspecting female. Dorian didn't know to either to cringe or laugh at this humiliating display.

"I get embarrassed when white people try to dance," said Henry.

"That's a racist remark," Adrian replied. "Have you ever seen *me* dance?"

"I thought you were having a seizure." Joked Hetty, as Henry gave her a high-five.

Immediately the main lights and music went off. Surprised gasps and murmurs swept through the crowd, and as everyone looked about in confusion, a voice called out from the front of the room, followed by thunderous cheers from the partygoers.

"Now the moment you all have been waiting for," called the emcee from the stage. The cheers from the crowd were growing higher and higher. "The Barca Lounge proudly presents Dextrose Coma!"

The stage lights surrounded a dark silhouette behind a massive sound system. Rhythmic scratches followed the synch of the lights.

"Yo, let's get this party started right!" Yelled Dextrose Coma, welcoming the applause.

The DJ spun up something wall-shaking.

A strobe light flickered over the dozens of bodies writhing on the dance floor a Hetty pulled Dorian out there. Above them the man of the hour called the shots and laid down the riffs from twin decks, grooving to the music himself.

Dorian gave into the rhythm and danced with Hetty. She has been dreaming to get this close to Dorian. She harbored such a crush on him since she first laid eyes on him. Dorian couldn't help to do the same thing to her.

"You look super slutty tonight, Het!" He said loudly, over the pumped up music.

Hetty laughed out loud. "Always the gentleman, dickhead."

"Whoa, ho-ho!" He taunted. "Oh, that just happened!"

Then he felt a tap on his shoulder. He turned his head to see Henry wearing the strange goggles and he looked quite antsy.

"You gotta try it out, Dor." He said, handing him the goggles. "These things are da bomb! Think Pink Floyd meets Slipknot!"

Geoff intercepted the handoff. "Love Slipknot…so 2003!" Then he lost his grip and the goggles fell to the floor.

"What the hell, Geoff?" Dorian barked at him, as he scrambled toward the antique eyewear before they are stomped by the dancers. "Do you know how much those are worth?"

"What do you care, Dorian?" Geoff scoffed. "You have enough money to buy the whole damn sweatshop operation, and get much back on the return investment."

Dorian waved through the dancers and found the goggles. He dove in to get him, but someone already picked them up. Dorian looked up to see Hetty holding the goggles in front of his face.

"Love me now, don't you?" She said, handing the goggles to him.

Dorian smiled. "More than you ever know, red." Then he slipped on the goggles.

Dextrose Coma was glowing in an aura of yellow energy. It was like a sun's corona during an eclipse. The energy was misty and its tendrils that wrapped around him and extend to his rig, especially the Victrola. Dextrose was pumping his fist in the air to the beat and the mist wrapped around his arm like barbed wire and it extended upward into the air and spread like an eagle's talons that were looking to gut its prey wide open.

The true mystery of the world is the visible,
Not the invisible

Dextrose said over the loudspeakers, and then he executed a record scratch on the Victrola. He lifted his head to look at the crows and settled his gaze on Dorian Gray who was wearing a pair of strange yellow goggles.

One's real life is often the life that one does not lead.

Dorian's mouth hung open in disbelief. Right behind Dextrose was the smirking face of a Morbus.

The very creatures Oscar Wilde had warned him about.

Now there was one with him here in the club. It was invisible to everyone else, except for Dorian and the lenses of the goggles.

It was a seething horror. A gaping, sucking maelstrom had phased into something *else* inside a misshapen, anthropomorphic outline. It was the smell of sulfur and death. It was the sound of a hive of bees inventing electricity and static.

The presence was completely and unknowably alien, and yet it had intelligence that Dorian felt could be comprehended in human terms. And it was ultimately malicious; hatred and contempt flowed over Dorian like waves of heat.

What in the hell is this thing?

He was frozen, watching with inner horror as the Morbus' face stared at him. Dorian was questioning his sanity more than anything else. There was no time for comprehension.

But the thing seemed to wordlessly reply to him, *I am everything you are not, and more you can hope to be. I am so much powerful than you.*

The presence and Dorian regarded each other for an eternity. It was like two gunfighters sizing up the strengths and weaknesses of their opponent, each hesitating to make a move until he better understood the nature and soul of the other.

For Dorian, who understood nothing of his opposite, it seemed that the presence was hesitating. This confused him; it seemed clear that the thing was more than powerful enough to outmaneuver and destroy him with very little effort.

But that line of thinking wouldn't do, he berated himself.

He cornered no fear for his physical wellbeing, but the fear of failure. If this monstrosity was going to give him the chance to crawl up off the floor, then he was going to press the advantage.

That was his only chance, he realized. He had to hope the thing had no idea he could and would attack. He had to count on the element of surprise.

A plan sprang to his mind, followed almost instantaneously by action, as Dorian launched himself at the pressure without hesitation, fearing that his nemesis would sense his intention if he delayed.

CHAPTER SEVENTEEN

Expose yourself to your deepest fear; after that, fear has no power, and the fear of freedom shrinks and vanishes. You are free.
Jim Morrison.

Squealing, hyper loud, painfully shrill feedback filled the room. It was beyond deafening, echoing back and forth between the walls as if it was hitting the face, over and over. Dorian clapped his hands to cover his ears, but the shrieking noise only increased in pitch, in volume, passing unbearable and reaching what had to be near-lethal intensity.

He hunkered down, putting his head between his knees, trying to block out the sound, wondering if he would come out of this with his hearing permanently damaged. It couldn't get any worse than this, he thought desperately.

It got worse.

Louder, higher pitched yet.

He writhed on the floor in agony, and then began to lose consciousness.

The Morbus was still studying him, collecting information, perfectly calm and convicted. Perfectly confident that it could annihilate him whenever it close.

It couldn't read his mind, Dorian was reasonably sure of that, but it did seem to have a pretty sharp understanding of his technique and tactics. Dorian had not been able to catch it by surprise.

Recognizing Dorian, knowing how many of its kind had been hunted by the young man's infamous lineage, the dark spirit snarled with such horrific fury.

Then a wind exploded toward Dorian, generated by demonic energy, making him sway and nearly fall. But the pain had not returned, and the presence that was still floated somewhere before him and it had an indefinable concentration of malignancy. His ears were still ringing from the sonic assault. His stomach was rolling with nausea.

The world went painfully white and vacant, the blinding strobe had flashed so quickly, even if he had been unable to avoid the full brunt of its awful glare. Dorian was blinded, his brain shocked and uncomprehending.

And the punishment began again. The high-pitched feedback assaulted him so loud he could feel rattling the bones of his head, vibrating in his chest, shivering his teeth.

Blood ran from Dorian's nose. Blood trickled from his ears.

Even so, his instincts served to protect him, his body unconsciously fighting to regain balance, his legs shifting direction, and landing him horizontally on a path at right angles to the one he had been on.

At the same time, Dorian struggled to shut the numbed lids on his watery eyes. But another blinding and agonizing light was blaring right at him.

Then there came another and another.

Stabbing, stabbing, stabbing him.

It was disorienting and blinding him.

His body slammed against the hard floor painfully. By chance, the angle of his head turned his eyes down and the impact carried his face into his upturned arms. Momentarily protected from the constant barrage of the strobes, Dorian squeezed his eyes shut.

It's a trap! His stunned brain finally acknowledged.

A sequence of extremely rapid strobe lights set to disable him. And he had stepped into it very neatly.

Then, horrified, he realized what had to be the aim of the ambush. He was lying there blind and vulnerable to that creature.

He kept his eyes squeezed shut, fearing the light barrage might still be continuing, knowing his dazzled eyes would that be of any help.

Pain laced into his skull like a lightning bolt.

White light, so bright it was almost blinding. Dorian blinked against it but was unable to shut it out entirely. Around him lightning flashed, somehow more intense than the white glare from which it emerged. Images from his life frozen in time sparked briefly into existence around him only to vanish as swiftly as they appeared. His vision cleared slightly.

Dextrose pushed the heavy stylus of the Victrola and it made a wince-inducing screech. There were some groans from the audience and Dorian could see at a glance that he wasn't going to be particularly popular. Everyone in the club looked up quizzically to see why the music had stopped.

Dextrose rose up and motioned to the crowd. "Yo, my sugar babies!" He called out, with a stern look on his face and his arms were crossed. "There's someone here, in this very room, that wants our party to stop!"

"No! No!" Yelled several members of the crowd, and booing and hissing accompanied it.

"Oh, yes, yes, yes!" Dextrose egged the crowd on. He paced around the stage, scanning the club. He stopped on the center of the stage and whipped a finger over at Dorian's direction. "One of those rich, trust-fund kids. *He* wants to shut us down!"

Everyone turned and glared daggers at Dorian. Some of them would have incinerated him where he stood if only they had the power. Dorian felt very exposed. Just his body language gave him away. Henry and Hetty cant tell that something bad was definitely going to happen if they didn't get the hell out of the club right now.

"Ain't no way, we gonna let this happen! Right?!" Yelled Dextrose.

"HELL, NO!" Every one started chanting. Henry and Hetty started pushing through the crowd as they tried to shield Dorian.

"And this is where we get off the A-train." Henry said to Dorian, urging him through the floor.

Beers, cups, and other debris started to rain down on the group as they tried to make an exit.

The demonic aura around Dextrose grew more intense. "Don't leave us so soon, Mr. Moneybags!" He sneered over to Dorian.

The large bouncer who was checking door stood in front of Dorian and his friends. He was blocking the only exit and it looked like he wasn't going to budge.

Hetty looked up to the brawny bald man with a relieved look on her face. "Oh, good. Can you help us get out?"

The bouncer cracked his knuckles and looked at Dorian with anger and fury.

"Shit." Dorian groaned, as he watched the bouncer cocked his fist. "Not in the face."

The bouncer's meaty fist caught him full in the face, shoving him back, knocking him to the floor.

And all hell broke loose in the club.

CHAPTER EIGHTEEN

*It's only after we've lost everything
that we're free to do anything.*
Tyler Durden, *Fight Club*.

The whole club erupted into a nasty brawl. Chairs were flying, and people were exchanging kicks and punches. Women were pulling each other's hair. Hetty gave one girl a vicious uppercut to the solar plexus. While Henry jumped on the back of the bouncer, and Geoff was busy biting some guy. All this time Dorian was standing incredulously in the middle facing Dextrose who remained on the stage and the Morbus was feeding him energy.

"Panic, instinct, genetics, impulse, focus..." observed Dextrose over the melee, "...This is my kind of night!" He laughed wildly.

Then a sudden hideous roar assaulted Dorian's ears.

"What's that?" Someone shouted.

Other voices jumped in, creating a chaotic chorus. People leaped to their feet, rushing toward the exit.

"We're under attack!"

"An explosion!"

"A bomb!"

The corridor was filled with smoke that stung Dorian's eyes and scratched the back of his throat. Flames had ascended the walls and were licking across the ceiling beams.

...And he felt a presence.

It was a tangible thing, a psychic weight, and an invisible malignancy, somehow centered on the platform.

Dorian became dimly aware that the sick hollow in his chest was more than a symptom of fear and despair. There was something physical, something right in this club, affecting him.

Then the assault came.

It was like the atmosphere pressure permitting the space surrounding him had suddenly crashed, leaving him nauseous and struggling to breathe, aching in his joints and chest like a case of the bends. He felt a buzzing, a *ringing*, in his skull.

Innate survival instinct screamed for him to leave—*now!*—but before his reflexes could respond, a surge of blinding pain washed over his mind, stabbing like a burning knife and crippling his ability to reason. More pain followed, rolling up like waves smashing into a beach, each one worse than the previous.

Each seemed to scream, *It's coming! It's coming!*

Strobes of brilliant multi-color lighting began to burst before his eyes, even though they were squeezed tightly shut in a grimace of raw agony. Through the haze of the hammering pain, Dorian was vaguely aware that the capillaries in his brain were about to explode.

He began to shake uncontrollably, but not spastically, not in a full-body heave. With an enormous effort, part instrumental, part blind panic, part desperate coming, Dorian forced his removing consciousness back to the state he had so really invoked. The world around him had become a hazy, distant mirage.

Hetty followed the other girl's attack with a double-fisted blow to the chest and jammed her fingers in and up below the rib cage.

Nothing seemed to faze the bitch.

The girl came back at her, hardly winded, and rammed her fist into her adversary's abdomen. Hetty doubled over, but managed to head-butt her as hard as she could.

They kept at it, maybe for five minutes, maybe for five hours. Hetty was way beyond tired. But gradually she began to get used to the clubber's fighting style, and she blocked more of her blows. Her open hand stopped a sock to her jaw. Then she used the meat of her hand to undercut the figure's chin, and threw in a quick jab to the other girl's cheek.

Still, way too many blows were hitting home. Sweat streamed down her face and arms as she kept up the killing pace. It was blazing hot in the club, and the heat was sapping her energy.

She wasn't the only one who was running out of steam.

Henry's arms felt like sandbags as he raised them up to block their attackers. He was trying to see what he could use as a weapon.

But the bouncer never gave him the moment he needed. And he only had one arm to work with.

The big man was laughing at them, slapping them around, and Henry, enraged, unleashing a punishing series of kicks, punches, and blocks, all with dizzying aggression. But the bouncer laughed in his face, his swollen features swelling even more, his eyes glowed much brighter. He blocked Henry and drove him back with pile-driver fists, so that he shattered against the brash rich kid.

Got to find a weapon, Henry thought. He glanced desperately around.

The bouncer saw him fumbling in the dance floor, stepped in, and backhanded him hard, sending him flying back. Henry managed to keep his feet but his head was still spinning, he tasted blood in his mouth, and he choked as he tried to warn Hetty, who was circling.

Henry started to turn away, as if he was going to run away— and then spun back, and clocked the bouncer hard in the face.

He'd caught him on the cheek, instead of the point on them man's chin as Henry had hoped, but that wasn't enough. He heard a loud crack and he held his hand in pain.

"Ow!" Henry exclaimed, nursing his fractured hand. "Seriously, ow!"

The bouncer whipped around and slammed Hetty hard in the chest with his right fist, sending her hurling backwards through the air till she came to a stop. Then the big burly man spun again and struck Henry—knocking him off his feet.

He lay there, trying to get the strength to stand…

The bouncer seemed to think Henry was done for.

He turned away.

* * *

Dorian got to his feet. He managed to use his fists to defend himself against some of the body blows that Dextrose Coma was raining on him.

Henry's eyes fluttered, and his head hummed—but he didn't want to move. He wanted to lie there and let the numbness that was gripping his limbs have its way. Every joint ached, and his damaged arm was screaming with pain.

But his friends needed him. Dorian and Hetty. And even Adrian, too.

Had to get up.

Get your ass up, Henry.

Gritting his teeth he placed his feet under him and stood, looking blinking around. He saw the bouncer stalking over toward Hetty.

She was slumped over a table, gasping for air.

Henry looked desperately around. There was only one thing handy—a fire extinguisher—which he could use as a weapon.

He picked it up and staggered, as quickly as he could, over to the bouncer, coming up behind him.

At the same time Hetty got shakily to her feet, seemed to gather her strength as the steroid addict loomed over her. She swung a haymaker at the man's face, but he caught her fist and tightened his grip.

Henry, slipping up behind the bouncer, could hear the bones breaking. Hetty gasped in pain and went to her knees. The bouncer towered over her, raising his fist to finish her off.

But Henry was within reach. He swung the fire extinguisher with all his strength, cracking the man's head.

He fell with a loud resounding thud.

"What the hell was that?" Henry said, sounding a tad disappointed. "Are we on *Gilligan's Island* where people get knocked out with a single blow to the head?"

Hetty smiled weakly at Henry. "Bet you three bucks and my left nut he wakes up with amnesia."

"You're on."

The panic had reached full proportions now.

Backstage, people were still rushing out, and Henry shouldered his way through them, shouting at Hetty.

"Come on, Hetty! Let's go!"

He headed for the door, moving against a current of hysterical people, trying to reach the main room.

Most important, the pain was gone. The devastating blindside attack had ended as quickly as it had came, and this was incentive enough to keep Dorian focused.

Despite the terror of the powerful unknown confronting him, Dorian, too, felt curious for this thing that apparently moved in and out of the world. He stared back at it and tried to define its shadowy form in his mind.

Up on the stage, it looked as if Dorian was losing his own battle.

His body went limp in Coma's merciless grasp. His head dangled forward like a rag doll. The enraged disc jockey was confident that he was going to win this fight, he was blindsided by a sucker punch right in the face from the struggling Dorian Gray.

Dorian hit him so hard, he didn't realize what had happened. Dextrose felt the back of his head as Dorian rammed it up into his chin, and the unexpected impact nearly knocked him off his feet.

Despite his bravado, Dorian was still weak. He managed to grab the microphone stand, holding it out like a weapon, and at the same time quickly assessed the stage to try and form another plan.

Dorian swung the stand at the steadily advancing Dextrose. He dodged it easily, bestowing him an evil grin in the process.

As the crowd panicked and shoved in all directions, the backstage door burst open. Henry stumbled out and nearly fell, but recovered himself at once. He took a quick look around, saw that the immediate vicinity had people herding out.

"Come on!" Yelled a bouncer.

As fast as he could direct them, the big man moved the panicking crowd through the door. His co-workers waited backstage to push everyone safely toward the exit.

Dextrose was closing in.

Dorian kicked him fiercely in the chest, sending him back against the wall. He landed hard, and seeing his chance, Dorian went in for the kill.

* * *

Henry kneed one man in the crotch, but one of the others cuffed him above the ear and another punched him in the mouth. Henry's lip burst against his teeth and hot blood poured over his chin. He recovered from the shock and he tried to pull away from the man, but they held fast.

Dorian twisted uselessly in Dextrose's grasp. He could feel the possessed DJ squeezing and squeezing—everything around Dorian was spinning, fading to black…

He coughed and choked, gasped desperately for air. From some distant place Dorian thought he could hear Dextrose laughing.

The celebrity DJ felt himself consumed by a hellish force, blasted by the spirit energy. His body turned loose of its slim frame, becoming something much, much more.

He looked out over the audience, hearing the fear in their voices and seeing the fear in their eyes.

Dextrose Coma was even more powerful now.

His whole being seemed to glow with energy and light, with undeniable strength, with eternal life.

Dorian found a wire and pulled on it hard. Sparks flew out of the end and he gripped it tightly. He bounced up on the stage and thrust the live wire at Dextrose.

Dextrose wrenched Dorian's arm that was holding the live wire behind his back trying to get it to zap the back of Dorian's head. Dorian rammed the back of his head into Dextrose's chin. Then Dextrose took Dorian by the back, trying to shove him far off the stage, but Dorian fell forward.

The live wire connected with the Victolas and it started to smoke. Dextrose wrenched backward screaming as if he was being electrocuted. The Morbus was being ripped from its grasp on Dextrose, and it began to burst into flames.

It let out a painfully high-pitched death shriek that made blood start from Dorian's eardrums.

Dorian leaped from the stage as Dextrose laid face down. Small wisps of smoke came for his body.

The clubbers were in shock and gave him a wide berth. Hetty grabbed Dorian with concern as Henry looked on.

"What the…?" Henry stared wide-eyed at his ghastly sight.

Dorian trembled. "I don't know…" he stammered, "…I just can't…anything right now. I gotta get outta here.

Dorian looked about at the carnage that surrounded him. Fire all around him, and he isn't going to be able to hold it together much longer.

The sirens were coming closer; everyone could hear the tires of police squad cars around the corner.

CHAPTER NINETEEN

Women are made to be loved, not understood.
Oscar Wilde.

A large fire was burning on the grounds of what was once known as The Barca Lounge. Preliminary reports indicate that the fire was out of control and the place was in the process of being evacuated. New York City police and fire officials were uncertain what was to be done with the club's population while the fire was brought under control, and it was also unclear how many people fled the scene without being questioned.

Emergency vehicles, news vans, and fire engines surrounded the club. Fire trucks and EMS filled the street. Police officers watched as firefighters hooked hoses to a hydrant and began to play powerful jets of water across the burning building.

One question emerged in the wake of the disaster was whether a single person was responsible, and if so whether it was the same person who started the disturbance with the special guest disc jockey. But the fire department and police investigators were walking closely to identify and arrest the person or persons responsible for this horrific act.

Outside of the club, several parents were taking their kids home, and the police were questioning and handcuffing others.

Lori had a death grip on Henry's arm, while a police officer was standing right next to her.

"Mrs. Lord, as long as your son promises to appear…"

"*Stepson*, officer." She said with venom in her voice. "And please, let me know about the damages."

The officer nodded and went back to the crime scene to take other people's statements. She looked right at her son with mean eyes and her lips curled into a hateful snarl.

"Were you, drunk, stoned or just plain stupid?"

Henry jumped back. "No, no, look I've got a pink wristband." He showed her.

"What the hell does that have to do with anything?"

"It means I wasn't drinking!"

"Enough!" She screamed. "Where is Dorian?" Lori couldn't keep the impatience out of her voice, and was beyond caring who heard it.

Henry hesitated. "I…I don't…"

"Goddammit, Henry Allen Lord! Where the hell is Dorian?!"

"I DON'T KNOW!" Henry screamed.

Lori Lord wasn't a happy woman. Henry had never seen that look etched on his mother's face before. It seemed very unnatural. He thought she wasn't even capable of displaying that frightening emotion. She usually let him and Dorian get away with murder. But as of tonight, there will be a brand new regime being established in the Lord household.

Less space, more discipline.

Without taking her eyes off her awestruck son, she reached into her purse to bring out her cellphone. Her fingers danced violently on the glass screen, scrolling down to Dorian's number. She hit "call" and waited for him to pick up the phone.

After five rings it went to voicemail.

"Hi, this is Dorian. I can't come to the phone right now. If you're Kate Upton, leave your number."

Lori clicked her teeth in disgust, whiling waiting for that obnoxious beep.

"Dorian, where the hell are you?" She spoke loudly into her stepson's voicemail. "You are in so much trouble, young man. Wherever you are, come home **NOW**."

She hung up her iPhone and covered her face with her hands. Then swept them up and over her head, smoothing her thick, occasionally unruly hair into momentary submission before clasping her fingers together behind her neck.

Dorian turned a corner, wondering how much further he'd have to go. The sidewalk stretched endlessly before him, camouflaged in shadows, and his footsteps echoed hollowly in the dark. He couldn't get the night's events out of his mind, all the people he'd met, and all the strange things that had happened. Lost in thought, he continued along the pavement until slowly it began to dawn on him that he wasn't alone.

Someone was watching Dorian.

It was someone who didn't want Dorian to see him following him.

There was another sound of footsteps now.

Footsteps behind him…footsteps walking where he had walked…

Dorian whirled around.

He could see a figure standing there, shrouded in blackness. Just far enough away so that he didn't feel quite comfortable confronting it.

The figure didn't move.

And through he couldn't actually see his stalker's face; Dorian had the distinct, unsetting impression that it was looking straight at her.

Turning quickly, Dorian went on.

The figure followed.

Dorian picked up speed. He could hear the footsteps again. Sure and measured behind him, taking their time. With a twinge of fear, he turned the next corner and went even faster.

The figure kept coming. Not hurrying at all…just keeping a discreet distance.

Dorian walked alone along the darkened streets. His hands were shoved deep into his pockets, and he kept his head down so people wouldn't recognize him. He spotted a coffee shop with its light still on down the street. He entered the building and ordered a small coffee.

The waitress looked worn and haggard, as she tended to be when she was approaching the end of her shift. Her straight black hair was tied back in a bun, but there were random strands hanging in her face.

She brewed the coffee and handed it to Dorian, who gave the tired barista several dollars. He turned around to survey the café and he surprisingly spotted Sybil Vane—the prima ballerina he met the other night—in the corner.

She was completely unaware that Dorian was standing right next to her with a steaming coffee in his hand. She was engrossed in a book she was reading. Dorian craned his head to make out the title; *A Woman of No Importance* by Oscar Wilde.

Great, Dorian seethed. *Him again.*

Sybil had just gotten out of a very grueling rehearsal. She couldn't concentrate on the book as she was relieving the day's events in her head.

Sybil found herself back on stage and dancing in a very crucial scene of the ballet. She was one with music and it carried her. The music vanished when she heard the director yelled, "CUT!"

All the performers stopped what they were doing. Sybil could hear the whispers of the tech crew and the costuming people as they dashed about doing their appointed tasks for the remaining run of the two-week production of *The Firebird*.

Then she saw Cecilia staring blankly at her. "Oh, my God," she winced, "I was supposed to come in and do a twirl, wasn't I? I'm *so* sorry. I'll get it right this time, honest."

Cecilia was tall and lean enough and her new hairstyle really stood out. Her agent had suggested she go with the new 'do since Zooey Deschanel was making a splash in the indie scene.

Cecilia hadn't been keen on it at first, but a few more gigs had dropped into her lap lately, so maybe the agent was right. She'd died as a plague victim on a recent *Fringe*, been killed on an episode of *Law & Order: SVU*, and showed up as a college coed on *Gossip Girl*.

If she concentrated more on her dancing than on her "budding" acting career, we wouldn't be stopping every ten seconds, groaned Sybil.

Somehow, she managed not to scream—which was more than could be said for Andre Romanov, the director.

"Cecilia, my darling—you are aware, are you not, that we have *nine* more performances?"

"I'm sorry, Andre," Cecilia said. "I'll try to—"

"No! No, no, no, *no!*" The Russian got up from his seat at front-row center in the one hundred-seat theatre and started pacing in front of the stage. "I do not want to hear no more excuses. The time for 'try' is past. The time is now for not 'try.' Time is now for 'succeed.' Okay?"

A male dancer whispered, "Thank you, Master Yoda."

Cecilia giggled.

Andre stopped pacing and stared at Cecilia—an effect diluted by the sunglasses that the director always wore, along with a black beret that rested on top of his balding head.

"Oh, this is funny, you think? My ballet is going to be turned into a goddamn dog and pony show, and you are laughing?"

"Sorry, Andre," Cecilia said, "I was—I was thinking of something else, honest. I wasn't laughing at you. Really, I wasn't, okay? Can we take it again?"

"Okay." Andre retook his seat and adjusted his cap. "From the top."

"Hang on a sec," said one of the crewmembers. "We're having trouble with the lights. Give me two seconds."

"I will give you five seconds, but no more!" Andre shouted.

Sybil knew *that* was a lost cause. The crew had been complaining about the stage lights since day one.

Andre withered a stream of words in Russian, none of which Sybil knew, though she suspected that their equivalents in English were mostly spelled with four letters. Andre had been effusive in his praise—which, for Andre, meant that he only told Sybil that she was awful and was ruining his show once or twice, as opposed to constantly. He was so frustrated at today's rehearsal; he actually succeeded in ripping his beloved beret in two.

Cecilia was annoyed at her self for not getting her moves right, and was taking it out mostly on the crew, who proceeded to take it out on the entire cast by screwing up cues and set changes. This is turn got the cast members annoyed and upset, which they took out on each other and Andre, who was aggravated at all of them.

Thank God we have tomorrow off, Sybil had thought.

When they were done with one scene, and the lights—were now functionally properly—went out, Sybil was stunned to hear clapping from the aisles.

The houselights came up, as they did after every scene so Andre could nitpick them to death before going on to the next scene, and she saw it was Andre who was applauding.

"Now *that*, my good friends, *that* is dancing, Sybil, for the first time in a week. I believe that you quite possibly might not be ruining my ballet."

"Gee, thanks, Andre," Sybil said dryly.

During her time performing under her Russian taskmaster, night had came swiftly to Manhattan, and it was the time of year when darkness arrived early and sunsets that crashed down like collapsing buildings. The skyscrapers glowed brightly red, then switched to their own feeble illumination.

Under any other circumstances, Sybil would have simply gone straight from rehearsal to his house. Or perhaps she would have taken up on Cecelia's offer to join the rest of the cast at some bohemian bar to decompress. The bar was kind of a dump. The patrons liked it that way. It meant that the idiot tourists tended to stay the hell away from it, and it could be some place for people who were in the know to hang out. Andre had put them through a brutal rehearsal, made worse by the fact that there were three understudies coming in.

So Sybil took a brisk walk across Manhattan to the Bowery where her favorite coffee shop was located. It was one of her many sanctuaries in the city. It was somewhere where she can be at peace and get some reading done.

After a moment, Dorian cleared his throat. Sybil continued on reading her book, turning her body slightly away from him as she turned the page. With one hand she stirred milk into her cup.

Dorian frowned.

Why was she ignoring him?

Perhaps he was intruding, but she had barely said a word to him since they met at the after party. Dorian felt that he should say something before the silence between them stretched much further.

He cleared his throat again, slightly louder this time.

"I hear it's a good book." He said to her.

"It's a play." She replied, turning a page nonchalantly.

Dorian took the chair across from her and sipped his coffee. It was still too hot. He reached for a non-dairy creamer container. Sybil barely acknowledged him.

"I was just, um, walking and thought I'd…and I saw…um, we met the other night. At your dance, I'm Dorian." He said, wrapping his hands over the Styrofoam cup and inhaled the coffee steam.

"Mr. "Trip the light fantastic."" She said, not taking her eyes off the page.

Dorian lowered his eyes and sunk in his chair. "Uh, yeah, right. I'm sorry, but I had a really weird night."

Sybil closed the book and held it in her small hands for a moment before setting it down gently on the table, next to her cooling cup of coffee.

"And I'm sure your psychiatrist will be fascinated." She replied, staring down at her cup.

Dorian reached out to touch her hand. Sybil trembled by the contact. He could feel her shaking.

"I don't mean to be forward," he assured her, and then he refrained. "No, that's bull…it's exactly what I mean. I just want to say, um, I like you."

Sybil looked at him as if he were crazy. "You don't even know me."

For the first time their eyes met. She offered him a tiny hint of sad smile.

"That's the point." Dorian replied. "I'd really like to."

"If you think you can save me…you'd have better luck with those debutantes who fawn all over you."

Dorian gave her a puzzled look. "Save you? I just wanted to walk you home."

"I've managed to walk those three blocks every night since I was twelve."

"You live around *here*?"

"It's called a dance scholarship, if that's what you're thinking." Sybil clarified. "I live with my sister. My father, well…just *don't*…" then she began to tear up.

Sybil closed her eyes, and bit her lip, not wanting Dorian to see any weakness in her. But inwardly she felt all the emotional pain fighting free, all the anguish she'd suppressed just to get through it all.

She got up quickly from the booth, leaving her book on table. "I need a moment." She told Dorian before gong to the ladies' room.

Dorian started to realize how much she's hurting. And he thought she liked him, or could like him. But she also desperately wants to be happy.

"An exciting night." Said a voice behind him.

Dorian spun around to see Marlowe Diamond sitting in the adjacent booth sipping tea.

"Especially in the light of the evening's events." He added, setting the cup on the table.

"What are you talking about?" Dorian asked him. He had just about enough of this guy. He started to ask himself if this creep was stalking him.

"The way you took out the VanderBraun Morbus." Diamond answered with a smile. "My employer took notice."

"What the hell is a Morbus?"

"Does it matter? You tricked it into destroying its totem."

Dorian was in no mood on shooting the breeze with this creep. "Listen, buddy, I don't know what the hell you're getting at." He said impatiently.

"You sent it back." Diamond explained. "And freed the VanderBrauns from its further influence."

Dorian got out of his seat and stared Diamond down. His hands were clenched into fists. "I don't know who you are or what you want, but if it's an ass-kicking, I'll be happy to oblige."

A disappointed look fell onto Diamond's face. "You know she's cursed as well." He sighed. "Just like the VanderBrauns."

Dorian raised an eyebrow. "Who?"

"Your girlfriend, Ms. Vane."

Dorian pointed his finger onto the crazy man's chest. Diamond looked almost bemused as the Pillsbury Dough Boy. "Listen, take your bullshit and…"

"*You* listen, Mr. Gray." Diamond said with such authority in his voice. "I can make all this hocus pocus go away. Sell me the Saligia and you can go back to screwing all the girls on the gymnastics team."

"What the hell is this 'Saligia' you have been bugging me about? What has this got to do with me?"

"Everything, Mr. Gray," Diamond's eyes narrowed. "The Saligia is your great-grandfather's diary. It's a collection of the seven deadly sins. They are used to educate and instruct Christians about humanity's tendency to sin."

"Well, no shit," Dorian scoffed. "Everyone has seen that Brad Pitt movie. What has this got to do with my family?"

"Your ancestor was a cautionary tale," Diamond replied, briefly glancing at his watch. "I take it you haven't read Wilde's novel about him."

"Well, I started to read it and it's no *Fifty Shades of Grey*, and then the new *Shades* book came out and—"

Diamond was no longer amused. He had been patient long enough.

"I grow weary of your snide remarks and uncooperative behavior." His tone was much more stern than Dorian's teacher Mr. Haskin. "Give me what I want and I'll go away and you will never see me again."

"I'm not giving you a goddamned thing. Stay away from me," Dorian warned, "and you stay the hell away from Sybil."

"Oh, it's a little late for that," Diamond replied.

The two men circled each other in some sort of macabre dance. Diamond took his time and seemed to be enjoying the slow-motion chase.

Dorian turned to see Sybil returning from the rest room. He picked up her book and took her by the hand, and led her out of the coffee shop. Diamond didn't move to stop them. He didn't even turn his head to watch them go.

"The pure and simple truth is rarely pure and never simple." He said to Dorian as they headed for the door.

"I know a place we can have some quiet." Dorian said to Sybil, putting his arm around her shoulder and then escorted her out of the café.

She had a worried look on her face. "Wait! I'm not sure."

"Come on," urged Dorian, "it will be fun."

INTERLUDE FOUR
FROM THE JOURNAL OF DORIAN GRAY

April 27, 1890

I have never been so humiliated in my life.

Sybil's failure to impress the audience has troubled me greatly.

For some reason, the house was crowded that night, and the fat stage manager was beaming ear-to-ear with a slithery smile. He escorted us to our box seats with a sort of pompous humility, waving his fat jeweled hands, talking at the top of his voice. I loathed him more than ever. Harry, on the other hand, liked him. Basil amused himself with watching the faces in the pit.

The heat was terribly oppressive, and the huge sunlight tamed like the theater had been set ablaze. Some audience members had removed their coats and hung them over the side. Some women were laughing in the pit; their voices were horribly shrill and discordant. The sound of popping corks came from the bar.

I told my friends that Sybil was divine beyond all living things. When she acts they will all forget everything they have ever known about fantasy and their own banality. And all of these common people in the theatre will become quite different when she would enter the stage.

A quarter of an hour afterwards, amidst an extraordinary turmoil of applause, Sybil stepped on to the stage. Yes, she was the loveliest of all creatures. There was something of the fawn in her shy grace and startled eyes. A faint blush, like the shadow of a rose in a mirror of silver, came to her cheeks as she glanced at the crowded, enthusiastic house. She stepped back a few paces, and her lips seemed to tremble.

Basil leaped to his feet and began to applaud, while Harry peered through his opera glasses and cheered in approval. I sat motionless, gazing on her, like a man in a dream.

The next scene was at the hall of the Capulet house, and Romeo had entered with Mercutio and his friends. The band, such as it was, struck up a few bars of music, and the dance began. Through the crowd of ungainly, shabbily dressed actors, Sybil moved like a creature from another world. Her body swayed, as she danced, as a plant sways in the water. The curves of her throat were like the curves of a white lily. Her hands seemed to be made of cool ivory.

The scene was very dramatic and moving moment; one Sybil had done many times. Each time, she had captured her adoring audience. But tonight, for some strange reason, she seemed dull and listless. She showed no signs of joy when, as Juliet, her eyes rested on Romeo. Her words were spoken in an artificial manner. The voice was exquisite, but from the point of view of tone it was absolutely false. It took away all the life from the verse. It made the passion unreal.

I grew pale as I watched her. Neither of my friends dared to say anything to me. She seemed to them to be absolutely incompetent. They were horribly disappointed and they dismissed her performance as of an amateur.

Yet they felt that the true test of any Juliet was the balcony scene of the second act. They waited for that. She looked charming as she came out in the moonlight. That could not be denied. But the staginess of her acting was unbearable, and grew worse as she went on. She over-emphasized everything that she had to say.

It was not nerves. Indeed, so far from being nervous, she seemed absolutely self-contained. It was simply bad art. She was a complete failure.

Even the uneducated audience of the pit and gallery lost their interest in the play. They got restless, and began to talk loudly and whistle. The only person unmoved was Sybil herself.

The play dragged on, and seemed interminable. Half of the audience went out, tramping in heavy boots, laughing, and there came a storm of hisses. The whole thing was a fiasco. The last act was played to almost empty benches.

I apologized to my friends as I asked them to leave so I could be alone with my tears. Sybil truly is a mediocre actress. I sat through the remainder of the show, and then rushed over to Sybil's dressing room. When I got there she was standing ther with a proud smile on her face.

"How badly I acted tonight!" She said it as if it didn't even matter. There was no remorse in her state of being at all.

Then she gave me all this rubbish on how she will never act again and how the craft of the theatre was nothing more than a sham.

I loved her because she was great. Because I thought she had such talent. Instead, I found her very shallow and stupid.

I cannot believe I was such a fool.

She killed my love. She used to stir my imagination. Now she doesn't even stir my curiosity. She simply produced no effect. I loved her because she had genius and intellect, because she realized my dreams of great poets and gave shape and substance to the shadows of art.

Now she had thrown it all away.

I was mad to love her. She is nothing to me now. I will never see her again. I will never think of her and I will never mention her name.

I wish I had never laid eyes upon her. She has spoiled the romance of my life. I would have made her famous, splendid, and magnificent. The world would have worshipped her, and she would have belonged to me. Now she is nothing but a third-rate actress with a pretty face.

In a few moments I was out of the theatre. I wandered through dimly lit streets, past shadowy archways and evil-looking houses. Women with hoarse voices and harsh laughter had called after me. Drunkards cursed and chattered to themselves like oversized apes. I had seen grotesque children huddled upon doorsteps and heard shrieks and oaths from gloomy courts.

After a while, I hailed a hansom and drove home. As I was turning the handle of the door to my house, my eye fell upon the portrait Basil had painted of me. The face on the painting had changed. The expression was different. There was a touch of cruelty in the mouth that had not been there before.

It was horrible!

What did it mean?

I turned around and drew up the blind to the window. The bright down flooded the room and swept the fantastic shadows into dusty corners, where they lay shuddering. But the strange expression that I had noticed seemed to linger there—more interested even. The quivering ardent sunlight showed me the lines of cruelty round the mouth as clearly as if I had been looking into a mirror after I had done some dreadful thing.

I examined the picture again. There were no signs of any change when I looked into the actual painting. There was no doubt that the whole expression had been altered.

Then I remembered that wish I made at Basil's studio.

I asked to remain young and for the portrait to grow old. Now my desire had come true. I would remain young and handsome and the canvas would bear the burden of my sins.

Has my wish been fulfilled?

Such things are impossible. It seemed even hideous to even think of them. And, yet, there was the picture before me, with the touch of cruelty in the mouth.

Had I been cruel? It was the girl's fault, not mine. I had dreamed of her as an artist and given my love to her because I thought she was great. Then she disappointed me.

What was the picture trying to say to me?

Then I suddenly realized that this macabre painting held the secrets of my life.

It's telling my story.

It changed already.

For every illicit deed I would commit, my portrait would pay the price. Would this painting teach me to hate my own soul?

From this day on, I will resist temptation. I will not see Lord Wotton anymore, and grovel for forgiveness to Sybil and marry her. I have been selfish and cruel to her. I'll make it all up to her and our life together will be beautiful.

CHAPTER TWENTY

To cure the soul by means of the senses, the senses must be by the means of the soul.
Lord Henry Wotton.

It was late at night and the moon was full in the sky, painting the exposed landscape with a wash of ghostly color. Dorian stood on the grassy bank for a moment, savoring the stillness of the night. The evening air was alive with the sound of nature going about its business, in a thousand tiny but important ways.

Dorian and Sybil were overlooking the Statue of Liberty at Battery Park. In the distance they could see that the ferry lines were all closed and it was deserted.

He thought he'd have to think quickly to keep up with her. But their conversation had followed as if they were old friends. She felt comfortable and relaxed right away.

Had she talked too much about herself?

He really hadn't given her a choice.

Dorian tried to get her to talk about her personal life, about her brother, about dancing, and how she became interested in the performing arts.

But Sybil seemed reluctant to reveal much. She kept changing the subject back to him, drawing him out, asking question after question, those bright eyes locked on his, appearing so amused by his answers, so fascinated and charmed.

"I just want to dance." Sybil said to Dorian, clutching her coffee as if her life depended on it. "It's all I think of." She lowered her eyes and felt her heart pound.

For all her light and litheness, there was a distant heaviness to her, thought Dorian, while watching her hair shimmering in the moonlight.

Dorian handed her the goggles. "Try these, maybe it'll give you a new perspective."

She pushed his advance away. "When I dance there's no one—nothing holding me. Not even gravity."

Like an unfulfilled wish, compared Dorian. He smiled at her as he placed the lenses over his eyes. *Something weighed her down.*

Then his smile disappeared.

A Morbus was surrounding Sybil. Its arms were crossed and it stared at Dorian sinisterly when it realized it was discovered.

Dorian quickly removed the goggles and his expression turned serious. "Uh, we should get home."

To his surprise, Sybil reached out and took his hand. Hers was warm and delicate in his, and suddenly he felt as if anything was possible. He couldn't take his eyes off her, and he was suddenly completely convinced that she was in the same predicament, unable to look away from him. He started to speak with absolutely no idea what he was going to say.

Then he felt someone tapping on his shoulder.

Dorian turned around to see Henry standing behind him, holding a flask. The stench of alcohol was in his breath and it looked like he did a little self-indulging .

"Who's up for a rave?" Henry slurred, waving his flask in the air. "I got some glow sticks."

Dorian was shocked to see Henry here.

"What?" Henry asked, trying to steady himself. "We're on the same cell plan. The magic of GPS!"

"It's late, H. Let's go home."

Opening the small silver flask, Henry took a gulp, grimacing as the amber liquid burned his empty stomach.

It's a good vintage, he observed. *I with I had more of it.*

"Don't make it that I snuck out for nothing. If I'm getting busted for something I didn't do—I should at least get the benefits of having done the crime." Then he looked over to see Sybil who was standing behind Dorian. She looked cold and felt a little tense. "Aw, crap, bro, I didn't mean to bogart your action." He held out the flask for her. "Sybil, would you like a blast? It's a '55 Glenfarcias. Straight from my dad's collection; worth about ten grand."

Sybil snatched the flask from Henry's hand. Sybil looked grim as a shadow crossed her face. "Where's the party?"

She took a sip. The dark red liquid felt good as it burned the back of her throat. She took another sip and smiled at Henry.

In all of a sudden an idea popped into Henry's mind. He jumped on the railing on the Brooklyn Bridge. He held the bridge wire with one hand leaning back on the walkway. With his other hand he took a swig from his flask.

"That weird shit I saw tonight?" He smiled over to Dorian. "Cops are blaming some bad Climax. But I wasn't high. Well, not yet"

Dorian motioned for him to get back on land. "Don't be an idiot, Henry."

"Everything is dangerous, Dorian." Henry replied. "If not, life wouldn't be worth living?"

"You consider a 150-foot free fall into icy water?"

Henry tossed Dorian the flask. "Show some stones. Come up here, then I'll come down."

"You know you're an asshole."

"Sphincterus giganticus!" Henry laughed.

Sybil looked up at the tangle of wiring. Wisps of the Morbus' aura circled around her.

Temptation can sink roots only when there is a void. Like a weed of sadness.

Then she began to take off her shoes.

Henry reached the ground and he gave Dorian a high-five. "Admit it, you love me." He said to Dorian, smiling. "I'm all the sins you don't have the balls to do." Then he looked up to see Sybil climbing higher. "You go, girl!" Henry shouted.

The wind roared in Sybil's ears, so that she had to strain to hear what Henry was saying. "Speak up!" She shouted. "I can't hear you over the wind!"

Dorian gazed up at Sybil in wonder. Stunned.

"Sybil!" He exclaimed in fear. "Are you friggin' nuts?"

The cold gasped into Sybil's bones, and she felt incredibly heavy and clumsy as a result. *Cold. The whole world is so cold tonight.*

The wind was blowing constantly, and that in and it was bad enough, but she also felt some degree of exposure that she couldn't understand.

Looking back onto the bridge, Sybil leaned out over the water hanging on with one hand. She was up on one toe like the graceful dancer she was. Dorian was scrambling up the lattice to get to her.

The Morbus that was floating around her was whispering in her ear. She listened to the vile and creature and a tear cascaded down her cheek. She could feel fear grabbing at her stomach.

Sybil took a deep breath. She wondered how long it would take her to hit the water if she jumped off the bridge at the exact moment. Even from where she was, Sybil could feel the heat rolling over her, and she knew that all the prayers in the world weren't going to transform this experience into a simple nightmare.

She wouldn't be waking up.

This was real.

This was happening.

She was going to die, and there was nothing that anyone could possibly do about it.

Sybil couldn't help it. She screamed as she plummeted toward the icy waters below.

The wind whipped her dress as she fell. She seemed to welcome the fall into the icy water. Below her Henry looked shock and he was frozen in his place.

Dorian, who was much closer, leaped to grab her.

"Don't worry, Sybil," she heard him say, again in that quiet, private voice that was for her alone, "I've got you."

Silence now. Sybil felt the hush in her heart. Even the wind seemed to stop.

Her eyes opened, and the tension seemed to slip from her shoulders. When their eyes met, she gave a start of surprise, her mouth forming a tiny "O" of amazement. She found something reassuring.

He smiled back. He had nothing left to say that he had not already said with his eyes.

Every saint has a past, and every sinner has a future.

INTERLUDE FIVE

London, England
1915

Dorian Gray had done many dreadful things in his life. He vowed he would not do anymore evil. He began conducting good intentions for several weeks.

He stayed at a little inn, knowing anybody can be good there in the country. There were no temptations there. That was the main reason why people who lived out of town were so uncivilized. Country-people had no opportunity of being either cultured or corrupt.

Dorian met a girl named Hetty, who was beautiful and wonderful as Sybil Vane. Dorian thought it was that which first attracted him to her. He loved Hetty—he was quite sure he loved her. He ran down to see her two or three times a week. Yesterday she met Dorian at an orchard, with hopes that they were to run away together, but Dorian released her and left the village.

He spared her. Spared her from revealing to her what he truly was, and the cruel gossip from onlookers who knew about his beastly and scandalous reputation.

When Dorian told Lord Wotton about his time in the country, he didn't share the same enthusiasm.

"You gave her good advice," he said to Dorian, "you broke her heart. This is truly the beginning of your reformation. Congratulations."

Dorian was taken back from this. "Harry, you are horrible! Hetty's heart is not broken."

Lord Wotton laughed. "Do you think this girl will ever be really contented now with any one of her own class? Hetty met you, and loved you, and her time with you will teach her to despise her husband. Besides, how do you know that Hetty isn't floating at the present moment in some pond like Ophelia?"

"Have you no shame, Harry?" Snarled Dorian, surprised by his friend's behavior. "You mock at everything, and then you suggest such unspeakable tragedies. I don't care what you say. I know I've done the right thing. This was the first act of self-sacrifice I have ever known. I want to be better. I am going to be better."

Then Dorian took a deep breath, and looked at Lord Wotton who was waiting for this little melodrama to end. It seemed that Dorian wasn't as much fun as he used to be. He watched as the bored aristocrat yawned.

"Let's change the subject," Dorian said, pouring some brandy into a glass. "What is the news in town?"

"People are still discussing Basil's disappearance." Lord Wotton answered, sitting back in his chair.

"I should have thought they had gotten tired of it by now."

"Dorian, they have only been talking about for six weeks," Lord Wotton seriously expressed. "The public is really not equal to the mental storm of having more than one topic than most times a man changes his shirt. Scotland Yard still insists that a man who fitted Basil's description who left on the midnight train on the 7th of November to Paris. The French police declared that Basil never arrived in the city at all."

"What do you think has happened to Basil?" Asked Dorian, wondering how it was that he could discuss the matter so calmly.

"If Basil needed to escape, it is none of my concern." Lord Wotton replied, stroking his chin in deep thought. "If he is dead, I don't want to think about it."

Dorian said nothing, but rose from his seat and let his finger stray across the keys. Then he stepped and looked over to Lord Wotton.

"Harry, did it ever occur to you that Basil was murdered?"

"Why should he be murdered?" Said Lord Wotton, as he almost lost his breath on that horrid notion. "The man was not clever enough to have enemies. He only interested me once, and that was when he told me, years ago, that he had a wild adoration for you."

"I was very fond of Basil," said Dorian, with a sad look in his eyes. "But don't people say he was murdered?"

"Oh, some of the papers do. However, it doesn't make any sense. I know there are very dangerous places in Paris, but Basil was not the sort of man to have gone to them. Now none of this tawdry business, it's really making me depressed. Tell me how you kept your youth, Dorian."

Dorian rose up from the piano, and passed his hand through his hair. He gave Lord Wotton a small smile.

"If I'd tell you, I'll have to kill you."

It was such a lovely night, so warm that Dorian threw his coat over his arm, and did not even put his silk scarf around his throat. As he strolled home, smoking a cigarette, two young men passed him.

"That's Dorian Gray," he heard one of them whispered.

He remembered how pleased he used to be when he was pointed out, or stared at, or talked about. He was tired of hearing his own name now. Half the charm of the little village where he had been so often lately was that no one knew where he was.

He had told the girl whom he made love he was poor and she had believed him. He had told her once that he was wicked, and she laughed at him, and told him that wicked people were always very old and ugly. What a laugh she had. She knew nothing, but she had everything that he had lost.

Dorian arrived home and found his servant waiting up for him. He sent him to bed and threw himself on the sofa in the library. People who came to stay at Gray Manor—Dorian, like his father before him, enjoyed having guests in the house, at least up until the last few years, when he seemed to spend for more time away from the manor than in it—often had a hard time getting comfortable. Dorian used to think it was due to the sheer scale of the place, but now he felt it had more to do with history, the associations that so many of the rooms had.

Dorian understood, intellectually, how so much history could be overwhelming, intimidating even, but it never had seemed the way to him. For Dorian, history, was something to be examined, prodded, its innermost secrets uncovered and brought to light.

At any rate, he'd grown up treating Gray Manor like somewhat of a museum. Much more of the house was open then, and he spent hours going from wing to wing, room to room, looking at the paintings, the statues, the furniture, and then returning to his father with a hundred questions:

Whose picture is that?

Who lived in this room?

Why is this there, that there?

Most of the time, his father had the answers, and if he didn't, he'd search the library for a book that did. His father had also hinted at the possibility of secret passageways, hidden rooms, and trapdoors running through the house. When he was younger, he used to go down to the basement, or into the sealed-off floors below the East tower, and rap on panels along the walls, listening for echoes. Now, of course, he knew he'd been having him on the whole time in what regard, but part of him still looked at Gray Manor as something to be explored, a place that just might hold a few surprises for him

The lord of the manor felt restless and agitated. He could not stop thinking about some of the things that his friend Lord Wotton had said to him.

He wondered: was it really true that one could never change? He suddenly felt a yearning for his lost boyhood—a time when he had been truly good. He knew that he had long since corrupted himself and that he had exerted on evil influence on others.

What was worse, Dorian thought, he had enjoyed ruining other people's lives. He had taken special pleasure in disgracing those who were most full of promise.

But was *his* life forever ruined?

Was there no hope?

What was responsible for his terrible ways?

He blamed Lord Wotton's evil book and Basil's portrait for everything. Now he knew what a monstrous thing he had wasted for in eternal youth and beauty. Why had he said those fateful words? If he hadn't prayed for his wish to be answered, he might have led a better life. All his failure had been due to this.

He hated his good looks—and his youth.

But for those two things, his life might have been truly happy. Instead, beauty had mocked him, and youth had spoiled him.

Dorian was finally confronting his own life—and he did not like what he saw. The woman he loved had poisoned herself when he treated her cruelly. Her brother was hidden in a nameless grave. Then Dorian's friend shot himself, but hadn't revealed his secret that he had been forced to keep.

Dorian had escaped being associated with all three of their deaths. Even the death of Basil Hallward had passed from public interest. He was safe there, too.

What weighed upon Dorian Gray's mind weren't the suicides or the murders, but the living death of his own soul.

He continually prayed for a new life, and he would never again tempt innocence. He would be fine and upstanding. Perhaps his decision to be good could change the ugly face in the painting. He would go and look. He took a lamp from the table and crept upstairs.

Yes, he would be good and the painting would no longer terrify him. He felt as though a load had been lifted from him.

As he unlocked the door, he dragged the purple covering from the portrait. A cry of pain and indignation broke from his lips. He could not see any change.

The thing was still hateful—even more than before!

The eyes had a look of deep cunning and the mouth was curved in a malicious sneer.

The scarlet dew that had spotted the hand after Basil's murder seemed brighter, and more like new blood.

Was the red stain larger than before?

It seemed to have crept like a horrible disease over the wrinkled fingers. There was even blood at the feet—as though the thing had dripped—and even on the hand that had not held the knife.

What did it all mean?

Did the painting want him to confess his many sins?

The idea was insane.

What if he did?

Then the whole world would laugh at him.

There was no trace of his guilt anywhere. He had gotten away with every one of his crimes. And if he told people the story of how the painting kept changing, they would call him crazy and lock him up in a lunatic asylum. And if he showed it to them, then who would believe such an outrageous tale?

But Basil's murder—was it to dog him all his life?

Was he ready to confess?

Never!

Dorian made a fateful decision. He refused to be burdened by his past. There was only one piece of evidence against him: the painting.

He would destroy it.

He had only kept it because it had given him pleasure to watch it grow old. Lately, he felt no such pleasure.

The damned portrait had kept him up at night. When he was away, he had been terrified that someone else might see it. The painting had brought sadness to his passions. Its very existence had destroyed moments of joy and happiness. It had been like a bad conscience to him. He would destroy that conscience and start fresh.

Dorian looked around and saw the knife that had stabbed Basil Hallward. He had cleaned it many times, until there wasn't a stain left on it. It was bright and it glistened. As it had killed the painter, so it would also kill the painter's work all that it represented. It would kill the past and when that was dead, Dorian Gray would be free. He would kill this painted monster and he would be set free.

He seized the knife and stabbed the picture with it.

There was a terrible cry—and a crash. The cry was so horrible that the frightened servants ran upstairs.

Two gentlemen who were passing in the square below stopped and looked up at the great house.

They ran to get a policeman and brought him back. They rang the bell several times, but there was no answer. Except for a light in one of the top windows, the house was all dark.

Inside, the servants were talking to each other in low whispers. The old housekeeper was weeping. The butler was as pale as a ghost. Still, he, the coachman and the footman crept upstairs.

The policeman and the other servants followed. They knocked on the door but there was no reply. Finally, they got on the rood and dropped onto the balcony and kicked in the windows.

When they entered, they found a splendid portrait of the 20-year-old Dorian Gray, with all his youth and handsome features intact.

"Whose house is this, Constable?" Asked the elder of the two gentlemen.

"Mr. Dorian Gray, sir," answered the policeman.

Lying on the floor was a dead man—with a knife in his heart! He was withered and wrinkled and horrible to look at. It wasn't until the servants examined the rings on his aged fingers that they realized it was their employer.

Dorian Gray had changed places with his own painting!

The separation of spirit from matter was a mystery, and the union of spirit with matter was a mystery also. A curse is like a prayer; arbitrary words, a collection of syllables only meaningful to the speaker. Being alive for only one fleeting moment. They are harmless because there is no such thing as magic incantations, summonings or divine intervention.

But curses exist.

To manifest and sink its claws it takes a willing victim… one who anchors faith to himself like an albatross. One was willing to give in to the basest of desires as easily as slipping a noose around his very own neck. In addition to being quite the oblivious until the rope snaps the neck.

Dorian Gray realized that now. But to what cost?

Living a life of paranoia, excess, and self-destruction. Thus leading to the alienation between him and his friends, and the tarnish of his once wholesome reputation.

In death, Dorian Gray was truly free.

PART IV
De PROFUNDIS

INTERLUDE SIX
FROM THE JOURNAL OF DORIAN GRAY

April 16, 1890

After I left Harry yesterday, I ate dinner at an Italian restaurant in Rupert Street and went to the theater. Sybil was performing that night and she was wonderful. She is a born artist.

When the performance was over, I went backstage and spoke to her. As we sat together, there came a look in her eyes. We kissed.

It was the most perfect moment of my life.

Of course, our engagement is a deep secret. I don't know what my guardians will say. All I know is that I love Sibyl Vane and I want the world to know she is mine.

I have become a different man when I am around her. She makes me good. When we are together, I forget all of Harry's poisonous ideas.

CHAPTER TWENTY-ONE

Those who find ugly meanings in beautiful things are corrupt without being charming. This is a fault. Those who find beautiful meanings in beautiful things are the cultivated. For these there is hope.
Oscar Wilde.

The bridge was filled with cops and firefighters. The ambulance arrived, and the paramedics scrambled away the onlookers. Sybil was lying on a gurney and she was being pushed into the back of the ambulance. A paramedic was walking both Dorian and Henry away with blankets wrapped around them. Dorian could feel the Morbus that followed Sybil was still there. Hiding in the bridge metal works, cackling at the destruction it caused.

A worried look was upon Dorian. He looked back to see Sybil, who was unconscious as the EMTs shut the ambulance doors and drove off in a siren wailing rush. A cold sweat was streaming from his brow.

"Why would she do that?" He shivered, remembering the sadness in her eyes before she jumped. "She seemed so happy. Why would she want to kill herself?"

Henry patted him in the back in an attempt to console him. "Just be glad you were there to grab her, man."

Dorian briskly turned away from him. This was all Henry's fault. If he didn't show being a jackass and goad Sybil into climbing the bridge, she wouldn't have thought about jumping.

Henry gave him a puzzled look. "Dor, what's—"

"*Don't.*" Warned Dorian. "Don't even touch me."

Henry and Dorian rode in a sparsely populated subway car. There was a pretty, disheveled woman on her way home from an embarrassing tryst. Over at the far side of the car was an old lady with a wagon basket of groceries. Right beside her was a very pudgy guy in an ill-fitting New York Knicks jersey, and a genial Asian man on his way home from the late shift at the docks.

Dorian looked with obvious concern at his best friend, who was leaning back in the train seat, who didn't seem fazed from what happened at the Brooklyn Bridge several hours ago. Dorian's blue eyes narrowed on his friend's face, studying him as if seeing him for the first time.

No words passed between the two old friends. Dorian couldn't even begin to imagine what must have been going through Henry's mind.

Henry felt Dorian's steely gaze burning into his back. Then there came a constant burden of his friend's anger and expectations. Chief among them was the expectation that they'd do things Dorian's way. An argument was the last thing he needed right now.

Dorian must really be pissed, thought Henry, as silence hung in the air between them like knives.

Dorian fumed. *What the hell did he think he was playing at? He's acting like this was no big deal, as though he didn't care what would happen if Sybil slipped. That stupid son of a bitch!*

"If we slip the doorman a twenty, he won't tell Lori about my escape." Henry said to Dorian, who paid no attention to him.

Dorian pulled out the copy of A Woman of No Importance he took from Sybil back at the café from his pocket. He opened it and started reading.

He wanted to ring off then, sitting back and trying to enjoy the ride back to the apartment, which meant that he let his mind wander back through the last several days. He was turning over ideas, picking up theories and shaking them to see if anything fell out.

"Sybil." He said out loud, hoping that Henry can see the seriousness of the incident. "She seemed so fragile."

He didn't get a response from Henry. Dorian looked up to see the subway car was completely empty.

All except for Oscar Wilde standing right across from him.

Wilde rested both his hands on the top of his cane. "There are several stages to awareness." He told Dorian, who rose to his feet. "Searching, knowing, awakening, remembering, becoming. But, my boy, you have come late to the party, so we need to skip to the end—*being*."

Dorian looked around the car, thinking whether or not he was dreaming. "I appreciate the hallucination," he said, walking toward the exit, "but I've had a long night. Why don't you go haunt a house or scare the crap out of some sorority girls playing 'Bloody Mary?'"

Wilde briefly glanced at the paperback copy of his long forgotten plan and squeezed out a small smile. "I'm surprised you are reading that," he said, crossing his arms. "It was considered the weakest of all the plays I had written in the late nineteenth century. Many of the critics noted that much of the first act-and-a-half surrounded the witty conversations of the members of the upper-class society, and the drama only began in the second half. They all found it similar to my previous play *Lady Windermere's Fan*."

Dorian closed the book. "But isn't that kind of lazy and cheap?"

Wilde's smile disappeared without a trace. After a long and lengthy pause he replied, "I was going through some very difficult times, Dorian."

Dorian scoffed. "They can't all be winners, can they?"

Wilde extended his cane across Dorian's body to stop his progress. "I'm taking a chance moving outside the safety of the book." Wilde said him, not appreciating the young man's attitude. "So I'd appreciate a bit of courtesy, old chap."

He led Dorian to the door of the train. He used his cane to press the button for it to open. The door opened wide, but it still looked as if the train was moving at rapid speed.

"Fine." Dorian finally caved in. "Clue me in. What's going on?"

"You know the old saying, "the greatest trick the devil ever pulled…"

"Convince people he didn't exist."

"Exactly." Wilde smiled, like a teacher hearing a correct answer from his star pupil. "Think of it. If the world knew of the existence of the Morbi, we'd witness an existential meltdown on a Darwinian scale."

Dorian, more confused than he was before, asked, "So we're dealing with God and the Devil?"

"Posh and piffle." Wilde gave a passé gesture. "Fairy tales. We are dealing with the true nature of mankind."

He picked up his cane and waved in around in the air like he was stirring a bubbling cauldron. Everything in the subway terminal became swirly and the background began to melt. It reminded Dorian of the Salvador Dali painting with the melting clocks but this wasn't anything he saw before.

Except when he was in the mirror training room with Wilde the other night.

The terminal disappeared and it was replaced by a dirty cloud that show the shadows of what have been where the Morbi were the ones responsible for mankind's failures and disasters.

Some of the prolific scenes Dorian witnessed started to bleed together as the memories crossed both time and space.

"By now you're a bright enough chap to recognize that you are dealing with the hypernatural." Wilde said to Dorian, showing him the past. "The Morbi, aren't your garden variety demons. They're created by a sickness in what *believers* call the soul. I simply call it self-actualization."

Dorian saw a group of Israelites being wrapped by the creatures' mist while they worship a golden calf. Over at the mountain there was a bearded man who was scaling down the summit. Dorian could clearly see the man wasn't happy on what he saw. He became so angry he shattered the two stone tablets he was carrying with them.

Dorian's eyes widened. "Is that…?"

"I've heard a tale that they leapt into existence during the time of Moses and that whole golden calf debacle." Wilde quickly retorted. "They infect generation after generation, like a family trait passed from father to son—a parasite sucking on the teat of the misery born from man's darkest desires."

Then it shifted to the death of Alexander the Great as his Morbus erotically caressed him as it wined and dined him. Pope Alexander VI was listening to his brother's advice as he was handed a bag of gold. But it wasn't really his brother, but a Morbi controlling him.

"It's what killed every Gray since your great-grandfather was felled by his own vanity." Wilde sorrowfully revealed to the young man beside him. "Although the Morbi are not of this world, they anchor themselves through a physical object. This totem is a manifestation of their influence."

Dorian seeing the stream of time from a particular angle, time for a human being like a tunnel made of human shapes, a flow of endless buildings up and collapsing to the ground, growth and death, lives passing in the flux of a single wave.

The time period jumped ahead to the year 1890 where a robber-baron watched in pride to see his first skyscraper being built, and it ended with the Vice-president evilly smirked while he watched his running mate being sworn into office as the leader of the free world.

Then all the pictures came together to form one giant image. Dorian saw the corpse of his ancestor that was lying on the floor—aged and grotesque. Then he saw a boy running into the room. It dawned on Dorian that it was his grandfather.

The pristine portrait loomed above them as it hissed with the energy of the Basil Morbus. The picture seemed to be staring at the boy. Dorian, Jr. hurled a small iron paperweight at the painting. Wilde ducked to dodge the object.

"Ever since the original Dorian was destroyed by the Morbus in the portrait, you and yours, made it a family quest to rid the world of the Morbi." Wilde explained, gripping his cane tightly. "But it is not easy. There are no silver bullets, no garlic draped crosses, no exorcisms or silly magic words."

Time skipped ahead thirty years later as Dorian II is fighting a Morbus in the beautiful home of Joseph Goebbels, the Nazi propaganda master. This generation's Dorian was trying to burn a copy of *Mein Kampf* while Goebbels fired a gun at him. The Morbus emerged from the book and it wrapped its misty cloud tail around Dorian's neck and began to strangle him.

"The only way to remove a Morbus is to destroy their anchor…their totem." Wilde revealed.

"Then why didn't my grandfather just burn the portrait?" Asked Dorian.

"I said it wasn't easy." Wilde replied. "Only a Morbus can destroy a totem. And believe, most of the Morbi are anathema to do so."

Then he waved his cane to show Dorian's father being blown skyward after trying to smash a 1920s film projector. A Morbus easily deflected the blow, while a mortified Howard Hughes watched on as he tried to reach his precious projector. The elder Gray scrambled backward from the demon, inches from its outstretched grasp—its sharp talons.

"Brute force won't work." Wilde rambled on. "The toys you found might temporarily suspend an individual from Morbi influence, but to send them back to their own dark hole, you must also sever the connection to the totem."

Dorian's father fought on so he could prevent the transfer the curse from a father to his son. The boy was wearing bellbottoms and rose-colored sunglasses. The old man was in his luxurious bed, as his son held his hand, waiting him to close his eyes and move on to the next world. Dorian and Wilde watched as the Morbus left the dying body and invaded the younger man. Dorian's father was pinned to the ground, while trying to destroy a ceremonial saber from the American Civil War.

"I'm no superhero." Dorian told Wilde. "How do I save Sybil?"

Wilde simply replied, "Cleverly."

With a snap of his fingers Dorian was back in the subway car, sitting with Henry. Everything was back to normal. Time had started up again and everyone there was doing their regular day-to-day things. Dorian checked his phone to find out what time it was and couldn't believe what he saw. He could have sworn he was gone for at least five minutes, but in reality it was as if he hadn't left the train at all.

Perplexed by this extraordinary discovery, he couldn't help to see the message icon on the cellphone's screen. He pressed the retrieval button and put the phone close to his ear.

"You have one unheard message." Said the female automated voice.

"Dorian, where the hell are you?" Exclaimed Lori Lord, sending Dorian back. "You are in so much trouble, young man.

Henry looked over to Dorian, who seemed to be vexed. "You okay?"

"Not when Lori gets her hands on me." Dorian replied, mulling over the forthcoming wrath of his stepmother.

CHAPTER TWENTY-TWO

Hell hath no fury like a woman scorned.
William Congreve.

Dorian and Henry journeyed all the way back home in silence. They didn't even look at each other. It was the most awful hour of Henry's life. They finally entered the building and saw the late night doorman coming up to them.

"Excuse me, Mr. Lord, Mr. Gray," said the balding middle-aged man, panting from his short hustle. "I have specific orders from you're mother to notify her on your return. I am not going sugarcoat it, but she is very, *very* angry."

Henry reached into his pocket to pull out his money clip. "We both appreciate you waiting up for us, Rick. It's very late and I don't see why we have to wake up Mom in the middle of the night." He said, handing the dutiful doorman a crisp twenty.

But Rick waved it away. "I'm not going to lie to your mother over $20."

Then Henry pulled out a hundred-dollar bill. "I think this will be more to your liking."

Rick took the money and looked at the face on it. "Oh, Benny Franklin. Does he have a twin brother?"

"You gotta be kidding me!" Henry said, surprised by Rick's sudden greed.

"You listen to me," Rick boldly retorted, "your mother is pissed off. Whatever you two did had to be so astronomical for her to act this way. Given the current circumstances only a hundred bucks guarantees one of you admission."

"This is bullshit!" Exclaimed Henry. "I'm not paying you another hundred bucks."

Rick started to walk to the front desk. "Well, let's see what Mommy Dearest is up to." He said, reaching for the phone.

"Okay, okay!" Henry reluctantly agreed. "Dorian, pay the man."

Dorian stuck his hands in his pockets. "Actually, H, I'm a little light. Can you front me this time?"

"Seriously?" Henry looked over to Rick who just picked up the phone and started dialing his mother's apartment. "All right," Henry broke down and handed Rick another C-note. "Here you go, you little extortionist. This will probably get you at least five hair plugs"

Rick shoved the bill in his pocket, and gestured them to the elevator. "You boys have a good night."

"Kiss my ass," Henry coldly remarked, entering the elevator with Dorian following him.

For the first time since before the incident at the bridge, Dorian smiled.

With a light hand, Henry unlocked the door to the penthouse. Taking a deep breath he opened the door slowly so it wouldn't make any noise when him and Dorian would creep in through the living room. As Henry walked in, Dorian silently followed and closed the door gently, tiptoeing into the lavish apartment.

Henry moved awkwardly into the living room, shoving his hands into the pockets of his baggy jeans. His sweater was torn at the collar. He thought he was going to get away with the perfect crime. But then he felt a presence. A presence he had known all too well.

"Where have you been?" Said a voice from the shadows.

Henry jumped and let out a loud yelp, as he turned around to see his mother sitting at the kitchen table, waiting for them to return.

"Geez! You scared me, Lori." Dorian said to her.

"Do you know what time it is?" She asked sternly, not batting a single eyelash.

Henry took a step forward, balancing himself on his drunken state. "Hey, Mom," he said, clearing his throat, "I know you're mad at me for sneaking out, but I—"

"Henry, go to your room." Lori growled, not shifting her gaze from Dorian. "Get to bed. We'll talk about you in the morning."

Henry seemed confused. "Mom, I only went out to—"

"**GO TO YOUR ROOM!**" She snapped at him.

Henry took a several steps back, feeling a slight chill. He quickly glanced at Dorian, who gave him the same frightened look and proceeded to go down the hall.

"Good luck, bro." Henry whispered to him, before leaving the kitchen.

Lori waited for the sound of Henry's door closing before she could even speak to Dorian. Once she heard it, she took a deep breath to steady her nerves.

"Do you know what time it is?" She repeated the question to Dorian.

"No."

"It's three o'clock in the morning."

"Seriously? Wow. Yeah—I—I was waiting on a train and—"

"Where were you?"

Lori noticed a blemish on Dorian's forearm that ran up to his bicep. Her jaw dropped, jumping at attention and ran over to him.

"Is this a bruise?" She frantically asked, rolling up his sleeve.

"I—"

"**Where were you?**" Lori repeated, with anger in her voice.

"No—no, I fell at school. I got this in gym. You know how physical the last two minutes of a basketball game can—"

"Tell me the truth, Dorian. Where were you?"

"I told you."

"I know a lie when I hear one, where were you?"

"Okay, all right, okay. I was—I was with Hetty."

Lori crossed her arms. "Uh-huh."

"I didn't want to get you mad."

"I don't care if you respect me or not, young man. But as long as you live in this house, you will respect the rules of this house!" She was clearly fighting tears. Thin rivulets worked their way down the crags of her face.

"No! I told you—"

"Hetty's house is the first place I called!" Her anger was akin to an intense downpour. It wasn't capable of sustaining itself for long.

"Do you think I'm stupid? Hetty was home hours ago, but boy, she was trying to cover your hide. She said you were with Adrian! So which was it, Dorian? Were you with Adrian—or at Hetty's? Which stupid, insulting lie do you want to stick to?"

Dorian couldn't breathe. He felt his heart race and his face felt hot like he was out in the sun all day. He couldn't tell Lori the truth. She was already angry with him for catching him in a lie but to tell her what really happened at the club and how he fought a maniacal disc jockey that was possessed by an ancient force wasn't going to do him any favors.

Tears were streaming down her face now. But her eyes had a hard gleam to them behind the little rivulets.

"Uh-huh. I swear to God, Dorian, if I find out you're in some kind of mischief with those idiot friends of yours at school."

Dorian lowered his head and chuckled softly.

"Oh, this is funny?" She glared at Dorian. Her face seemed to shift within itself.

"No." He answered, clearing his throat. "I just…they *are* idiots, aren't they?"

"Haven't I been through enough for one night? The police calling me in the middle of the night and telling me you were involved in a brawl, Henry sneaking out to find you, and I had to sit here and wonder what happened to you! It's funny that I have to sit here and wonder if you're dead lying in a gutter somewhere?! This nightmare of a city!"

"No, I—"

She swiped her hand viciously to silence him. Dorian suddenly became speechless. This was an entire different side he saw his guardian. She was both angry and heartbroken.

Lori took a deep breath. "I can't imagine how hard it was to lose the only family you have," she began, stifling tears. "I tried to give you space to respect your privacy but I can't go on like this. Until you can figure out how to get home at a responsible hour and how not to lie to my face—you are grounded." She didn't wipe away the tears then. She just appeared to shut them off through willpower alone.

"What?" Reacted Dorian, trying to understand the meaning of the term "grounded."

It seemed foreign to him. Never in his life has he heard the phrase "you're grounded." Not even his biological mother uttered those dreadful words. But he wasn't talking to his mother, but his entrusted guardian and she was pissed. This was a different side he ever saw of Lori. Dorian didn't even consider she would be capable of such fury. And something told him that she was just getting warmed up.

"That's right! No more clubs!"

"What?"

"No more one-on-one time with that Merton tart. You go to school and you come from school. A straight beeline to and from—no side stops whatsoever. And I will be calling your headmaster to inform him of this a well."

"Come on!"

"Yeah? 'Come on?' And if you can't figure out how to do this I will call the cops on you myself! Is that understood?!"

Dorian lowered his head in shame. "Yes, ma'am."

"Now get out of my sight until you can figure out how to tell the truth."

And with a ferocity that startled Dorian, she slat back. He looked at her as if he wanted to tell her something. She waited for a response, but all he did was lower his head and marched somberly to his room. Lori put her hand gently to her face and lolled her head back wondering what she did wrong and silently cursed that her husband George wasn't there to share much of the stress. The one thing Lori Lord knew since high school was that stress caused wrinkles. And now she could feel crow's feet forming around her eyes and strands of her shimmering black hair were turning gray.

"Damn you, Dorian."

Dorian sat on the edge of his bed, back straight, hands on his knees, waiting for the sun to rise. Despite the lateness of the hour he was still fully clothed, clad in his jeans and T-shirt.

Henry was in bed next door, sleeping off his aches and pains. Dorian's body was tired, but he would not allow himself to succumb to sleep. He needed to stay alert.

Dorian stated at the patch of moonlight on the wall in front of him, letting it soak through his retinas and fill his senses with crisp light. In the background, his subconscious hummed with white noise, processing and sorting the information he had learned during his visits with the late great author Oscar Wilde, and the encounter with Dextrose Coma's Morbus.

He blanked his mind of all conscious thought, giving his subconscious free reign to sort out the tangle of new facts. Usually this form of therapy worked well, and in the morning, he would arise as refreshed as if he'd had a full night's sleep.

Unfortunately, all that he had succeeded in doing this time was giving himself a headache.

There was too much he didn't know. He needed to find out more.

Dorian blinked, and the state of his subconscious faded away to be replaced by the warm glow of his conscious mind. He blinked again and looked around him, licking his dry lips. There was the faint sound of activity coming from next door, the clink of coffee cups and the splash of running water, followed by the muted sound of voices raised in greeting. It looked like Dorian wasn't the only one who couldn't sleep.

Dorian got to his feet and stretched mightily.

It was time to go and find that missing piece.

CHAPTER TWENTY-THREE

Know your enemy and know yourself and you can fight a hundred battles without disaster.
Sun Tzu.

It was as if Lori was waiting for him. As if she knew he'd came sprinting across the hall—which he did—heading for the door at top speed—which he was. She was seated in the living room, reading a fashion magazine, but it seemed as if it was just a pose as she waited for Dorian to appear.

With his backpack slung over his shoulder, Dorian said, "Hey, Lori, I know I'm grounded but I got to go to the library. I have to write a paper and my teacher instructed the class to use other forms of research material besides Wikipedia. I think he called these things 'books', or something. Ever heard of them?"

"If it's for school, it's acceptable to temporally lift your punishment."

Yes! Dorian silently exclaimed in triumph.

"I'll drive you there," Lori said getting up from her chair.

Shit.

"What are you talking about? I have my own car."

But Lori was already taking her jacket off the coatrack, and Dorian could tell by the jingling coming from the pocket that the keys were already in there.

"I'm thinking about heading there myself. I heard that Jeffery Deaver wrote a *007* novel. Everyone says it's good. We can go together and save gas."

"Lori, I can safely assure you that given our current financial status we don't have to worry about the astronomical gas prices that are threatening our present economy."

Lori spoke in a surprisingly firm, take no-guff voice. "I said I'd drive you. Get in the car!"

Taken aback by the sharp tone, Dorian meekly climbed into Lori's Bentley. To his surprise, most of the ride passed in silence. He couldn't figure it out. He'd hoped Lori just wanted to spend some quality time with him, and talk about what was going on in his life. Truth be told, Dorian hadn't much been looking forward to it. Because of course there was only one thing of the significance that had been going on in his life. He didn't want to lie to Lori, and to a great degree it was easy to avoid doing so.

After all, unless Lori said, "So, Dorian, did a deceased author from the Victorian era tell you that you are mankind's last hope against a race of ancient demons that make Faustian deals?" Dorian wouldn't be put on the spot.

Dorian firmly believed in concepts such as sins of omission. The very fact that he wasn't being completely forthcoming was, in and of itself, deceitful. Anything less than a honest answer to a question as straightforward as "What's been going on with you lately?" was going to be a lie.

He hated the idea of lying to Lori. She had such an open, honest face. He should have told her the truth and what was happening. But if he did, he knew that Lori would never have let him do what he was planning to do. Instead she'd probably take him to a doctor or a specialist to question his sanity. And then it really would have all been painful.

Dorian Gray breezed into the city library and passed row after row of bookshelves and tables until he reached the reference desk in the history department. Behind it were several carts stacked with books and magazines, but no one was around. As he waited, his thoughts drifted back over the last couple of days.

"Excuse me," he said, waving a hand at a middle-aged woman who was prowling around in the stacks with a pile of books under her arms. "Can you help me with something?"

The librarian peered over her glasses at him, and then carried her load of books up to the front desk where she set them down. She was thin and pale and her shoulders slumped, as if she'd been carrying too many books. She looked like she didn't want to be bothered.

"What is it?"

"This is the reference desk, I believe," Dorian said, annoyed by the woman's attitude. "I'd like some help with research I'm doing on Oscar Wilde." He spelled the last name for her.

Dorian was sure that whatever was available would cross-reference what he read in his ancestor's diary. Somewhere in those documents would be a description of the supernatural force he was warned about.

"Well?" Dorian asked impatiently.

The librarian, whose tiny, cheap name tag read Gladys, said, "Literature or historical?"

"What?"

"I said do you want literature or historical reference material?"

"Oh, both. I want everything you have."

Gladys nodded and slipped away, as silent as a ghost she crept through the many rows of books for the subject the young man had requested.

If I'm going to dance with the devil, it would help to know the tune, thought Dorian, watching the librarian return with several books.

"Is this for a school report?"

Dorian paused. Instead of telling her the truth he simply nodded.

"It's good that someone your age is into the classics." Gladys said, handing him the books. "Most kids usually do their book reports on vampire romances or children going to wizard school."

"Well, I'm not most kids," Dorian chuckled nervously.

"No, you're not." The librarian replied. "You're more of an old soul."

Dorian looked through several titles; one of which was *The Picture of Dorian Gray*—the tale of his ancestor and his encounter with the Morbi. But the line between fiction and truth would always be a very thin one. He wondered how exact this text was, and if Wilde had hidden clues on ways to beat the Morbi.

"Will there be anything else?" Asked Gladys.

"Um…yeah," Dorian said, clearing his throat. "Do you have any books about deals with the devil, like *The Devil and Daniel Webster*, and "*Feist*?"

"You mean, *Faust*?"

"Yeah, yes, I do."

Gladys gave him an inquiring look. "Does this tie in to your school project?"

Dorian hesitated, and then held up a copy of Wilde's *Dorian Gray*. "In this book, the guy makes a deal with the devil to stay young forever, and I thought it would be a very interesting sidebar on how this type of genre is popular among classic to modern literature."

Gladys laughed softly. "I'll be back with those two books. Would you like for me to get some of the movies that were based on them as well?"

An image of the Wilde-demon's claw bursting out of the Saligia flashed before Dorian's eyes. He felt a slight shiver down his spine.

"No, thank you." He gulped. "I get so much more out of the book than I do on the screen."

Gladys smiled. "Bless your heart."

Dorian prided himself on his knowledge of history, but more and more he was realizing that history was filled with obscure episodes that had faded into legend. Until a few days ago, he had never heard of wither Oscar Wilde or the Morbi. He probably never would've heard of them, wither, except for the odd fact that seemed to contradict the article.

Dorian sensed someone standing beside him and jerked his head around to see the librarian.

"Oh, Gladys, you scared me," he said, placing a hand below this throat. "I'm just about done here."

"Take your time, I won't be leaving for another hour and a half. Meanwhile, is there anything else I can get for you?"

After her slow start, Gladys had become impressively cooperative. "No, I don't think—wait a minute." He showed her the article that mentioned the Morbi. "Can you look for something about them?"

She pushed up her glasses and read the article. "The Morbi, hmmm…sounds like a legend. But I'll see what I can find."

Several minutes later, the librarian returned with this heavy leather bound tome. Years of wear and tear had affected it through time. Judging by the amount of dust and cobwebs, this hasn't been checked out in many, many years.

"Here you are," Gladys said cheerfully. "Anything else?"

Dorian's eyes widened in awe by the very sight at the girth of the book that lay before him. "Yeah, can I get a dolly to wheel this thing out of here?"

"Happy reading."

After an hour of reading that gigantic volume, Dorian thought it was enough. He had what he needed, and proceeded over to the checkout to bring some of these books back home for further study.

"Did that help you?" Gladys asked him.

He looked up. "Yes, but I think the big book needs to be updated." He thought about what he'd read and about what he knew. "Then again, maybe it's best just the way it is."

He stood up, thanked Gladys, and left. He felt intrigued by what he had discovered, but disappointed by what he had not.

He walked over to the Bentley to see Lori reading behind the wheel. He opened the passenger door carefully so he wouldn't startle her. He set his books in the backseat of the car and then buckled himself in.

"You found what you're looking for?" She asked, not taking her eyes off the page she was currently on.

"More than I realized."

"Good." She said pleasantly. "Now you have something to make the time go faster during your incarceration."

"Don't remind me." Dorian groaned, as Lori shifted the car into drive and headed for home.

Stacks and stacks of books were piled up in his room. There were multiple translations of the Bible, the Koran, and the Bhagavad-Gita were mixed in with volumes on voodoo, spiritualism, witchcraft, astrology, exorcism, reincarnation, and other occult topics. Post-its flagged specific pages. Tarot cards were used as bookmarks.

Henry scanned the titles of some of the books.

The Necronomicon. The Book of the Damned. The Tragedy of Doctor Faustus. Visions of the Vishanti. The Satanic Bible. The Dark Side for Dummies.

He shook his head. What the hell did Dorian see in all this crap? What exactly was he looking for?

"Doing a little light reading, bro?"

"Huh?" Dorian said, looking up from a book.

"Are you gonna be pissed at me all day?" Said Henry, crossing his arms. "You haven't said a word to me since the subway. And all through breakfast this morning."

Dorian didn't give him an answer.

Henry held a video game controller in front of Dorian, waving for him to take it. "You wanna give it a shot?"

"Give what a shot?" Dorian asked him.

Henry motioned for him to follow him to the living room. On the giant television there was a zombie video game paused on the screen.

"Can you believe the coin this d-bag is making from the piece of crap game?"

"Who?" Asked Dorian.

"Friggin' Alan Campbell." Henry answered, turning the game back on. "His last few games were badass, but this one is terrible. Looks like he got lazy on the A.I. and the motion configuration. I haven't seen him yet. But when I do, I'll tell him his game is shit and he owes me fifty dollars."

Something about the name peaked Dorian's interest. Then he made the connection.

"I gotta go." Said Dorian, running back into his room.

He put the goggles on his face and poured through the pages of the Saligia. He was flipping through the pages like his life depended on it.

"The name has got to be here." He said out loud. Then he found a list of names and scrolled his finger down the column.

Cyril Vane
Born 1868, taken 1902. Deceased 1929.
Heirs—Robert K. born 1926, deceased 1951.
Harrison D. born 1928.
Known totem—unknown Degas statuette Ange En Vol.

Without any delay, Dorian shoved a bunch of the weapons he sorted through the container into his backpack and ran out the door.

INTERLUDE SEVEN
FROM THE JOURNAL OF DORIAN GRAY

May 5, 1890

The day after Sybil's suicide, I decided to hide my tortured painting. I was in constant fear of someone discovering it. Worried about what they would think. I ordered my servant to take the painting to the third floor of my townhouse and store it in my old playroom.

I had given him strict orders that no one was allowed to enter the room. With the only key to unlock the door, I knew in the utmost confidence my dreadful secret would be safe from the world.

My eyes fell on a large 17th century purple satin cover my grandfather had found in a convent in Italy. It had often wrapped the dead, and now it would hide something that had a corruption of its own. But it was far worse that it would breed horrors and it would never die.

Shortly after, I picked up a copy of the St. James Gazette. The newspaper was full of reports of Sybil's death. However, I was so relieved that I had avoided any bad publicity or any connection to the deceased. I was more determined to think only of my own pleasure in the future.

A messenger came by and delivered a package from Harry. He had given me a little yellow book. It was the strangest book I had ever read in my life.

It chronicled all the sins of the world. The novel had no plot and only one character—a young Parisian man who spent his life trying to realize, in the nineteenth century, all the passions of every century before his own. It was a book of evil.

I was so fascinated that I could not stop reading. The hero, who was romantic and possessed several scientific temperaments, resembled me in such prolific detail. He was so much like me, and it seemed that this strange novel continued the story of my life—even before I had lived it!

The good looks that had been captured in Basil's painting of me captivated others as well. Even those who heard the most evil things about me would not believe them.

Yet I began to live the life written about in Harry's book. And it was so easy. I had wealth, my handsome features were well known by everyone I had ever met, and I knew joy and cruelty. I could do whatever I want.

Sometimes I would creep upstairs to the locked room and stand in front of the portrait that Basil had painted. There I would look at the evil, ugly, aging face on the canvas. I grew more and more taken with my own looks, and more and more interested in the corruption of my own soul!

All the sins I had read about in the little yellow book became real to me. I indulged in every mood, every whim, and every want and desire. But hanging on the walls of the lonely locked room where I had spent my childhood, I had hung the terrible portrait whose constantly changing features showed me the real degradation of my life.

I had draped the purple and gold Italian curtain over it to hide it from view. For weeks I would not go to the locked room and I would forget the hideous painted thing. For a time, I would enjoy a light-hearted and joyous existence.

Then at night I would go to dreadful places near Blue Gate Fields and stay—day after day—until I was driven away. On my return, I would sit in front of the picture—sometimes hating it and myself. My obsession took over my life.

What if the painting became stolen? Or what if, while I was away, someone gained access to the room, in spite of the bars, and learned my secret. It terrified me than death itself.

What if the world already suspected?

After all, there were people who distrusted me. I was nearly blackballed at a West End club. Women who had admired me, now shunned me. Respectable men would leave the room if I entered their club.

I had been poisoned by Harry Wotton's book.

Evil was now beautiful to me.

CHAPTER TWENTY-FOUR

All great ideas are dangerous.
Oscar Wilde.

Throughout the entire morning, Dorian prepped on what he was going to say to Marlowe Diamond. He hadn't put this much work into something since his oral report on the Magna Carta for history class. Dorian felt confident on what the result the proposal he had in store for the creep. He had watched *The Godfather* so many times and he finally came up with an offer Diamond couldn't refuse.

With the backpack on his back, Dorian walked down a nice Greenwich Village street. He pulled out a small card from his pocket and looked over the address. The business card had a gold embossed logo icon that represented the Old Dutch East India Company.

* * *

VEREENIGDE OOST-INDISCHE COMPAGNIE
VEREENIGDE IMPORT & EXPORT
MARLOWE DIAMOND
600 WASHINGTON SQ NORTH
NEW YORK, NY

The address led Dorian to an old 19th century brownstone. The entry was unassuming, but there was the card's symbol on the door. Dorian pressed the doorbell, waited in vain for an answer, and pressed it again until he heard a voice from the intercom.

"A pleasant surprise, Mr. Gray." Said Marlowe Diamond from inside the house. The iron bars behind the door slid open. Dorian could see Diamond's silhouette opening the locks. "Can't be too careful, even in this neighborhood."

Dorian opened the door and let himself in. Although it looked crowded, the showroom was very clean and orderly. It was filled with artifacts and antiques from the floor mounted with elephant tusks, a gold gilded bird cage, Greek statues, glass cases full of jewelry, paintings, and very old books.

Minutes later, Dorian found himself waiting in an opulent study, surrounded by antiques and heirlooms he was almost afraid to touch. He fidgeted upon a well-upholstered chair, still wondering if he was doing the right thing. He had rehearsed this visit a thousand times in his head, but it was one thing to imagine it, and another thing to actually go through with it.

What if he was making a tremendous mistake?

Dorian moved across Diamond's expensive office, his feet sinking into a carpet so thick that it was like walking on an immense sponge.

The office was a glass cave high above the city. Everything this Diamond guy needed was here or just a phone call away.

Dorian stopped at the window and stared out over the New York skyline, admiring the skyscrapers.

"You have reconsidered my offer for the book, the Saligia?" Asked Diamond, entering the office.

"No," Dorian replied, sending a frown on the broker's face, "but I do have a deal in mind."

Dorian stood behind a chair that was adjacent to a large wooden desk. Diamond, had his back to him putting an ancient, leather bound book onto a bookshelf.

"I want to trade." Dorian proposed, holding his backpack in front of him. "I want to release the Vane family from their situation."

"What are you talking about?" Inquired Diamond, taking a seat behind his desk.

"I want the totem that controls the Vanes destroyed." Dorian demanded.

"What makes you think I could do that even if I wanted to?" Replied the strange dealer, giving Dorian an uninterested look. "But that aside, what would you offer in trade?"

"Me." Dorian answered, his face was serious and his eyes were desperate.

Diamond laughed out loud, suddenly struck by the sheer ridiculousness of the situation. "A very noble, but empty offer. You're already bound by an object d'art…the portrait."

Dorian didn't seem to mind being laughed at. He assumed he would get that kind of reaction anyway.

The young man turned his backpack upside down and spilled its contents all over Diamond's desk. "Then what about any of this crap? Something's got to have some value."

Diamond's laughter died upon his lips. He curiously picked up a spiked mace about the side of a man's forearm. "Not to my employers."

Diamond found it amusing as two curved daggers sprang from the side of the mace. Dorian looked on as he unzipped and reached into the front of his backpack.

"Then what about this?" Said Dorian, holding out a video game controller.

Diamond studied the controller in front of him with increasing displeasure. He was old, older even than he looked. And he knew he looked *very* old. His hands had withered over the passage of time. But he didn't mind that, he had power, and power made up for a great many of what other beings might term shortcomings. He wore his thin blond hair pulled back, coated with gel to keep it in place.

Diamond maintained a neutral expression. "I am sorry, Mr. Gray, but we do not conduct any business with video games. Unless you have an Atari that is mint in box that is. I have a gentleman in Brighton who would pay a king's ransom for one and a copy of both *Space Invaders* and *Asteroids*. I even threw in *Custer's Revenge*. It's a very rare video game. Despite its crude animation and gameplay, the object of the game is to evade raining arrows in order to get across the stage to literally rape and pillage the Indian tribe's women. It was the first banned video game in history with *Death Race 2000* following it. I'll give you ten dollars for the controller."

"But you don't understand…"

"I think we are done here, Mr. Gray." Diamond rose up from his chair. "If you decide to sell the Saligia you know where to find me."

Dorian looked at him as if he didn't care at all. "I don't know what to…"

"**Good day, Mr. Gray.**" Diamond said flatly.

Dorian let out a defeated sigh and gathered all the weapons and equipment he spilled on Diamond's desk. Without anything else being said Dorian showed himself out.

CHAPTER TWENTY-FIVE

Love cannot save you from your own fate.
Jim Morrison.

Dorian jogged across the ambulance bay at Roosevelt Hospital while two attendants were taking a person out on a gurney from an ambulance. Then he walked into the nurse's station.

There was never any doubt Diamond would reject the deal. Dorian rationalized, as he approached the front desk. *But that was never the point. However, he unknowingly disclosed a trade secret. That deals CAN be made.*

Walking past the waiting area, with several rows of plastic chairs, he proceeded to the long, high desk, behind which set a harried-looking man in his twenties wearing light blue scrubs, though he didn't seem to be a doctor or nurse. He didn't have the usual arrogance that every doctor Dorian had ever met carried, nor the seen-it-all look that must nurses had. The desk was at Dorian's neck level, and the receptionist was seated, so he had to peer down at the man.

The receptionist was on the phone. "Excuse me," Dorian said.

Holding up a finger, the guy said, "No, Manny, we need them down here *now*. Yeah, I know they're backed up, but we got a serious situation here. It's sixty degrees out, Manny; we really don't need the AC on full blast. Look I—"

"Excuse me," Dorian said a bit more forcefully. "I need to see a friend of mine."

Again the receptionist held up a finger, this time mouthing the words "just a second."

"Manny, I've got Dr. Kaling crawling up my ass, and he ain't gonna leave there until this gets fixed. Can you *please* just send some body—any body. I don't even care if they fix it just have someone *show up*, okay? Thank you." He hung up the phone and looked up at Dorian. "Sorry 'bout that, it's crazy here. Now who—"

"My friend—Sybil Vane."

Even as the receptionist started typing something onto his keyboard, the phone next to him rang again. He picked it up.

"E.R. Yeah. Yeah. No. No, she's not on right now. No, she's not due back until tomorrow. Yeah. Yeah. Yeah. I really don't know that, you'll have to ask her. *Really*, ma'am, you have to ask her. Yeah. Sorry. Bye." The receptionist let out a long breath. "Sorry 'bout that. What's your aunt's name again?"

Through clenched teeth, Dorian said, "It's my friend, Sybil Vane."

"Could you spell that, please?" Before Dorian could, the phone rang again. The receptionist picked it up. "Hang on. E.R."

Dorian was only two steps shy of reaching down there and yanking the phone out of the floor jack it was plugged into when the man finally got off the phone. No jury in the world would convict him.

"Who was it you're trying to find again?"

"*Sybil Vane*," Dorian impatiently replied. "V-A-N-E."

The receptionist clicked several keys on the keyboard and looked up to Dorian with a patronizing smile. "She's at room 2017, on the second floor."

Dorian breathed a sigh of relief. "Thank you."

Without any further delay, Dorian took the elevator. When he got to his destination, he saw the nurses' station. He silently prayed that he wouldn't have to go through the runaround like he did with that jerk back at the lobby. He marched right over with his best foot forward and gave the nurse a polite smile.

"Hello," he said to the nurse, "I'm here to see Sybil Vane."

"Sorry." The nurse replied, never taking her eyes off the computer monitor. "Only family is allowed to visit."

"Can you at least tell me how she is?"

The nurse turned her gaze from the gleaming screen to face Dorian. "I'm sorry, but that's between family."

"Oh," Dorian said, lowering his head, "Well, thanks anyway."

He walked down the hall and as he passed Sybil's room, he was able to get a glance of her. Dorian was genuinely concerned and even a bit sad that he felt partially responsible.

Now Sybil Vane lay helpless in a hospital bed, hooked up to machines. Blinking medical equipment monitored her vital signs, which were stable. An I.V. fed fluids into her arm. Her vocal cords were shot. She had screamed so much when she fell off the bridge.

Dorian felt a long-burned anger building in his chest.

He loved Sybil.

And he felt guilty that she ended up here. Also he was angry with someone else.

Henry.

Dorian stepped into Sybil's room, and the sight that confronted him instantly bothered him.

Flowers.

There were lots of flowers. No. They were tons of flowers.

It looked like someone had defoliated a section of the Amazon rain forest in order to acquire enough blossoms for this display, and Dorian knew without question or hesitation who the "someone" was.

Jim Vane—Sybil's brother.

Dorian leaned forward, and kissed Sybil on her forehead. "I'm sorry this happened to you."

The doctor looked at him guardedly for a moment, clearly not sure how much he should share of his patient's condition. He knew who Dorian was and also his reputation. But Dorian wasn't a family member and there were such things as doctor/patient confidentiality.

After silently weighing his options, the doctor said, "Stable. Vitals are strong."

To the physician's clear annoyance, Dorian took the clipboard with Sybil's chart on it out of the man's hands. He didn't notice the glare the doctor was giving him, however, for he was much too focused on its observations.

"We knew what we're doing," the doctor said simply. "Twenty-four hours of observation and she will be free to go."

As he spoke he took back the clipboard that Dorian had been studying. He tucked it under his arm and walked out, giving Dorian an irritating leer as he did so, Dorian didn't notice it, though, since his focus was entirely on the sleeping Sybil.

He approached her again and said quietly, "Sybil…I want to tell you…I'm…"

"What the hell are you doing here?" Said an angry voice behind him.

Dorian turned to see Jim Vane, Sybil's brother, standing in the doorway and he was very angry. So angry he had dropped his backpack filled with several textbooks and soda that he had gotten from the vending machine.

"Jim!" Dorian gasped, holding his hands out in defense. "I'm just here to—"

"Get out." Jim snarled, his hands turning into fists.

"Look, I'm sorry for—"

"**NOW!**" He yelled. "Have you already done enough?"

"It wasn't my fault." Dorian explained, hoping to reach out to him. "It was an accident. If there's anything I can do, please let me know."

Jim stood silent for a moment, and then he spoke. "There is something you can do for me."

Dorian gave him his full attention. "What's that?"

"You can bleed." Jim answered, punching Dorian in the face.

CHAPTER TWENTY-SIX

*And wrath has left its scar—that fire of hell has
left its frightful scar upon my soul.*
William Cullen Bryant.

Jim Vane brought textbooks to keep current with his studies, but they sat in the backpack near his feet. He knew he'd get around to them, eventually, but at this point he was afraid to take his eyes off Sybil, lest she step away into oblivion while he turned away even for a moment. At the end of visiting hours, the nurse who ran the ward tried to get him to leave.

He ignored her. He simply sat in the chair, not moving.

Annoyed, she called the doctor, who came and told Jim pretty much the same thing. He had to leave, visiting hours were over, Sybil's condition had stabilized, and he wasn't going to accomplish anything by taking up room. Besides, it was hospital policy. That was all. And such policy was well known. Carved in granite and not to be trifled with.

Jim didn't acknowledge him, didn't even glance at him.

He...just...sat.

The doctor summoned a burly orderly, who endeavored to pick Jim up bodily. Jim ignored him too. He didn't fight back; didn't have to. He simply didn't budge when the orderly, who outweighed him by a good hundred pounds, finally forced Jim out of the room with him still in the chair and threw Jim out of the hospital.

The next day went more smoothly. Jim came back from the lobby, grabbing some snacks from the vending machine, and returned to Sybil's room, ready to read the textbooks that were taking up space in his backpack. He nodded to the nurses who came in every so often to check on her. They'd stopped worrying about him, apparently coming to think of him as one of the fixtures, no different than a chair or a bedpan. Perhaps they even thought it was kind of sweet.

He gave a friendly smile over to the nurses at their station. They smiled back and waved him through so he could see his sister. He opened to door and to his utter horror there was someone standing over Sybil's bed. Jim recognized the figure all too well.

Dropping his backpack and soda from shock he said, "What the hell are you doing here?"

It startled Dorian Gray as he turned around to find him standing with blood in his eye. Jim didn't wait for an explanation. All he wanted to do was to pound the shit out of this guy.

Dorian turned to face Jim on an attempt to calm him down, but a fist suddenly exploded against his jaw. Dorian dropped hard in front of Jim, pain whitening his face. He breathed in though his mouth in panicked breaths, gasping. Jim Vane felt no remorse at all for the damage he'd inflicted. If he hadn't care enough about Sybil to not want to kill the man in her hospital room, it would already been done.

"Get over here," Jim dragged Dorian to his feet and looked at Sybil, who was still sound asleep.

Before Dorian could make a sound, Jim smashed a blow into the boy's face, breaking off the scream before it started. He hit Dorian, again, knocking him to the floor.

Dorian still moved, but his nervous system seemed disjointed. He had no more crawling ability than even a newborn.

Jim picked him up and flung Dorian out of the room and into the hallway. The anger was on him now, and he went with it, hoping it would burn out his unaccustomed feelings.

Across the room, Dorian tried to rise, stretched a hand toward the door.

Crossing the room, Jim kicked him, driving the air from Dorian's lungs again. And he kept on kicking, and enjoying the anger because it was the only emotion he was feeling right now. Before Dorian could get up, his attacker kicked him in the stomach.

"This is all your fault, Gray!" Jim yelled at him, hearing the sounds of rushing footsteps of the hospital orderlies. "If it wasn't for you, my sister wouldn't be here!" Then he sent another devastating kick.

Dorian wasn't even trying to fight back. He just took whatever Jim dished out to him. Dorian felt he deserved every ounce of punishment. He was with Sybil at Battery Park. It was his friend who goaded her to climb the bridge. It was his curse that made her jump.

It was his fault—all his fault.

Now he was going to pay.

"Stop!" Screamed one of the nurses. "You're going to kill him!"

Jim ignored her cries. He picked up Dorian by the collar of his shirt. Jim balled up his fist and reeled it back.

"You're not going to be pretty anymore," he threatened, about to send the punch on a collision course across Dorian's bruised face.

Before his fist made contact, the same burly orderly who threw Jim out the other day caught it.

"I expected better from you, man." Said the gigantic caretaker. "I thought you were a decent dude, but you're not doing your sister any favors beating up this guy."

"Let me go!" Jim demanded, trying to break free. "This is all his fault!"

Dorian wiped the blood from his mouth and looked at Jim with eyes filled with sympathy.

"I'm sorry," he said softly, as he slowly got off the floor.

Security soon arrived to settle the dispute and apprehended Jim. Two of the guards held him down while the others helped Dorian.

"Sir, do you wish for us to call the police so you can press charges?" Asked one of the guards.

Dorian gave a world-weary sigh. "No," he answered, adjusting his coat, "I had it coming."

The guard looked confused. "Sir, he could have killed you."

"I think he got what he wanted. Let him go."

The guard shook his head and gestured to his men. "You heard him. Let him go."

The guards released Jim, who still hasn't taken off that look of hatred and bloodlust on his face. The nurse gingerly approached the angry young man with a very serious look.

"Your sister is scheduled to be released today, Mr. Vane." She said, crossing her arms. "I think it's best that you should wait for the doctor in the waiting room. Sybil has been through a lot, and it's imperative that she doesn't need any more stress."

Jim nodded, not taking his eyes off Dorian. Dorian knew that expression all too well. If James ever sees him with Sybil again, he will finish the job. Jim turned around and started to walk down the hall. The nurse gestured over to the two security guards to make sure he makes it there and stays there until Sybil is ready to leave.

The head guard shifted his gaze over to Dorian. "If I were you, sir, I would leave."

Dorian sucked his teeth. "Would it be okay if I—"

"I am not asking you," the guard said strongly, "I am *telling* you."

"Oh," realized Dorian, taking the hint. He dusted off his coat and prepared to make his trip to the elevator.

The nurse shot Dorian a disapproving look. He smiled with bloodstained teeth and waved at her as he stuffed a piece of paper in his pocket. He sneakily removed the front page of Sybil's hospital chart.

Sybil stared at the ceiling, waiting for the doctor to show up with his personal stuff and tell he could finally go the hell home.

She wiped her clammy hands on her bed sheets. Thinking about that night still made her sweat, still made her stomach tighten and her legs tremble. She could still see the sweat-soaked paramedics breathing hard as they labored over her on a gurney in the back of the ambulance. There was an IV set up and it shook with the vehicle's motion. They had given her a shot, but she was persistent enough to be aware of everything going on in the ambulance even though she was unconscious.

He caught me, she realized, shifting her position on the bed. *Then I snapped out of it, came to my senses or something.* She lowered her eyes. *I thought I was going to die. Everything was spinning. I couldn't tell what was sky and what was water. It felt my lungs had burst. My chest—it burned like it was on fire. I gasped in breath after breath. I couldn't get enough air.*

Then a small smile appeared on her mouth. *Then he held me. Just held me. And then he let out a cry, in a strange, hoarse voice. And he started to hug me, tighter and tighter. And I still couldn't breathe. I just wanted to breathe again. I thought I was going to drown above the water.*

I was so cold, so frightened. Dorian had his friend call an ambulance and never left me—not even for a moment. I felt so weak, so shaken.

Then the doctor came in with a warm smile on his face. Sybil knew that it meant she was finally going to go home.

About damn time.

"Hello, Sybil," the doctor said, smiling. "Good news, you're getting out today. But you need to take it easy for a couple of days. You need to avoid stress and get plenty of rest."

"Can do, Doc," she yawned with a big stretch. "When is my brother going to pick me up?"

The doctor hesitated and looked a little sheepish. "Oh, he's here. He's at the waiting room."

Sybil frowned. "What did he do this time?"

So much for avoiding stress, the doctor thought.

JOHN GRAVAGLIA

INTERLUDE EIGHT
FROM THE JOURNAL OF DORIAN GRAY

February 18, 1915

A cold rain fell and the streetlamps looked eerie in the dripping mist. The moon hung low in the sky like a yellow skull. I hailed a cab and told the driver to take me to the docks. On the way, we passed public houses that were just closing and men and women who were clustering in broken groups around their doors. From some of the bars came sounds of horrible laughter. In others, drunks brawled and screamed.

Lying back in the hansom, I watched with dull eyes the sordid shame of London. I repeated the words Harry had said to me when I first et him at Basil's studio.

"To cure the soul by means of the senses, and the senses by means of the soul."

Yes, that was the secret.

There were opium dens where once could buy oblivion. The hideous hunger for opium seized me. Suddenly, the driver drew up the horses with a jerk at the top of a dark home. Over the low roofs the jagged chimney stacks of the houses had risen up like the black masts of ships. A wreath of white mist clung like ghostly sails to the shipyards.

I gave the driver the extra shillings I had promised him. I quickly walked in the direction of the docks. In less than ten minutes I reached the opium den and performed the secret knock that gained me entry to the establishment. In one corner, a sailor was sprawled over a table. Then there were two tawdry women over at the bar, and at the far end of the room was a little staircase that led to a darkened musty chamber.

When I entered the room, I saw Adrian Singleton who was bent over a lamp lighting a long thin pipe. He was thin, washed, with a look of doom about him. I didn't even think he would be here. But where else would he be? The man has no friends whatsoever. I thought he would have left England, but he had found solace by consuming the milk of the poppy.

I winced and looked at the other people on the floor. They were lying on the mattresses in grotesque, strange, positions. The twisted limbs, the gaping mouths, the staring eyes, made them look like creatures from another world.

But I knew what I felt. And what had driven them to this terrible place to escape their own thoughts and deeds.

I kept seeing the eyes of Basil looking at me. I needed the opium to help me forget, but yet something bothered me. The presence of Adrian Singleton in the corner, a man Basil had accused me of destroying, troubled me. I wanted to be where no one knew who I was. I wanted to escape from myself.

I turned around and walked to the door with a look of pain on my face. Then I heard a hideous laugh from one of the women by the bar. She called me "Prince Charming"—the name Sybil had given me with affection.

Then a drowsy sailor leaped to his feet as she spoke and looked wildly. I hurried along the quarry through the drizzling rain. My meeting with Adrian had strangely moved me, and it made me wonder if I really did ruin his life. Each man lived his own life and paid his own price living it. The only pity was one had to pay so often for a single fault. One had to pay over and over again, indeed. In her dealings with man, destiny never closed her accounts.

There are moments, psychologists tell us, when the passion for sin, or for what the world class sin, so demonstrates a nature that every fiber of the body, as every cell of the brain, seems to be instinct with fearful impulses men and women at such moments lose the freedom of their will. They move to their terrible end as automatons move. Choice is taken from them, and conscience is either killed, or, if it lives at all, lives but to give rebellion its fascination, disobedience and its charm. For all sins, as theologians weary not of remind us, are sins of disobedience. When that high spirit, that morning star of evil, fell from heaven, it was as a rebel that I fell.

Callous concentrated on evil, I quickened my step as I went. Then somebody took me from behind and threw me up against a wall. Before I had time to defend myself, I was thrust against the wall with a brutal hand around my throat.

In a second, I heard the click of a revolver, and saw the gleam of the barrel pointing straight at my head.

"If you move, I'll shoot you dead." I heard the sailor say, smelling the smoke from his breath. "You wrecked the life of Sybil Vane—my sister. She killed herself and you are responsible for her death."

I recognized my assailant as James Vane. He must have recognized me when the woman at the opium den was calling out my old pet name.

I told him I had never heard of her and he was gravely mistaken. But he was hell-bent on putting a bullet in my skull. I was paralyzed with terror. I did not know what to say or do when suddenly a wild hope flashed across my brain.

I asked him how long ago his sister had died. James replied it was eighteen years ago when she committed suicide. I told him to look at my face, showing him there was no way I would have known his sister. I have the face of a twenty-year-old therefore it would be impossible for me to be his quarry. I convinced him that I was a babe when his sister died.

James Vane hesitated and dragged me to the light. Dim and watering as was the wind-blown light, yet it served him as he studied my face and I saw the horror on his face that showed him the terrible error he was about to make. James seemed had fallen for the face he had sought to kill had vanished, and it was replaced by the unstained purity of youth. To him I appeared to be hardly over twenty years of age.

He loosened his hold on me and stood in the pavement as he broke down into tears. While he was distracted I ran away as fast as I could, vowing never to venture to this side of town ever again.

CHAPTER TWENTY-SEVEN

The bravest man amongst us is afraid of himself.
Oscar Wilde.

Michael Steele was in the gym and he was doing his eighth set of bench press reps. He had increased the bench weight to three hundred pounds and it was feeling like he couldn't do a seventh set without tearing something. As it was, he felt like his chest was going to explode with the thudding of his heart and the aching labor of his lungs. Sweat dripped from his forehead, burned his eyes.

His muscles hurt like a son of a bitch. And that was good. Serious workout pain, short of snapping a tendon, was Michael's friend. It meant he was pushing the envelope, reaching the absolute outer limit of his endurance—and going beyond. He had to attempt the impossible. It was because his former life as a soldier was impossible. It was him versus every enemy in the free world.

He heard the door open, figuring it was another early riser about to break a sweat before he or she had to go their office. But he was thrown off by the voice that called to him.

"Hey, Mike."

Michael set the barbell on the rests and sat up to face the newcomer. He couldn't believe who was standing in front of him.

"Dorian," he said, wiping the seat off his brow with a towel. "Usually you are not up and about before the crack of noon."

"Crack of noon," Dorian chuckled. "That's very funny."

"Are you supposed to be in school?"

"I'm taking a personal day."

Michael frowned. "Does your stepmother know about this personal day of yours?"

Dorian paused. *Oh, great. Lori got to him.*

"She told me you're grounded and you won't be making to our afternoon sessions." Michael elaborated, getting off the bench. He stood before Dorian, dwarfing him in both size and girth. "She also said you're only supposed to go to and from school—no side stops."

Dorian brushed his hair back. "Mike, I'm in some kind of a bind."

Michael raised his eyes. "What kind of trouble are you in?"

"It's nothing I can't handle but I could use some help."

Michael crossed his arms in a disapproving manner, like a teacher hearing an excuse from a student who didn't do their homework. "If you're using what I taught you to hurt others I don't want you here."

"It's not like that, Mike." Dorian pleaded, as his mentor turned his back on him. "It's not just me, there's also another."

Michael craned his head back. He used his peripherals to glance at Dorian.

"Why don't you call the police?"

"They probably own the police."

"Who's 'they?'"

"*They.*" Dorian stressed.

Michael studied Dorian's expression. His eyes never wavered from his, and his breathing was normal. If Dorian were lying he would be staring at the top of Michael's head.

"If you are serious—"

"I *am.*" Dorian promised, showing fear for the first time.

Michael took a moment to process this and clapped his hands together. "Then let's get to work."

Michael flipped Dorian flat on the mat, making a loud slamming sound that reverberated throughout the whole gym. Dorian quickly got up and threw a punch at his teacher's head, but missed with a swift dodge and weaved in with a right cross. Dorian flinched, setting up a block.

"The most important," said Michael, "is not to show them any fear. If you hesitate, or look like you don't know what you're doing, even for a second, they'll sense the weakness. They'll eat you alive."

"No fear," Dorian said to himself, delivering a punch. "No getting eaten. Check."

"I'm serious." Michael bellowed, catching Dorian's fist and twisted his arm. "You're outnumbered. They're faster, most of them are stronger, they can run you into the ground, and if you're going to keep it under control, you're going to have to win the battle here." Dorian slipped through the hold, did a spin and faced Steele who touched a finger to his forehead. "You get me?"

"Mind war," Dorian acknowledged. "Wax on. Wax off."

Michael frowned at him. "You are not taking this seriously."

"People always think that about me," Dorian replied. "I'm not sure why." Then he charged straight at Steele with a war cry.

The teacher took Dorian's arm and performed another judo flip.

"See, that's what I mean," Michael Steele crossed his arms in a grave demeanor standing over his brash pupil. "You go joking around with them like that, and that's it. You've lost control."

"Quite the contrary," Dorian replied, "I have you right where I want you."

Then with a swift sweep, he tripped Michael off his feet and landed face first on the ground. Michael tried to get back up, but Dorian tackled him and put him in a chokehold, never letting up—not even once.

"Tap out." Dorian ordered.

Michael grunted and struggled.

"Tap out!" Dorian repeated.

Michael could feel Dorian's hold tightening up. Without any other option, Michael Steele tapped out, finally losing to Dorian Gray.

He was expecting Dorian to cheer and brag about his victory, but all he saw was him breathing in and out and not saying any smartass remarks. Dorian offered Michael his hand and he gladly accepted.

"Good," Steele panted, "very good."

"Do you think I'm ready?" Dorian asked, looking at him as he felt both fear and doubt tingling in his spirit.

"Not yet." Michael replied, rubbing his temples. "I haven't taught you the most important lesson."

"What's that?"

"Always attack a man's strengths."

Dorian wasn't sure if he heard him right. "Don't you mean always attack a man's weaknesses?"

"No," Michael said with conviction, "always attack a man's strengths. No one expects a full on attack in front of the fort."

Dorian nodded in response. "Thank you so much, Mike."

"You be careful whatever it is you're about to do." Michael replied, shaking his hand and hugging him.

CHAPTER TWENTY-EIGHT

And how can man die better than facing fearful odds, for the ashes of his fathers, and the temples of his gods?
Thomas B. Macaulay.

At dawn, the sun was a brilliant orange ball of fire rising in the pale blue sky above New York City. It hovered for a few brief moments at the point where the horizon merged with the East River, casting a ghostly silver tint across the water that separated Manhattan from its sister boroughs, Queens and Brooklyn.

The city was slowly coming awake. From Inwood and Washington Heights at the island's northernmost reaches all the way south to Wall Street's narrow canyons, people were stretching and yawning and shaking off sleep. Uptown, the runners dripped with sweat as they pounced the track that circled the Central Park Reservoir. On the Upper West Side, along the length of Broadway, the Korean greengrocers rearranged their sidewalk displays of fresh fruits and flowers. Delivery trucks dropped off bales of *The New York* Times at the sidewalk kiosks so news-hungry New Yorkers could get their daily fix of politics, culture, sports, and disaster.

Dorian walked past Central Park West and he was on his way to the Dakota apartment complex. The building is widely known as the home of former Beatle John Lennon as well the location of his murder. The architectural firm of Henry Janeway Hardenbergh was commissioned to create the design for Edward Clark, head of the Singer Sewing Machine Company.

The building's high gables and deep roofs with a profusion of dormers, terracotta spandrels and panels, niches, balconies, and balustrades gave it a North German Renaissance character, an echo of a Hansectric town hall. Nevertheless, its layout and floor plan betray a strong influence of French architectural trends in housing design that had become known in New York in the 1870s.

According to often-repeated stories, the Dakota was so named because at the time it was built, the Upper West Side of Manhattan was sparkly inhabited and considered as remote as the Dakota Territory. It was more likely that the building was named "The Dakota" because of Clark's fondness for the names of the new western states and territories. High above the 72nd Street entrance, the figure of a Dakota Indian that was constantly keeping watch.

But it wasn't enough to save the life of one of the most beloved pop music stars of an era that has nearly been forgotten. As John Lennon and his wife Yoko Ono walked to their limousine, several people seeking autographs approached them, and among them was Mark David Chapman. It was common for fans to wait outside the Dakota to meet Lennon and ask for his autograph.

Chapman, a 25-year-old security guard from Honolulu, Hawaii, had previously travelled to New York to murder Lennon in October—before the release of Lennon's latest album *Diamond Fantasy*—but had changed his mind and returned home.

On the evening in question, Chapman silently handed Lennon a copy of *Double Fantasy*, and Lennon obliged with an autograph. Chapman had been waiting for Lennon outside the Dakota since mid-morning, and had even approached the Lennons' five-year-old son, Sean, who was with the family nanny, when they returned home in the afternoon.

The Lennons spent several hours at the Record Plant Studio before returning to the Dakota. Lennon had decided against dining out so he could be home in time to say goodnight to his son, before going on to the Stage Deli with his wife. Lennon liked to oblige any fans that had been waiting for long periods of time to meet him with autographs or pictures.

Chapman stated that he was incensed by Lennon's "more popular than Jesus" remark, calling it blasphemy, and the songs "God", and "Imagine", because of the lyric "Imagine no possessions" and Lennon's personal wealth. Chapman even sang the song with the altered lyric: "Imagine John Lennon dead."

Dorian was going by the address he got from Sybil's hospital chart under the insurer's list. As Dorian crossed the street, he saw Geoff and Adrian coming toward them.

"Dude, you're gonna miss Haskins' class!" Adrian yelled out to him, as both he and Geoff grasped Dorian's arms to guide him back to the sidewalk.

"I can't stand the windbag either." Admitted Geoff.

"So we thought we'd go roust some bums."

Dorian shook his head. "Sorry, guys, I got some place to be."

"C'mon," begged Geoff, "it's gonna be epic!"

"Maybe next time." Dorian replied, crossing the street.

"Forget him, Geoff," said Adrian. "Maybe he's doing a *house call.*"

Geoff's lips stretched to a boyish smile. "*Oh…Dorian, you dog!*"

The wind cut sharply around the building. Dorian pulled up the collar of his jacket. His dark hair flattened around his face.

Dorian sneaked past the doorman who was busily helping an old lady with her groceries.

Boy, that was easy, he disappointedly observed. *I was expecting maybe another doorman, or a laser grid security system.*

"Hold it right there," said someone behind him.

Dorian turned around to discover it wasn't a security guard who had busted him. But it was Hetty Merton.

Dorian was very surprised to see her standing in the lobby. She was wearing a very sexy alter version of her St. Paschal uniform. Her white blouse was unbuttoned halfway down and her skirt was raised a little higher. What got Dorian going were those long black knee-high socks she wore on her long slender legs. She pushed her damp red hair back over her shoulders with both hands.

Hetty charged straight at him, giving Dorian a wet kiss and a warm embrace.

"I was hoping you'd come by."

She dreamed of this for God knows how long.

"Oh, Dorian," she moaned.

Again, she pictured his blue eyes. They were so open and warm, and then she thought of the white curve of his teeth when he smiled.

Oh, wow. Why am I thinking about him like this? Am I losing it totally?

She gave him that dazzling smile of hers again, shifting position beside him so that her skirt rode high enough on her thigh to flash some skin above the top of her stocking and her breasts brushed against his chest. She seemed to lose her balance just a little, forcing him to catch her with his arm suddenly tight around her waist, and she giggled like it was all a big joke.

But first—

The embrace.

Dorian's strong hands stroked her body through the tawdry outfit. Then his left hand was in her hair. It was gentle and warm.

I'm ready, she thought. *I've never felt like this before…*

Her breasts pressed against his sculpted chest—she could feel his heart beating deeply within, and it seemed to beat for her. Their souls seemed to fuse through each ravenous kiss, and soon she felt tingling all over, flushed with heat and desire.

She didn't flinch when he pushed up her white blouse, popped the black bra and was about to feel the contours of her body.

"I've been saving myself for you, Dorian," she moaned. "You can do whatever you want to me. All I ask is that you won't be gentle."

The anticipation shocked her. She rose up on her tiptoes to kiss him harder.

He pulled away, feeling guilty about kissing Hetty whereas his heart belonged to Sybil. "Listen, Hetty, I know what you're feeling but I can't do this. The temptation alone is far too great."

She focused her eyes on him. Licking her teeth with the tip of her tongue lecherously she replied, "The only way to get rid of temptation is to yield to it."

Dorian couldn't believe what she did next. Hetty reached down, pulled her skirt back and spread her knees. She put Dorian's hand on her knee and moved it briskly up her thigh and under her skirt. She was wearing nothing underneath.

She let out a sudden gasp of ecstasy and stiffened, as she rolled her eyes in the back of her head. Dorian saw her mouth open as she clutched at his wrist, and her lips formed the words "oh, God." Her eyes were closed and her face was twisted with pleasure.

Dorian gently pushed Hetty back, surprised at her approach. "It's definitely on my bucket list, but I just can't…"

Hetty clawed at Dorian, hating him for stopping the ecstasy that had filled her. It was more powerful, more potent then any feeling she had ever experienced in her life.

"Don't stop!" She begged, throwing herself at him.

Dorian gripped her by the shoulders, shoving her back.

"I'm sorry," he said, backing away.

He smiled embarrassingly and waved as the elevator doors closed while Hetty tried to stop the doors from closing but it was too late. The elevator door opened and there was Henry waiting for him.

Dorian looked from Henry and behind him in the elevator car and back again. He couldn't understand what was transpiring. There was some sort of weird dynamic going on between his two friends, at which could only guess.

"Of course, I get it now."

Henry put his hand on Dorian's chest preventing him from moving forward. "You can't go in, Dor."

"So says you or the puppet pulling your strings."

Henry was looking right into Dorian's eyes.

But his were black, solid black without whites.

Henry was possessed. By something powerful…and Dorian suspected he knew what it was.

The Vane family's Morbus had enchanted his best friend.

Great, Dorian sighed disparately, *her old man lives right in the middle of spook central.*

Dorian tightly gripped Henry's wrist in which he could easily twist and break his arm.

"Hurtful." Henry winced.

"You can let me pass, or I can knock you on your ass." Dorian offered, tightening his hold on his enchanted best friend.

"Just trying to prevent your funeral." Henry groaned, as Dorian grabbed him by the shirtfront and slammed him against the wall.

Dorian looked confused that Henry was even bringing it up. The topic was clearly of no relevance to him at all, even though it really wasn't his best friend talking. But Dorian loosened his grip slightly, and when he spoke, he didn't seem angry so much as sad or even tired.

"I knew it's not you talking, Henry. But this is way beyond your own understanding. Sybil is in danger, Henry. You have to let me through."

Henry stared right through Dorian, seeing nothing. All he heard was the voice of his old friend disconnected from the visual of the current reality.

"What are you waiting for, then?"

Dorian nodded, and dashed through the hallway. He adjusted the shoulder strap on his backpack and proceeded to carry out on his mission.

Henry remained there by the elevator. He let out a heavy sigh.

"Dead man walking."

Dorian turned left in the hallway, toward Harrison Vane's apartment. Still, he couldn't resist a quick glance behind him.

The deserted emptiness of the corridor hit him like a physical blow. He realized how far he was from Vane's door. Dorian lengthened his stride and walked with more haste.

These guys are incorrigible, scowled Dorian, thinking of none other than Henry and Hetty coming after him.

The sound of footsteps behind him grew closer, faster.

Unable to stand it anymore, he whirled around to face his stalker with the strange pistol he pulled out of his backpack, clutching it tightly in his hand.

Only—no one was there. The hallway was empty.

He'd imagined it. He sighed in relief, silently cursing Henry and Hetty.

Dorian finally reached Vane's apartment. He took a deep breath and placed the gun back into the backpack. All he wanted to do was to talk to the man. If he showed up wielding a gun it would only escalate this confrontation with dire consequences.

A plump Hispanic maid answered the door. She was in her late forties and her frizzled brown hair was in a bun.

"The mister isn't receiving nobody." She told Dorian. Her voice was low and her English was quite broken.

Dorian shoulder passed her brusquely. "Sorry, I don't deal with the help." Dorian barged through the living room, while the maid hustled right behind him. "Mr. Vane?" Dorian called out to the man of the house.

He entered the apartment, stepping into the waves of demonic energy was like stepping into a sauna. But there was something unusual about this emotion. It was more intense, clearer, the wavelengths crystalline—sharp. Powerful.

He walked into the sitting room, which was just as expensively furnished as the rest of the apartment. Something caught Dorian's eye at the left side of the room on top of the fireplace. He approached the mantle and found a set of framed photos that occupied a place of honor.

The first frame held a portrait of a man and woman in wedding attire. Dorian figured it was Cyril Vane and presumably his wife. The next picture was of Jim and Sybil as young children. The last one caught Dorian's attention because it was the playbill to *The Firebird.*

For an estranged parent he sure does follow his daughter's success, Dorian silently acknowledged.

Dorian tried to open a door, but his hand was swatted by the maid's broom.

"Don't talk to him," she snapped at him. "He will not hear you."

The apartment became second nature to him—almost instinctive. It was reaching out with the part of him that couldn't be touched physically. He suspected the entity hadn't identified him yet. He didn't know what he was dealing with.

The door stood ajar. He'd have known it anyway—he could feel fury as pure energy coming from it in waves, like heat from a house fire.

Dorian turned the handle and entered the room. Once he walked in eh found a frail old man who was hooked up in an I.V. machine. It was the image of a defeated man.

Beyond was a chair, and in that chair sat something that could only be charitably to be called human. At first glance, because the body was so shriveled and emaciated, the presumption was that it was someone extremely old. The way the head lolled to the side was further evidence of the lack of any effective musculature. There was a water tube close by his mouth, which he constantly licked, but that was just so he could keep his tongue and lips from going dry. Fluids and nutrients flowed into him intravenously, through permanent junctions in the major blood vessels of the leg up close to his groin. The site was mercifully hidden beneath a blanket, but Dorian assumed that permanent catheters were likewise employed to deal with his waste products.

The study was a man's place, with many sofas and chairs and bookshelves crammed with volumes in a dozen languages. Tables were scattered about, some being bottles of wine and brandy, others covered with maps, and one with an open book on western civilization. Tall windows of thick leaded glass let in filtered light, which was warm and colored by the flow glow, a thick knot of logs in the fireplace.

Dorian put his hand on the doorknob—and the thing inside sensed him.

It wasn't sickness and age that ground him down, Dorian observed. *It was the unending burden of being a Vane. Of being a cursed man.*

Dorian gingerly approached the sickly man with the utmost of ease. "I need to tell you about your daughter, Sybil."

"Don't you have no manners?" Said the maid, who violently threw Dorian toward the door and out of the room with superhuman strength.

A look of wither hatred blew apart the last semblance of the maid's human façade. Bestial and inhuman, she revealed the sheer malevolence that lurked at the heart of evil itself. Eternal rage twisted her face into the true image and likeness of the menacing Morbus. The sight of the creature's face sent adrenaline coursing through Dorian's system. His paralysis had lasted only an instant. In one hand she held a mop and her other fist was clenched. Her body seemed to be oozing the signature Morbus cloud.

CHAPTER TWENTY-NINE

The gratification comes in the doing, not in the results.
James Dean.

The maid's whole body contorted. She seemed to swell up, her clothing splitting at the seams, and her natural chestnut eyes began to glow with an eerie yellow. Dorian's attention focused on her, and he took the opportunity to run.

Before he had gone more than a step, the maid spun and viciously backhanded him, knocking him back. Dorian fell heavily to the floor, stunned.

Dorian scrambled to open his backpack. He frantically searched weapon after weapon. Anything he could use to send the bitch back to hell.

It's these moments where I ponder on what would Bruce Willis do.

Dorian was utterly shocked as the maid hurtled through the air straight at him. He had about a split second to react; which wasn't remotely enough time. The heavyset Hispanic woman slammed into him, sending the table crashing to the floor. The combatants fell over the chair upending it, as both Dorian and the demonic maid tumbled across the room.

Dorian twisted, sending her flying overhead. She slammed into a set of shelves upon which various curios had been placed.

The top shelf was jolted loose, fell onto the one below it, which feel onto the one below that, and so on until they all hit bottom, causing all the objects into dust.

Staggering to his feet, Dorian raggedly said, "I hope you're insured."

The maid wasn't listening. Instead she covered the distance between herself and Dorian in one leap, sending the two of them flying backward and crashing into the mirror hanging on the wall.

With superhuman strength, the maid took the opportunity to grab an iron poker from the fireplace and swung it around like a baseball bat. It struck Dorian in his side, staggering him. The maid brought it sweeping back in the other direction…but Dorian grabbed the weapon, yanked it from the psycho bitch's grasp, and tossed it aside.

He swung a punch at the woman, who ducked under it and came in fast with several quick blows to Dorian's gut. He faltered, recovered, and swung a vicious roundhouse that damned near took the maid's head off.

She was flat on her back, and Dorian gave her no time to got up. He landed heavily atop her and, with an unbelievable ferocity, started hammering her in the face.

Now she was on the receiving end of as brutal a pounding as anyone had ever endured. Dorian wasn't letting up for even a second. The blows came fast and furious. The maid couldn't even begin to mount a defense. Her head slumped back, and

Dorian cocked a fist, looking ready to punch it straight through her head and into the floor below.

Reveling on tormenting her, Dorian let down his guard for a second, and the cleaning lady from hell seized the opportunity. She brought a fist around and slugged Dorian in the side of the head, then hit him again, and a third time.

Dorian fell sideways off her, and she crab-walked backward.

Dorian saw the muscles begin to tense all along the maid's shoulders and he felt his own muscles growing taut in response.

"Something tells me that you're not on PCP." Dorian said, after watching the maid perform such athletic feats that were highly incapable for such a robust woman.

Dorian battled furiously with the Morbus controlled house lady. The two combatants demolished furniture and shattered windows as they sparred, bare-fist fighting in a whirlwind of attack and counter attack. For her size, the maid was remarkably fleet-footed, striking at Dorian again and again as he drove her back, trying to find a gap in her defenses.

He was too busy on finding an opening he forgot to protect his exposed body from a quick jab. It was right in the same spot where Jim Vane kicked him. The pain was much worse.

Dorian fell to the floor as the maid laid into him, pummeling him with a rapid-fire volley of uppercuts. He'd managed to block her attack with a vicious head-butt that earned him a howl of rage and a bone-cracking slap. Now she had him by the throat and was beating the life out of him.

The lights above him seemed to spin as he tried to focus on the maid. She loomed above him, her eyes shining with anticipation.

Dorian groaned and climbed to his feet, weaving like a drunk. Then he feigned a clumsy punch at her and lunged downward and scooped his gun off the floor as she danced backwards, out of reach.

Dorian's legs, which generally loped along with ease and spring, now seemed weighted with lead. There was an agony of fatigue throughout his body that was something more than muscular. His body pleaded that every step be his last. His mind forced his legs to pump faster, every step *faster*. There was no time to maintain, no place to backslide, no alternative but to run *faster*.

Failure is not an option.

And then the maid hit him again.

First with a right cross, and then followed with a left hook that was just as hard.

Dorian staggered.

The maid reared back and swung again. This time, Dorian had the wherewithal to duck.

The demonic maid's fist went though the wall—and stuck.

Dorian grabbed a nearby chair and in a single fluid motion swung it at her head.

Except that somehow, miraculously, the maid grabbed his wrist with the free hand and stepped Dorian's attack just before one of the chair's legs made contact with the side of the monster's face.

That's not possible, Dorian thought. *No one that big can move that fast.*

The maid then pulled her stuck hand free of the wall, wrenched the chair from Dorian's grasp with her other hand, and slammed Dorian all the way to the other side of the room.

Dorian screamed in pain.

The maid smiled, and advanced toward him.

The woman had her right hand raised, with an open palm—and Dorian knew what that meant. The death-strike. Dorian was shooting, trying to destroy the creature—but not hitting it straight on enough.

And then…Dorian was within reach. He tried to block the blow, but failed, and it slammed him in the chest, open handed with precision and power.

Dorian gasped—and fell to his knees, choking blood seeped from between his lips.

The muzzle of his weapon flared as he gripped the weapon with both hands. Two double-taps, and four bullets came speeding out of the barrel. All good hits, but they didn't even slow her down. Angry growls assailed his eardrums. Moving with unexpected speed, the maid was on top of him in a blur. Dorian didn't even have time to squeeze off another shot.

A powerful hand seized his right arm.

Sharp claws dug into his skin, drawing blood.

Dorian can hear the bone crunching and he knew it was from his own scream. Excruciating pain raced up his fractured arm.

The gun went flying.

A swipe of the maid's arm cracked his ribs and sent him tumbling across the room. The titanic blow knocked the breath from him. He crashed down onto the hard marble floor, landing amidst the jumble of priceless objects.

The maid's extended claws remained wrapped around Dorian's throat as she yanked the stunned human from the floor. Dorian's feet dangled in the air, his face was inches away from the femme fatale's snapping jaws. She snarled at the intruder. Drool dripped from its jagged fangs. The inhuman beast was only seconds away from biting the boy's head off.

Dorian struggled as he dug frantically through his backpack for a weapon.

He was losing the battle.

The maid held him flat against the floor, and as he stared up at her. Dorian's attacker's teeth lowered menacingly toward his neck.

He was almost unconscious. The maid was taking her time, savoring Dorian's death, making it last a few seconds longer— and yet another few seconds later. The maid was gloating about it, though Dorian could not hear what she had to say.

"Here, little boy, have some air—then I'll choke you again! I can do this all day!"

Dorian was so weak…he was ready to give up.

Gasping for air, desperate to keep his advantage, Dorian rolled over and flung himself atop the maid, clocked her across the face with another punch, and another, and another.

WHAM!

Dorian was hit full in the chest by a hundred and fifty pounds of demon-possessed housemaid. He flew backwards, limbs cartwheeling, and cracked his head on the glass-covered windowsill before falling to the ground in a heap. His pistol clattered to the floor and slid away from him across the tiles.

Gasping, Dorian raised his head to see the maid stalking toward him, hackles raised, lips drawn back from her wickedly curving teeth. He felt the heat of the maid's fetid breath blast over him, evaporating the sweat on his face.

Time seemed to freeze as they stared at one another.

Dorian's gaze ticked sideways to where his pistol lay several yards from him.

The spell shattered.

The maid lunged at him, her attacker all the more terrifying for it being completely silent. Dorian threw his arms up to protect his face as the maid hit him like a ton of bricks, crushing him back against the wall. He yelled at the top of his lungs as he saw her mouth open wide, and grabbed the maid by the scruff of her neck, digging his fingers into the psychotic woman's skin in an effort to prevent her from ripping his face off. With his other hand, he groped blindly for his dropped pistol.

The maid twisted and bucked, jaws snapping closer and closer to Dorian's neck as his grip pulled away, inch by inch. Dorian yelled out in frustration, letting go of the demon's neck and slamming his elbow into its unprotected throat.

The maid yelped in pain and recoiled, buying Dorian enough time to curl his knees up to his chest. As the monster lunged for a second time, Dorian jammed his booted heels up into the maid's soft belly, bracing a foot either side of the hard bone of the woman's pelvis. Pushing with all his might, he slowly lifted the pudgy housekeeper off him.

Her hand flicked out, faster than he could follow, and he felt a hiss of pain along his jaw.

He retaliated with a roundhouse swing that missed her by a mile as she ducked beneath it and came up like a jack-in-a-box, unleashing a powerful side-kick to the belly that pitched him backward through several pieces of antique furniture, upending them on top of him as he tumbled to the floor.

With a horrific screech, she leaped after him, trying to slash him with both her hands, but instead only managed to break the table in two like a karate student delivering a devastating chop on a two-by-four.

Harrison Vane heard the sounds of battle and struggled to get out of his chair. Time, now more than ever, was of the essence.

* * *

Legs pumping, Dorian rounded a corner.

Dead end.

Dorian's mind went into overdrive, scanning the short corridor before him.

He turned away, the wound in his side aching—but what hurt worse was the pang of uncertainty, his fear for Sybil. He wasn't used to this—he was used to being confident in himself, trusting himself to make the right move.

This was uncharted territory.

His instincts were strong, and he would defend her to the death.

The maid speared Dorian in the gut with her large meaty hands, and the contents of the bag scattered all over the floor like candy being thrown from a parade float. Catching his breath, Dorian made a mad dash to pick up any weapon he could to defend himself with.

When faced with surrealistic death by demonic domestic staff—fly a car up a ramp and destroy a helicopter in midair.

Dorian smiled gleefully when he grasped a steampunk-looking pistol. He took aim and fired at the maid.

Click.

No bullets.

"Oh, shit." Dorian groaned, watching the maid stampeding straight at him.

Then a ring of sonic energy came from the pistol blew out of the barrel and it knocked the crazy woman back. The demonic maid toppled the books from the bookcase and made a hole in the wall from the impact.

Dorian grinned. *Nothing like on the job training.*

The glass that surrounded the Degas sculpture shattered.

But the benefits suck.

The salary's a joke.

The maid swung hard, but Dorian slapped her aside. Before he could take advantage, she hurled herself clear of him, running straight at the wall and using it as a springboard to flip herself up and over.

Dorian scoffed in disbelief. "Oh, come on!" He complained, looking at the woman's plump figure. "There is no way you were able to pull that stunt off!"

The insult threw her fractionally off balance; she didn't quite land where she wanted to, or as smoothly.

It was the opening Dorian had been waiting for.

He tackled her, and together they crashed through a glass wall into the foyer. Lamps, electronics, and vases crashed and shattered around them as they struggled. Dorian had speed and a fair share of agility, but the maid possessed strength he couldn't hope to match. For every blow he landed, he took a dozen.

She hit him again, and again, using her feet this time more than her massive fists, choosing her blows with care so that she connected with soft tissue instead of bone. She wanted to wear him down, to strip him of the ability to defend himself, to remove all hope before she came in for the kill.

She sent Dorian crashing backward into a cabinet, and he tumbled into it, rearing up immediately only to collapse against the opposite end. He was clumsy and dazed, he had to be at the end of his rope.

Dorian showed fear in his eyes, which was exactly what she wanted to see.

The maid's mop swung at Dorian again, knocking him to his knees. A meaty hand with long fingernails locked around his left wrist. Another gripped his right shoulder.

A shockwave ripped between the two points, slamming up his arm and across his chest. He could feel his bones begin to hum as his muscles convulsed. In another moment his teeth would explode like firecrackers.

His right arm was still free. He reached up and grabbed the woman's wrist, wrenching her hand loose from her grip on Dorian's shoulder. Now she had it by one wrist and she had it by the other.

Dorian put every ounce of strength into a lunge to the side. He took the maid with him—and both her gigantic hands hit the marble floor.

Dorian's body stopped shaking itself apart, and the ground began to shudder instead.

He had a stitch in his side. Or maybe it was something far much worse. The pain was increasing, was viciously throbbing, burning…he reached down, felt his left side—and found hot blood pumping out. He was wounded. He was cut during the scuffle.

He pressed his hand against the wound, trying to stem the flow of blood and encourage clotting.

It hurt like a son of a bitch. And every step made it hurt worse. But he kept going.

He always did.

Dorian charged at the snarling demon and proceeded to pummel it into submission. He hit the possessed maid again and again, and with each blow Dorian shouted:

"This—!"

WHAM!

"—is!"

WHAM!

"—for!"

WHAM!

"—Sybil!"

WHAM!

Dorian's right arm was sagging with fatigue, so he switched over to his left fist and went on punching, over and over, with each punch feeling that he was striking deeper into the demon's spiritual core.

At last he had to stop, winded, gasping for air, and he was sweating buckets a plenty.

The maid fought back with incredible strength, lunging again and again, her sharp claws scraping on the floor as it fought for control. Seeing Dorian react to strikes against the wound on his side, the maid grinned sadistically and began to aim more and more blows there, making blood spurt freshly once more from the ruptured dressing. Dorian blocked a blow of her fist—but couldn't stop the mop handle from striking home.

The handle broke in half, sending Dorian to the floor. This was not what Michael Steele prepared him for. He wasn't dealing with a mugger or a school bully, but a tenacious wraith that was bent on killing him and taking her sweet time doing it.

She pounced right on top of them and started strangling him again. This time she wasn't playing around. She was out for blood.

"I have grown very tired of this," she snarled. Her broken English accent was laced with an otherworldly entity. "It's time we end this farce."

She stretched her mouth to reveal razor sharp jagged teeth and a forked tongue that slithered in and out of the gaps like it was snake. She let out a god-awful shriek.

Dorian scrambled furiously for something he could use as a weapon. His free hand searched for something nearby and he found one of the broken handle pieces from the mop. In one swift move he thrust the stake into the maid's neck as blood spurted out like a water fountain.

She quickly released him and held her neck in pain. She was gargling with her own blood. She was screaming and crying hysterically, trying to find something to stop the bleeding.

Dorian breathed greedily for air. He was expecting his attacker to die right away, but she was running around like a chicken with its head cut off.

Then he realized that only the worst was yet to come.

CHAPTER THIRTY

The only thing we have to fear is fear itself.
Franklin D. Roosevelt.

The pain hit him like a strike of lightning, making him arch his back, rising up through his spine to flood his brain with red glare, and then he fell to his knees, pitching forward, almost losing consciousness.

Behind him he heard a terrifying wail, like a shrill siren. It rose over the crack and thud of shattering glass, rose over Dorian's desperate shouts.

The maid's cry, revealing so much pain, so much horror, forced him to stop and turn around. She crouched at the entrance to the hall, head tilted back, eyes bulging wide, mouth open in her endless wail.

She dropped to her knees. Raised her hands and clasped them in a prayer position.

Dorian started toward her, back through the broken hallway, his shoes crunching over shards of glass.

He stopped as her wail was cut short. The maid appeared to choke. Raised her hands to clutch her throat—as her tongue shot out of her open mouth.

No. Not her tongue.

Something that was much wider than a tongue.

It was a hand!

Then another one burst out. Two hands.

Stretching from the maid's mouth, and they were reaching out to Dorian.

"What the hell?" He said in amazement.

She smiled, but it wasn't a human expression. In fact, nothing about her seemed human or any at all connected, it was like she was some different species entirely forever gazing at the world from the outside. She was a predator, while all others were prey. That was the natural order of things.

The maid fell onto her side, clutching her throat with both hands, making ugly choking sounds.

Dorian stared in disbelief at the twisting, hands pushing out farther and farther from the woman's mouth.

She withered a choked groan as strange foam pushed out of her mouth behind the exposed forearms.

No. Not foam.

A head. A spongy, wet orange head.

Two red eyes opened. The hand poked through the maid's open mouth as she gagged and choked, her hands flailing the air wildly now.

A sour odor rose through the narrow hallway, heavy and rank. The air grew colder. Dorian felt a sour dew on his cheeks that made his skin tingle.

Orange shoulders slid up past the maid's lips, the flesh appeared glisteningly wet. The red eyes opened and shut rapidly, focusing on Dorian. The maid's eyes, ears, nose and mouth started to bleed heavily and the Morbus entity was shoved out of her body.

The maid lay sprawled on her back now, arms flying wildly, helplessly above her, feet kicking, had tilted back as the red-eyed demon and slid the rest of the way out from the woman's mouth, making a soft *plop* as its clawed feet splashed on the floor.

The smell. Dorian couldn't bear the smell.

He tried to hold his breath. But the heavy, fetid odor seemed to wash over him, creep into his pores.

The demonic foot made wet sucking sounds as they moved over the hard floor. The creature stood upright, as tall as Dorian. It raised its spongy, wet arms as it made its way heavily down the hall, leaving a thick mist behind it.

One step. Another. Another. Its red eyes were glowing even brighter now.

It's real, Dorian thought. *Oh, my God. It's real.*

Staring in horror and amazement, it took Dorian a few seconds to realize that it planned to attack him.

The sour stench rolled over him.

Dorian staggered back. Turned. Tried to run the other way, toward the living room. Away.

Away.

But it was too late.

He felt the Morbus' meaty hand wrapped around his neck. Pulling him back. Tightening around his throat. Tightening like a boa constrictor.

Then there was the smell—the putrid god-awful smell.

With a groan of disgust, Dorian reached up, tugged, his hands sliding over the bumpy, wet flesh, struggled to pull the hand off.

I...I can't...breathe. Can't...breathe.

An instant later he was aware that he was being lifted up into the air. Dorian was jolted into consciousness at the sight. He grabbed the maid's wrists, and struggled to pull the demon's hands off his neck. The pressure was making flickers appear before his eyes, cutting off his breath.

He let go of the Morbus' wrists, resisting only with his lower body, reaching downward.

The Morbus chortled, certain the demon had won. It started to dangle him out the window like a worm on a fishhook. He was hanging over fifty stories high above the pavement.

"Oh, no, not this again." He groaned, remembering how the Basil Hallward Morbus held him in midair from the bedroom of his penthouse.

The cloud was like a giant python squeezing him was now consuming Dorian. Another cloud-like appendage had Dorian by the throat. He was trapped next to Harrison Vane.

"Listen, I don't want to destroy you." Said Dorian, trying to reason with the demon. "I've a way for you to move beyond the Vanes."

I just hope the Christmas party rocks, Dorian thoughtfully complained.

Dorian could see Vane's vacant face. He was helplessly shedding a tear. Dorian was being strangled and the tail brought him just an inch away from the Morbus' face.

"You just need to let them go."

The Morbus drove Dorian out the window shattering the glass and held him aloft fifty stories above the ground. Black and blue from numerous cuts on his face grasped through the smoke of the Morbus' non-corporeal arm. His eyes began to bulge.

"Are you still certain you want to talk about 'letting go?'" The Morbus sadistically asked Dorian, as it loosened its grip around the boy's throat.

"The Vanes are done for." Dorian said, struggling with the demon. Looking up from how high he was lifted up, and he kicked his legs trying to get a toehold. "They're already fragile. Once they're broken, you'll have nothing. You need to trade up. Cash in on a new family. Be the first on your block to terrorize the nouveau riche. Be the envy of all the other ugly monster things."

The Morbus threw Dorian back into the room. The would-be monster hunter tumbled like a rag doll.

"Don't take this as an act of mercy." Cautioned the Morbus, floating back into the apartment. "But it would be bad form if I did not hear your plea…before ripping out your throat."

Dorian got up, wiping a trickle of blood from his mouth with the back of his sleeve. There was a glint of larceny in his eye.

"He's a guy who creates, um…*electronic dreams*. He's kinda like you, man. He gives guys like me all the things they could want in this virtual world." Dorian handed the video game controller to the cloudy claw of the Morbus. "We're talking thousands of people."

The Morbus inspected the crude device with such scrutiny. "And this is his totem?"

Harrison Vane slowly got up with great pain from his chair and pulled the oxygen tube from his nose. Then he sneakily picked up the bleeding Degas statuette.

"I know Diamond didn't want you to have it." Dorian said to the Morbus.

"I am the arbiter of my own fortunes." The demon corrected the lowly worm.

"What a trophy he would make, huh?"

Vane stepped onto the window ledge and took a very deep breath. "For Sybil," he whispered before he jumped off the ledge.

The Morbus noticed Vane was gone and the cloud's essences rushed out the window.

"Your ruse is comical." It said to the old man. Then it returned with the statuette. The creature was still bleeding, and the smoke coiled around Dorian in a threatening manner. "So transparent and, need I say, gauche."

"Think it through!" Dorian pleaded to the demon. "Now there's just Sybil. Weak. Not worthy of your influence. And when she's gone. Zip! You're done, boss."

The Morbus looked tense. "I am not a fool."

Fool, no, Dorian thought. *But we're banking on "chump."*

"No doubt. But think of the challenge; all the worlds you can conquer through technology."

The Morbus released the statuette, and it stopped bleeding. "After 110 years this family no longer offers anything of value."

Close the deal, Mr. Trump!

"Then it's a win-win, right?"

The Morbus looked as if it was being duped, but he wanted to know where this was going. Then it considered the infinite possibilities about this new medium, or perhaps this strange new virtual lifestyle, which seemed to be its competition. For a small fee, men and women could live out their vivid fantasies through these "electronic dreams" the brash young man had suggested. Deep down in its core, the Morbus knew this offer was too good to decline.

"It is done." The ancient demon said, with a wave of its gigantic hand. "My arrangement with the Vane family is now null and void."

Dorian threw a paperweight at the statuette and it cracked in half. "I did forget to mention one thing." He grinned.

The Morbus tried to infuse his influence on the game controller, but it became frustrated that it wasn't working.

Dorian got to his feet. His legs were like jelly under him. He found a pistol from the backpack. He held it in his shaky hand—and didn't think he could fire it accurately. Not yet. Anyway, it seemed to be too late.

"Technology's an abstract. Ones and zeros really." Dorian explained, picking up the gun from the floor. "There's no anchor to hold you here."

Ice water was circulating in Dorian's veins. His teeth were grinding. The pressure returned to the trigger finger. He took aim and fired.

"Yippie-ky-yae, motherfuh—"

The Morbus roared in rage as it was being shattered into a million pieces like an ice sculpture. Dorian shielded his face from the blast. He grabbed the wall, his temples were throbbing, his entire body was convulsing in a shudder that stopped his breath.

He forced himself back to his feet, scanning the area around the room for any sign of the demon. Dorian raised his gun, holding it at the ready as he moved down the last few meters to the apartment. Dust and debris swirled away from him, caused by the motion of his feet.

Dorian swore colorfully and drove himself onward, ignoring the burning ache in his legs as his bruised muscles complained.

After a long and terrifying pause, he learned he had won the bloody battle. The curse has been lifted on the Vanes. Dorian surveyed the apartment to find it all in shambles. It definitely looked like a bomb went off in there.

The superintendent is going to be pissed.

"Now that's how you clean house," Dorian boasted, twirling the gun like a cowboy in an old Western he once saw on TV.

Like a paintbrush or a sculptor's knife, a controller is a tool. It's not art itself, he realized, wiping some blood off his mouth with his sleeve. *It couldn't be the embodiment of the lust or greed that binds a Morbus to a family. Not sure if it was inspiration, wishful thinking or a wild guess. But I'm sure; they won't make the same mistake twice.*

It was late at night and Dorian was feeling completely drained. He felt as if he'd started the day a hundred hours ago.

He walked past the slightly open door of his stepmother Lori. He'd he chosen to do so, he could have moved with such stealth that Lori would never have detected his passing. But considering the array of ups and downs—mostly downs—he'd experienced on this, the worst day ever, he simply strode in knowing that he would hear exactly what he did.

"How was school?" Lori's voiced calmly down the corridor.

Dorian stopped in his tracks as Lori opened the door wider. Her TV was playing some reality housewife show.

Crap! Dorian exclaimed through the caverns of his mind. *I forgot I was grounded.*

"It was exhausting," muttered Dorian.

"Michael called," Dorian could feel fear tingling in the back of his head. "He said you had to stay after class for further tutoring and he helped you with your math homework."

A cool sensation came over the sweating teenager. Michael Steele had come through for him in his darkest hour.

"Did you get a lot of work done?"

"Well, the hard part is over," Dorian sighed.

Lori didn't appear impressed. "You're still grounded."

"I know."

"All right then," Lori said, losing the door and then she smiled. "Now, go to sleep, you little creep."

"Thanks, Lori," replied Dorian, even though he didn't know what he was thanking her for, and closed the door of his room behind him.

He flopped onto the bed. Dorian started to drift off into sleep. It was the rain's fault. A cold fall shower had started up sometime after midnight, and the persistent beating of the raindrops against the windows was like a lullaby. Like a gentle, soothing lullaby…

His head drooped back against his pillow. Too many late nights and not enough caffeine made it hard for Dorian to stay awake. His eyelids sagged. He pulled the pillow over his head and fell into a restless slumber.

He was so tired…

He closed his eyes. Sleep came. A troubled sleep.

EPILOGUE

Dream as if you'll live forever, live as if you'll die today.
James Dean.

The next day started with a cavalcade of aches and pains. Dorian climbed slowly out of bed. He staggered over to the stereo and hit the *POWER* button. Foster the People's new album blared to life, and Dorian turned the volume up to ten in hopes of drawing out the early-morning capacity outside.

It worked, a little.

A hot shower helped bring him back to life. Dorian stood in the stall, letting the pelting water massage his aching muscles. His body was a world-class collection of bruises, scrapes, fractures, and hematomas.

After the shower, he wandered over to his closet, where his school uniforms and designer suits were hanging. Out of instinct he picked out the uniform that was neatly pressed and then he proceeded to get dressed.

Eli Weinstein looked at the clock on the wall, smiled, and said, "We've got a few minutes, so let's go to the next chapter: "The Periodic Table of Elements."

A roomful of teenagers moaned and whined.

Weinstein smiled to himself, remembering hearing similar moans in science class when he was a student over at Crown Heights and the teacher jumped ahead. Of course, Weinstein never indulged those complaints himself—he was always three steps ahead of the rest of his classmates, especially in the science classes, whether it was in physics, chemistry, biology, or the general sciences that he now, years later, was himself teaching.

"Now, now," he said chidingly, "the periodic table was part of the reading you were supposed to have done by *yesterday's* class. So you all *should* have it down pat by now." He walked over to the side of the classroom, to the bulletin board situated between the room's two doors on the right-hand side from where the kids sat. "Besides, it's been up on the board all year."

"Dude, I thought it was a movie poster," Adrian Singleton muttered. Several of the kids around him tried, and mostly failed, to swallow a laugh.

"Well, it has been coming soon to a *classroom* near you." Weinstein winced even as he made the bad joke. "All right, who can tell me why the isotopes are in the order they're in?"

This was a ridiculously easy question, and one that anyone who had actually *done*, the homework would know. He looked out over the class to see who actually did the work.

Actually, only a few were looking at him. Most of the twenty kids were studying either their notebooks, or the window, or the floor, or the clock in the hopes that it would move faster. Weinstein's general science class was scheduled for last period, and it was always different to hold kids' attention during the final class of the day, particularly in a required class that most of them didn't give a damn about.

Still, he was there to teach, and they were there to learn. Slowly, Dorian Gray raised his hand. Weinstein looked surprised. Not once since the school year started Dorian had volunteered for anything. Why the hell would he start now?

"Mr. Gray, you can visit the men's lavatory after class." Then Weinstein looked around the room for anybody else who might know the answer.

"I know the answer, Mr. Weinstein." Said Dorian, waiting for the teacher to allow him to speak.

"Okay, Mr. Gray," Weinstein replied, waiting for Mr. Too-cool-for-school's answer. "Why are isotopes in the order they are in?"

"They are classified by atomic mass."

The class went silent. They all stared at Dorian as if he revealed the meaning of life.

Weinstein nodded. "That's right."

Indignantly, David Harrison said, "No, it's *not*! The book says it's atomic *weight*!"

Dorian retorted, "Scientists prefer the term atomic mass now."

"Thank you, Bill Nye the Science Guy." David mocked him, leading everyone into laughter.

At least he didn't call me "Dorie," Dorian seethed, resting his hand on his cheek. *Good thing he grew out of shooting spitballs at my head.*

"Actually, you're both right," Weinstein said, overlapping David. "Unfortunately, the textbook we're using is about eight years old—or, to put it in simple terms, the same age that Mr. Harrison is acting—" That got a quick laugh from several kids, with the notable exceptions of Dorian and David. "—And since then, as Dorian said, scientists have come to prefer the more precise term 'atomic mass' to 'atomic weight.'"

Let's hear it for budget cuts, Weinstein thought with a sigh. The text they were using wasn't much farther along them the one *he* had used as a fifteen-year-old.

Looking out over the mostly apathetic faces of kids desperate to get out of school as fast as possible, he let out a long breath and walked back to the front of the class, away from the chart, and sat on the edge of his desk.

"Look, I know this all seems meaningless—but look at what we're talking about here." He pointed at the chart. "This is *what everything's made* of. You, me the desks, your books, the pavement outside, the lockers, the trees, the cars, the buildings, your clothes, your cell phones, your video games—this is what it's all made out of. These are the building blocks of the world. How can you not be excited by that?" Quickly holding up a hand, he said, "Don't answer that." Several chuckles followed. "I know, you don't think this is a big deal, but it really is." He glanced at the clock. The bell would be ringing momentarily. "Any other questions?"

Geoff Clouston raised his hand.

"Yes, Geoff?"

"Kr stands for Krypton, right?"

Weinstein nodded.

"I thought that was a planet."

Before Weinstein could give that the answer it deserved the bell rang. "We'll pick this up tomorrow."

His words could barely be heard over the din of books and notebooks closing, desks sliding on the linoleum floor, and classmates talking to each other.

"And don't forget," he said louder, "there's a test on chapters four, five, and six on Wednesday."

That was met with predictable moans and whines.

As Dorian left the classroom Hetty who shyly turned to the side confronted him. "And we will *never* speak of it again. Right?" She blushed.

"Speak of what?" Henry stepped between them. "What?!"

Dorian smiled wryly. "The final." He said to Henry. "I caught her looking on your paper."

Hetty closed her eyes in relief and her cheeks turned almost as red as her hair. "Yeah. That's right."

Henry looked disappointed, and then wagged his finger in front of Hetty's face. "You musta been desperate."

They met up with Adrian and Geoff at Dorian's car. He was putting his key in the door and noticed Sybil in the distance.

"Who's my ride to the Red Cup party tonight?" Geoff asked the lot.

"Guys, gimme a sec."

Dorian and Sybil looked at each other knowingly.

"Hi." He said to her. *Just as eloquent as ever.*

Sybil smiled, and strode across the few feet that separated them. "Hi," she said right back at him.

Dorian wrapped his arms around her, and she let him. In fact, she more than let him. After a moment's hesitation, she returned the embrace, hugging him tightly to her.

A slow smile appeared on her face. "Thank you, Dorian Gray." Sybil said, her voice barely above a whisper. Her face was pressed against his.

He moved his hand close to her face, and tears sprang from her eyes as static electricity made the fine hairs of her cheek stir. She clenched her fists, feeling her body tighten from head to toe as though she were being stretched on a medieval rack. His breath touched her mouth—first warm and tempting, then chill enough for her own breath to leave a cloud of condensation in the air between them, then warm again, so inviting that she couldn't hold back any longer.

She pressed her lips to his, arms around his neck as he went around her body, and felt a sweet spark of contact as their tongues touched.

For a moment, it was bliss.

He took her in his arms and a moment that seemed like an eternity finally arrived. Their lips pressed together and Sybil almost melted into him.

The warmth between them became fire, a torrent of raw lava coursing along her nervous system.

Dorian's friends watched as Dorian and Sybil embraced in the distance.

"Aw right!" Geoff exclaimed. "Brown chicken, brown cow!"

Hetty slugged Geoff very hard in the arm.

"Ow!" He screamed, nursing his wound. "What the hell is your malfunction?"

"You are truly a Shakespearian." Henry said, putting his hand on Geoff's shoulder.

Dorian closed the front door behind him and ran to answer the phone. "Anybody home?"

Why didn't someone pick up the phone? He had heard it ringing from the hallway as he fumbled with his keys.

Breathing hard, he picked up the receiver. "Hello?"

He heard a click, then the steady drone of a dial tone.

Whoever it was had given up.

His shoes were treading dirt on the floor. He bent to pull them off. The cold clung to his coat, to his skin. He shivered as he dropped his book bag to the floor.

He turned to the living room. "Where is everyone?"

It was dark in the apartment. Lori must not be home.

Dorian took off his coat and tossed it into the front closet. Then he made his way back into the living room and turned on a light. His eyes quickly surveyed the room. Sections of the morning newspaper spread over the couch. The vacuum cleaner was against the wall, and a bottle of Windex on the coffee table.

Frambroise.

She must have gone somewhere without finishing.

Shivering again, unable to get warm, he checked the thermostat on the wall in the front hall, then walked into the kitchen for a Coke.

A note on the refrigerator caught his eye. It was in Lori's flowery handwriting, informing Dorian and Henry that she would not be home this evening. Lori was having dinner with a woman she worked with, and they were also going to a poetry reading.

Dorian picked up his backpack, walked into his room and threw it on the bed and sat on the foot of it. He looked up at his ancestor's portrait to discover it has a black eye and cuts just like the kind Dorian received during his fight with the Morbus at Sybil's father apartment.

"That's gotta come down." Dorian said, rubbing his temples.

When he opened his eyes he saw something spewing from the portrait. Dorian jumped out of bed and searched furiously for a weapon. This must be his family's Morbus. He scrambled around his room trying to find his gun.

"I think it's time we were formally introduced, Dorian Gray." Said the Morbus, who was emerging from the painting. "I am Basil Hallward."

The name rang a bell for Dorian.

He looked at the painting and on the bottom left corner there was Basil's name written in red letters. This was the man who painted this portrait over 120 years ago. The ghost's eyes were strangely milky, lacking iris and pupil.

"Consider me an old family friend."

THE END.

CPSIA information can be obtained
at www.ICGtesting.com
Printed in the USA
FFOW02n1953230318